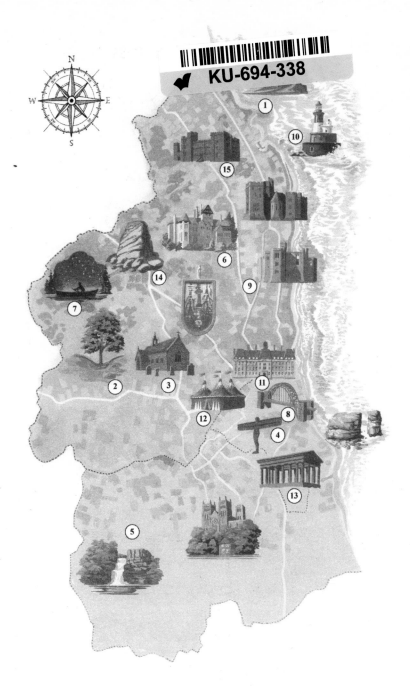

# PENSHAW

A DCI RYAN MYSTERY

# PENSHAW

## A DCI RYAN MYSTERY

## LJ ROSS

*"When there is no enemy within, the enemies outside cannot hurt you."*

—Winston Churchill

# PROLOGUE

*21ˢᵗ August 1984*

*Penshaw Village, County Durham*

Anger was ripe on the air that day.

It sat like a heavy cloud, blanketing the village of Penshaw with a noxious blend of fear and fury, hope and despair. It had been months since the pitmen had walked out of the colliery and dug their heels in for the duration of the strike. Free cafes had been set up by the miners' wives and flying picket lines were drawn up as the community rallied around. Across the country, other union men did the same and, under Arthur Scargill's leadership, the British coal industry came to a shuddering halt in one of the largest industrial actions the country had ever known.

But spring turned into a long, hot summer, where tempers frayed and resolve wavered with every sticky day. The Union was divided, with some continuing to work while the rest watched the news reports on boxy television sets in their front rooms, hoping to learn that the battle had been won but finding no radio broadcast from the Queen, nor any quivering message of regret from the Prime Minister.

*Oh, no.*

Like them, Maggie Thatcher had settled in for the duration. She might have been the daughter of a greengrocer, but any affinity with the working classes she'd once been a part of ended there. *The enemy within,* she called them now. They, the people who had built the country she governed.

And so, turbulent days stretched out into months as people fought for their heritage; to be heard and to be valued. They saw the future stretching out before them, one they were not part of, and grieved.

And, while their hearts quietly shattered, the bus arrived.

A sleek, blue-painted thing put on by the government, designed to carry dissenting miners back to work, promising cash bonuses for those who broke with their comrades and stepped on board. For three days it crawled through the streets, empty but for a sinister, ski-masked driver, while Alan Watson watched from the steps of the Colliery Club.

*Scab,* he thought.

The bastard was right to wear a mask, to cover his cowardly face.

"Mornin', Al."

He didn't bother to turn but gave a distracted grunt when his son-in-law came to stand beside him and leaned against the charred, red-brick wall.

"Bus been through, yet?"

"No," Alan replied shortly.

After a brief internal debate, he reached for the pack of cigarettes he kept in his back pocket. The way things were, he needed to ration himself, but a man couldn't be expected to live without the bare necessities in life. After another debate, he offered the pack to Michael, who snatched one up with muttered thanks.

"They're wasting their time, here," the lad declared, once they'd set the nicotine fizzing. "No man in Penshaw'll get on that bus."

Alan said nothing but took a long drag of his cigarette as he glanced at his friends and neighbours who had gathered on the pavement nearby, banners resting in the crooks of their arms.

*United we stand!*

*Coal not dole!*

He knew the majority of the men were down at the colliery entrance half a mile away, their picket line forming a human barrier to prevent any wayward union men from entering the colliery grounds. So much depended on faith and solidarity.

Without it, the strike would fold.

"I heard there was a bloke on the bus yesterday, over at Easington," Mike continued, and Alan gave him a sharp look.

"Keep your bloody voice down," he growled.

He'd heard the news too, of course. A man over in Easington Colliery had boarded the bus, becoming the first in the area to break with the Union. Unless they were careful, he wouldn't be the last. People over in Easington were growing restless, with a heavy police presence on the streets only making things worse, and an emergency meeting had been convened the night before to discuss the best way forward.

There'd been a lot of big talk, a lot of hard words and bravado, but not a lot in the way of fresh ideas. The truth was, all they really had was the hope that strike action would lead to a national fuel shortage. Without fuel to power homes and businesses, the government would surely see sense and reverse its present course, working to preserve the industry that fed and clothed communities rather than smashing them apart.

Alan took another fortifying drag.

Men like him were expendable, he thought. Just part of the so-called masses, the bloody *proletariat*, whose worst crime had been to try to retain the dignity of a profession, the only one they knew. He ground the cigarette beneath the heel of his boot and turned to look at the younger man standing beside him.

Mike Emerson was what he would have described as a *gobshite*, always looking for the quickest, easiest way to get a job done, rather than the best way. Always the loudest mouth in the pub, full of the blarney. He'd married his

4

daughter, Sally, the previous month—in a hastily-arranged affair. As far as he could tell, Mike spent an unnatural amount of time preening himself in the bathroom mirror and considerably less time tending his wife but, for all that, he was an easy-going lad who could stomach a few pints and was always eager to please.

"Here it comes," he muttered, and nodded towards the vehicle turning into the village with a full police escort.

The sun was high in the sky that morning, its rays bouncing off the windows so they could hardly see inside but, as the bus rolled by flanked by four police cars, a collective gasp rippled through the crowd.

*No!*

*I don't believe it!* they whispered.

There, on the bus, was a single passenger.

Angry shouts rose up in a crescendo and the crowd charged forward, uncaring of the police armed with batons and shields. More people spilled out of their houses and joined those on the streets, the treachery of a single man almost too great to bear. There followed grunts and cries as they met the blunt force of the law, then the twist and groan of metal as cars were overturned.

Through it all, Alan watched with a heavy heart, tears rolling unchecked down his proud, working-man's face.

# CHAPTER 1

*Friday, 7<sup>th</sup> June 2019*

*Thirty-five years later*

Joan Watson's nightgown was soaked with sweat.

It covered her from neck to ankle and clung to her body, which was comfortably rounded after eighty years of living. Her hands plucked at the cotton material, but nothing helped; the air in the bedroom was as thick and hot as a desert summer, despite it being June in the north of England.

With a sigh, she swung her feet off the bed, wincing as her bad hip protested at the movement.

"Alan?" she called out to her husband, but there was no answer.

*Typical.*

"Alan!"

Joan began to cough, eyes watering as her fingers groped for the bedside light. A weak glow illuminated the room, with its peeling floral wallpaper and elm wood furniture they'd bought on finance years ago and never found the money to replace. She blinked a few times, trying to clear the haze that was clouding her vision, so she could read the time on the carriage clock.

*Two-fifteen.*

*Or was that three-fifteen?*

It was still dark outside; she knew that much.

Coughing harder now, Joan felt around for her slippers and heaved herself off the bed. The springs gave a protesting whine and she reached for her dressing gown before padding towards the door in search of water. Her throat felt parched, and her head was throbbing so badly it was almost crackling, like twigs snapping in the undergrowth.

The air was even hotter when she opened the bedroom door, and she threw up an involuntary hand, as though the action would help her to wade through the heat. She began to worry as the crackling grew louder, like log fires in winter...

*Fire!*

She clung to the bannister and peered downstairs.

"Alan!" she croaked.

Through the stifling darkness, she saw the first lick of flames.

Fear coursed through her body and she stood frozen at the top the stairs. The crackling became a roar as the fire took hold and black smoke oozed beneath the living room door, pumping through the narrow hallway and rising to where she cowered against the wood-chipped wall.

*Alan!*

Her husband rarely made it past the sofa these days; not once he'd settled in for the night with a bottle in his hand. Joan's eyes closed, a single tear escaping as she imagined him fumbling with his cigarette lighter and being too drunk to care.

Suddenly galvanised, she staggered across the landing to the bathroom, hands shaking as she ran a flannel beneath the cold tap. She caught sight of an old woman with wild, frightened eyes in the cabinet mirror, but there was no time to stop and stare.

She hurried back onto the landing, clutching the flannel to her face as she made her way downstairs. Her legs felt stiff, but she forced herself to move, and by the time she reached the bottom step she was coughing uncontrollably, lungs bursting as the smoke grew heavier.

Helplessly, her eyes strayed to the front door, where freedom and fresh air beckoned.

*Not without Alan.*

Trembling, heart racing with terror, she burst into the living room and into the very mouth of hell.

# CHAPTER 2

*Monday, 10<sup>th</sup> June 2019*

*Newcastle upon Tyne*

The morning sky was a perfect canvas of cornflower blue, unbroken except for the wispy trail of an aeroplane making its way to the Mediterranean. Detective Constable Jack Lowerson watched its progress from his bedroom window, eyes narrowed against the blazing sunlight which broke through the unwashed glass. He thought of all the people inside that metal bird and wondered what might be occupying their minds.

*Sand and sea; suntans and sangria.*

He might have laughed, if he could remember how.

Instead, he reached for a pale blue shirt hanging on the back of the door and eased his arms into the sleeves with slow, painful movements. Next came the suit trousers, which took longer since he was forced to bend over.

He considered knocking back another paracetamol to take the edge off, but he'd come to rely too heavily on those little white pills over the past few days and didn't want to become dependent; he'd seen what happened to people like that.

Jack turned to look at his reflection in a mirrored wardrobe. The man who faced him was of medium height, slimly-built with light brown hair and shadowed, bloodshot eyes.

*Purplish-yellow bruises covered his ribs and torso.*

A tremor ran through his body, like an echo, reminding him of how they'd come to be there. He wished he could run; far away, where nobody knew him, and nobody would find him. There would be no talk of the man who'd once been Jack, and of what he'd seen and done. The thought was seductive, and he allowed himself to wallow in it for a moment before reality crept back in.

There was nowhere to run, and nowhere far enough, or dark enough, to hide.

He buttoned his shirt with shaking fingers, drawing the material over the bruises until they were completely hidden. Then, he touched a hand to the back of his head, feeling for the wound beneath his hairline. Thankfully, the bleeding had stopped days ago, and the swelling had reduced so it was unlikely anyone would notice. His suit trousers concealed more fading bruises, but his gait had returned to normal. If he was careful, nobody would notice.

Jack schooled his features this way and that; practising the normal, everyday expressions people would expect to see when he returned to the office. Squaring his shoulders, he found he could manage a pleasant sort of neutrality, but the effort left him grey and clammy. Staring into his own eyes, he saw stress and fear writ large across his face and wondered how he was ever going to pull it off. The men and women he knew, the people he called *friends*, were no fools. They were trained observers of human behaviour, experienced in picking up the tell-tale signs of when something was badly wrong.

*When somebody was lying to them.*

His eyes strayed to a chest of drawers, on top of which sat a small burner mobile phone, next to his regular smartphone, his keys and wallet.

And his warrant card.

Jack sank down onto the edge of the bed and held his head in his hands.

---

Thirty miles further north, Detective Chief Inspector Maxwell Finley-Ryan covered the ground at speed, long legs eating up the worn pavement as he jogged around the picturesque village of Elsdon, in Northumberland. It was early yet, and mist from the surrounding hills curled its way through the valley and around his pounding footsteps as he passed through the quiet streets.

He sucked in a deep breath ahead of the final uphill leg that would lead him through the fields to the house he and his wife had built. There was a dewy, earthy scent of wild garlic on the air and the hedgerows on either side of the single-track lane had grown tall, providing shelter for the rabbits who'd made their burrows beneath. He dodged their scampering bodies and wondered, not for the first time, how he had come to be so lucky.

Soon enough, the house came into view at the top of the hill. Ryan had chosen the spot himself, having fallen in love with the panoramic views across the valley, and gifted the land as a wedding present to Anna. He could remember the first time he'd brought her here and asked her to put roots down with him, just as he remembered every happy memory they'd shared together. He hoarded them, tucking them inside a special corner of his mind to sustain him during the darker moments of his daily grind. The job of a murder detective was a far cry from bunny rabbits and pretty views; it was the province of death and destruction, the very worst side to humanity that most people could only imagine.

As if she had read his mind, Anna stepped out of the house and onto the veranda overlooking the garden, where she could follow his progress along the lane. She raised a steaming cup of coffee and fanned it in the air, like an aircraft marshal steering a plane on the runway, and Ryan grinned, quickening his pace.

"I thought I'd have to send out a search party," she called out, as he rounded the corner. "Did you run all the way to Scotland?"

"Har har," Ryan said, and leaned down to bestow a thorough kiss. "I had a bit of energy to burn off."

"I can think of other ways to help you with that," she said, with a glint in her eye.

"Oh?" he said, recovering himself in record time. "Like what, for example?"

She leaned back against the patio table and took a leisurely sip of coffee, pretending to think about it.

"Well, for starters, there's plenty of weeding to do in the garden," she replied. "And then, there's that mirror to go up, in the spare room…"

She trailed off as Ryan walked slowly towards her and set his palms on the table, leaning down until his mouth was inches away from her own.

"Anything else?" he whispered.

Anna raised a hand to his chest and took a fistful of the damp material, drawing him closer before looking up to meet his silver-blue gaze.

"Now that you mention it…"

The rest of her sentence was lost on the morning wind.

---

Back in the city, Ryan's sergeant was enjoying a very different kind of morning routine; one that did not involve runs in the country or spontaneous bedroom workouts, more was the pity.

"I don't want to wear a tartan dress. I'm not even *Scottish*!"

At the sound of the mutinous voice wafting downstairs, Frank Phillips rolled his eyes and decided to add another spoonful of sugar to his morning tea.

He had a feeling he was going to need it.

There came the sound of galloping footsteps and, moments later, the newest addition to their family entered the kitchen with a stubborn look in her eye.

"Why do I have to wear this stupid dress to school?" Samantha demanded, gesturing to the blue and green tartan with obvious disdain. "How am I supposed to run around, if my knees keep getting caught in the material?"

The precocious ten-year-old they'd agreed to take into their home and treat as their own looked him squarely in the eye, clearly awaiting a response.

Phillips cleared his throat.

"Well, now, all the other kids will be wearing the same thing—" he began.

"No, they won't! The boys get to wear trousers. How come I can't wear trousers—or shorts, since it's summer?"

Phillips opened his mouth and then shut it again, because she had a point.

"It's…tradition," he finished, lamely, and made a mental note to raise it with the teaching staff. If his girl wanted to wear shorts, why shouldn't she, in this day and age?

"Seems a daft tradition to me," she muttered, taking the words right out of his mouth.

"Daft or not, that's the school uniform, young lady."

This last remark was delivered by Phillips' wife, Detective Inspector Denise MacKenzie, whose lilting Irish tones preceded her entrance into the kitchen. She set her briefcase on the countertop and brushed his lips with her own, before pouring herself some tea from the pot. They prided themselves on having a relationship of equals, albeit MacKenzie happened to be his senior in the police hierarchy, which was something Phillips didn't mind one little bit.

"Some schools don't even have a uniform," Samantha continued, never having been to one herself. She'd grown up in a travelling circus community and her education had been patchy at best.

"Well, this one does," MacKenzie said.

She took a fortifying sip of tea, then placed a hand on Samantha's shoulder and steered her gently towards the breakfast table.

"What'll it be? Cereal or toast?"

"Can I have a bacon sandwich?" she asked, hopefully.

"There's a girl after my own heart!" Phillips let out a rumbling laugh. "And, it just so happens, I made one earlier."

He opened the oven door to retrieve the plates he'd been warming, then set them on the table for the two most important women in his life.

"Thanks, Frank!"

"Can't have you going hungry on your first day, can we?"

Phillips gave Samantha's ponytail a playful tug and winked at his wife.

"What if they don't like me?" she asked, having munched half the sandwich in the time it took most people to draw breath. "Everybody probably has friends already. They might not want any more."

"Why wouldn't they like you, sweetheart?" MacKenzie replied. "Just be yourself, and you'll make lots of friends."

"What if they're into stupid stuff? I don't want to talk about boys and make-up all day."

MacKenzie couldn't help but smile.

"Why don't you tell them about your horse, Pegasus? You could bring your new friends to meet him, one day?"

The little girl's face lit up.

"That'd be good!"

Then another thought crossed her mind.

"What if they all know what happened to my mum and dad?"

"Even if they do know about it, they probably won't say anything," MacKenzie soothed, thinking of how cruel children could be. Samantha's parents had been murdered by the same hand, eight years apart, and the news had been full of it over the past few days. As her new foster parents, she and Frank had discussed things at length with Social Services and had come to the conclusion that it was best for the girl to make a fresh start and put down some roots.

"If anybody is unkind, just ignore them or tell the teacher," MacKenzie decided.

"Stick up for yourself, if you have to. Just remember to keep your guard up," Phillips threw in, and earned a hard stare from his wife. "I mean to say…"

"Oh, don't worry," Samantha assured him, taking another mouthful of bacon. "I'll remember to go for the sides, first."

MacKenzie sent him a fulminating glare, following which Phillips took a hasty gulp of builder's tea.

"Nearly time to head off!" he said, cheerily.

"I'll take your head off, in a minute, Frank Phillips."

# CHAPTER 3

The ignoble lines of the Northumbria Police Headquarters lay to the east of the city of Newcastle upon Tyne, in an area known chiefly for its association with two great fallen empires: shipbuilding, and the Romans. 'Wallsend' took its name from the latter, being located at the end of Hadrian's Wall nearest the North Sea. Thus, when it came time for the Powers That Be to relocate their constabulary offices, it had been decided that what was good enough for the Romans was certainly good enough for the Criminal Investigation Department.

Which was appropriate, Ryan thought, as he crossed the tarmac towards the main entrance, when you considered their stock in trade.

"Hold up!"

He recognised the unmistakable sound of his sergeant's booming voice carrying across the forecourt and turned to find Phillips and MacKenzie making their way towards him. Superficially, at least, theirs was an unlikely partnership.

Denise MacKenzie was a smart, capable woman in her mid-forties with a mane of flowing red hair and an army of admirers. In the end, she had chosen Frank Phillips; a man ten years older than herself, with a short, boxer's physique and salt-and-pepper hair that grew thinner by the day. He boasted an unhealthy relationship with carbohydrates and karaoke, as well as a razor-sharp eye for police work.

He was also the best friend a man could ask for.

"Frank, Denise." Ryan greeted them with an easy smile. "Everything go off smoothly, this morning?"

The other two exchanged a telling glance.

"Yes…and no," Phillips replied, as they ambled towards the automatic doors. "We had a call from the headmaster on the way here. Apparently, Sam's set up a petition to allow the girls to wear summer shorts instead of dresses. It's been signed by more than half of them already!"

Ryan checked his watch, which read eight forty-five, and let out a bemused laugh.

"She doesn't waste any time," he said, with a trace of admiration. "What does the headmaster expect you to do about it?"

"I suspect he wanted us to clamp down on any political activism," MacKenzie drawled. "However, I pointed out that it was an excellent demonstration of lateral thinking, which put a different complexion on matters."

"You've got a wonderful way with words," Phillips cooed.

"Don't think flattery will get you anywhere," MacKenzie warned him, swiping her card across the door scanner with unnecessary force. "I still haven't forgotten the little pearls of wisdom you gave Samantha, this morning."

Ryan's lips quirked.

"Teaching the kid bad habits already, Frank?"

"Aye, and don't you start," his friend muttered. "I'm just lookin' out for her, that's all. Don't want people thinking she's a push-over."

Ryan thought of the fiery little girl they'd more or less adopted, and nearly laughed out loud. Instead, he clapped a bolstering hand on his friend's shoulder.

"Frank, I don't think there's any danger of that."

---

When Trainee Detective Constable Melanie Yates entered the open-plan office space which housed the Criminal Investigation Department, she immediately scanned the room, anxiously seeking out one face in particular. Jack Lowerson wasn't anywhere to be seen, but she spotted his suit jacket hanging limply over the back of his desk chair. He hadn't been into work on Thursday or Friday, having been afflicted by a stomach bug—or so he'd told her, in the measly couple of texts he'd sent over the weekend—and she'd been worrying about him for days.

Dropping her bag on her desk, she bade a hasty retreat into the corridor. Ryan had called a briefing at nine o'clock but, if she was quick, she might catch Jack before it began.

She found him in the break room, staring listlessly at the kettle.

"Jack!"

When he spun around, she thought he looked hunted. Then, his face cleared.

"Hi, Mel. Are you heading to the conference room?" He made a show of checking his watch.

She blinked in astonishment. From his impersonal tone, anyone would think they'd never shared a...a *moment*, in his car the week before.

"Jack," she hissed, and reached out to grasp his arm as he made for the door. "What's the ma—?"

Her grip was light, but he jerked as if she'd struck him. Melanie dropped her hand in a combination of shock and surprise.

"Sorry, I didn't mean—"

"It's nothing," he said, angling his body away from her. "We need to get going, or we'll be late for the briefing."

She didn't budge.

"How are you feeling?" she persisted. "I wish you'd let me help you. I could have brought chicken soup."

"I'm vegetarian, remember?"

She flinched at the abrupt tone.

"Look, thanks for the concern but, as you can see, I'm fine," he said, focusing on a point somewhere just above her head. "Actually, a bit of time off work has given me a chance to think about things. About us."

"Us?" she queried.

"Maybe we were a bit quick off the mark, last week," he said, affecting a bored tone. "You're a great girl, but I don't really have any space in my life for a relationship at the moment. If things went wrong, it'd be pretty awkward around the office, wouldn't it?"

Even as he said the words, his heart yearned for her to tell him he was wrong. He wished she would argue with him, tell him he was a hypocrite—tell him *anything*, so long as she stopped looking at him with those big, all-seeing brown eyes.

But Melanie Yates was a proud woman.

"If that's how you feel about it," she said, softly. "From now on, you can rest assured, it'll be strictly business."

Lowerson felt his stomach plummet, but he managed to work up an empty smile.

"Great. I knew you'd understand. See you at the briefing."

Melanie watched his retreating back for long seconds, trying to make sense of it all. What had gone so badly wrong? How could he have been so warm a few days earlier, and yet so cold to her now?

*What had she done?*

Tears threatened, but she would not allow them to fall.

# CHAPTER 4

"Crikey, we'll need a cattle prod to get through this lot!"

Phillips made his delicate observation from the doorway of Conference Room A, where a sea of law enforcement personnel had gathered ahead of the nine o'clock briefing.

"Standing room only," Ryan agreed, and his eyes scanned the room.

There was a smorgasbord of police staff in attendance, ranging from his own team of murder detectives from the Major Crimes Squad to representatives from the Drugs Squad, Intelligence and Organised Crime, Digital Forensics and Cyber-Crime Units; not to mention the regular detail of support staff and crime analysts who mingled with the rest. The air hummed with friendly chatter, interspersed with an occasional burst of laughter as his colleagues chewed the fat. Each team was possessed of its own internal hierarchy, and the room had already divided into smaller clusters of people who kept to themselves and spoke in undertones.

"We're going to need coffee," he decided. "A *lot* of coffee."

"Or a pair of fast horses," Phillips shot back.

"Chance would be a fine thing. C'mon, Frank—let's go and catch some bad guys."

"I reckon we can collar a few of 'em before I have to do the school run," Phillips replied, and then laughed richly when Ryan looked at him as though he'd sprouted three heads.

"What's next?" he demanded. "Bring Your Kids to the Office day? A bake sale for the school gym?"

"The thought never even crossed my mind," Phillips said, gravely, thinking of the school raffle tickets tucked inside his breast pocket.

Ryan eyed him with suspicion, and stepped inside the conference room.

"There'll be no raffles or tombolas, either," he threw back over his shoulder, leaving Phillips to wonder whether he had x-ray vision.

---

As Ryan made his way to the front, a quiet hush spread throughout the assembly. It was interrupted only by the late arrival of Chief Constable Sandra Morrison, who shuffled to the back of the room in a vain attempt to remain inconspicuous, the effort serving only to draw more attention. There followed the predictable rustle of papers and scraping of chairs as people sat up a little straighter in their seats, never more conscious that their boss was in attendance.

"Alright, settle down," Ryan began, in crisp, well-rounded tones. "Before we get into it, I want to thank you for being here so promptly. We all have full caseloads, so the last thing any of us wants or needs is more work. That said, it's my hope—my *belief*—that, if we work together in a co-ordinated way, we'll save ourselves a lot more work further down the line."

Ryan paused, allowing that to sink in, then took a marker pen and wrote the name of the operation he had been tasked to lead in block capitals across the whiteboard behind him.

"OPERATION WATCHMAN is a new initiative," he explained, turning back to the room. "Some of you may already know what it's all about, but here's the gist for the benefit of those who don't."

He leaned back against the desk at the head of the room and spread his hands.

"WATCHMAN is a cross-constabulary effort, which means we'll be working alongside our colleagues in Durham and Cleveland to tackle a new wave of organised crime in the region. As you know, 'organised crime' includes burglary, drug-dealing, cyber-crime, fraud, vice and, of course, *murder*," he said, nodding towards each respective team. "Within each constabulary, those units falling under the remit will be required to share intelligence, resources and allow reasonable access to active, closed and cold investigations—"

"Look mate, I don't mean to piss on your bonfire, but isn't that what we do already?"

Ryan's head whipped around, seeking the source of the interruption, until his eyes clashed with those of a heavily-overweight man in his early-forties he knew to be one of the detective sergeants from the Drugs Squad.

"Tim Gallagher, isn't it?"

"*Detective Sergeant* Gallagher," the other enunciated.

"Right. Well, sergeant, I'm delighted to hear you've been doing your job and I'll look forward to hearing your insights as the operation progresses," Ryan said, with the ghost of a smile. "You say you're already exchanging information with the other units in a co-ordinated way? I say, there are too many cases that drag on for longer than they should, because one unit didn't contact another. We need to work together with Specialist Ops to tackle a new breed of criminal—"

"Oh, aye? And who gets to notch one up for the quota? Major Crimes?" Gallagher sneered.

"We all do," Ryan said, taking the wind out of his sails. "This isn't about who gets the collar, *sergeant*. If we can drag a few more dealers off the streets or, better yet, disrupt their supply and eliminate the source, it's a win for all of us and for the people we serve."

He pushed away from the desk, speaking to all of them now.

"There's a new gang operating in the area, and it's crossing police boundaries. I've been in touch with the National County Lines Coordination Centre, who tell me the 'Smoggies' have been assessed as one of the most serious threats to community safety, not just here in our region, but on a national level."

Ryan referred to the street name that had been given to the most powerful gang in the area, the shadowy leader of which was rumoured to have been born in Middlesbrough. 'Smoggie' was derogatory slang, coined by rival football supporters on account of the factory smog that once hung over the streets of that city. It seemed that whoever was in charge had appropriated the term for their own use.

"We've been approved for a special grant from central government," Morrison chipped in, and a roomful of heads turned in her direction. "This operation will form part of a nationwide crackdown, and I'll do my bit to ensure you have all the resources necessary to get the job done."

Ryan nodded his thanks.

"If there's one thing we can learn from the past, it's that we work best when we work together. For once, this isn't about hitting targets, or winning Officer of the Month," he said, pointedly. "The Smoggies are highly-organised, well-funded, and their leader doesn't play by the old rules—"

"Used to be, they'd deal in Newcastle, Gateshead and Sunderland," Gallagher put in, grudgingly. "They'd squirrel their gear into the clubs and pay off the bouncers through a syndicate. Nowadays, supply's outweighing demand, so they're pushing out into the villages to shift the goods, and it's getting ugly. We're not talking about coke anymore; they're cutting dangerous mixes full of all kinds of crap and we can't keep up with it."

Ryan nodded his agreement, fighting the instant, impotent rage as he thought of all the men and women who slipped into the cycle of drugs. Down and down they went, until they died on the streets or in a filthy doss house somewhere for Ryan or one of his team to discover.

"Two years ago, the Moffa brothers were in charge of the ruling gang, and the youngest brother, Jimmy, was its leader," he said, casting his mind back. "He was brutal, but he had his own code. Since Jimmy died, there's been a turf war waging across the North East and we're dealing with the consequences of that. Cyber-crime, money-laundering and fraud are all on the up, trafficking has sky-rocketed and, most obviously, the death toll from gang-related crime is the highest it's been in years."

"It's getting harder to trace the money, too," said one of the members of the Fraud Squad he recognised as DI Anika Salam, who he'd worked with many times before. She might have been softly spoken, but Ryan knew her to be a first-rate detective with a solid track record. "They're recruiting kids to act as go-betweens, so the dealers don't have to touch the money. They send ten-year-olds to do their dirty work, then find some poor, vulnerable person's home and move themselves in."

"Cuckooing," Gallagher added. "Happens all the time."

Ryan nodded, and then looked around the room with stormy eyes.

"The buck stops here," he said. "It's up to us to put an end to this."

"As soon as you pull one weed, another one springs up," one of the Vice Squad muttered. "Today, it's the Smoggies. Tomorrow, it'll be something else."

Ryan couldn't argue with that. At times, he'd battled his own crushing sense of disillusionment, and had lain awake wondering why it was human nature for some people to inflict misery and destruction while others worked to prevent it. He still didn't have the answer to that question, but he knew that apathy would never be an option.

"There'll always be something or somebody new," he said, with quiet conviction. "There'll be other weeds to pull, but that's the job we signed up for. We agreed to be the constant gardeners."

He nodded towards the words he'd written on the board, in black and white.

"We agreed to be the watchmen."

―――――――

While Ryan battled outmoded attitudes and internal politics, Joan Watson awakened to a world of pain.

"Mum? Can you hear me?"

Her eyelids fluttered and her head turned towards the sound of her daughter's voice.

*Is she alright? Did she hear?*

"I—I can hear," she croaked.

"Mum! Oh, thank God. Thank God."

Joan opened her eyes and immediately shut them again, finding the light inside the private hospital room unbearably bright.

"Shut the curtains!" Sally barked out another brisk order, and dabbed at the tears which leaked from her mother's eyes. "Mum? The curtains are closed, now. Try opening your eyes again."

Taking comfort from her daughter's strong, authoritative voice, Joan blinked several times until the faces huddling around her began to come into focus.

"How are you feeling?"

This, from her son, Simon, who was seated on the visitor's chair on the other side of the bed.

"Everything hurts," she said, trying to swallow the ash in her throat.

"Pass her some water," Sally demanded of her brother, barely stifling a sigh as he made a clumsy grab for the jug of lukewarm water and sloshed some of the liquid into a cup. "Can you go and find a nurse? We need to see about increasing her pain medication. Mum's obviously in agony."

Simon Watson mumbled something beneath his breath and left the room, presumably to do his sister's bidding.

When Sally turned back, her face was deliberately cheerful.

"You're doing *so* well," she said, fiddling with the covers on the bed. "The doctors weren't sure…they said it might take much longer for you to come around. But I told them, you're as strong as an ox."

If Joan had been in any doubt before, her daughter's artificial cheerfulness was all the answer she needed.

*Alan was dead.*

"How's your da'?" she forced herself to ask.

Sally's eyes filled with tears, and she shook her head. She reached out to cradle her mother's hand, stopping short as she remembered the bandages protecting her burnt skin.

"He—Dad didn't survive the fire," she choked out.

Joan's eyes glazed for a moment, confusion warring with grief, then let out a harsh sob that ricocheted around the bland, hospital walls.

*Alan.*

*Oh, Alan.*

Just then, Simon re-entered the room. He was joined by a nurse and another man she recognised as her daughter's husband, Michael Emerson.

"Looking good, Joanie," he lied, with his usual aplomb. "You'll be out of here in no time!"

"Shut up, Mike," Sally muttered, and blew her nose loudly. "Nobody wants platitudes at a time like this."

"I'm just trying to keep things light," he said, defensively.

"Light?" Sally was incredulous, and then her face set into knowing lines. "You took your time getting here, didn't you? What was it this time? Traffic?"

Mike reddened, just a fraction.

"Yes, as a matter of fact," he said, forgetting that it was mid-morning and no longer rush hour. "I got here as quickly as I could."

Joan cast her son-in-law a weary glance, cataloguing the unremarkable attributes of a middle-aged, portly man who'd gone prematurely bald soon after his twenty-fifth birthday, as she recalled. For all that, he was part of their family, and there was nothing more important to her than family.

"I—I tried to get Alan out," she gasped. "I tried—"

"Shh, Mum. Don't upset yourself," Simon murmured, while the nurse fiddled with the drip next to her bed. "You did everything you could to save Dad. It's a miracle you got him out and survived."

Joan's hands began to shake as her body remembered the trauma and exhaustion of dragging Alan's inert body through the flames and out of the house. The smell was still in her nostrils, the stench of burning wood, burning plastic and…

*Burning flesh.*

"I thought it would be the mine that killed him," she whispered, so softly the others strained to hear. "Thirty years down a pit bringing up coal was dangerous, back-breaking work. But, when the mines closed, that's when I knew."

She fell silent.

"What did you know?" Sally prompted.

"I knew it would be the drink that killed him, in the end."

The others exchanged a glance, hardly knowing what to say. Eventually, Simon broke the silence.

"We don't know how the fire started," he said. "The police are still looking into it."

Joan's mind began to float away, as the new dose of pain medication started to kick in.

"I told him to be careful," she slurred. "I told him—"

Her voice faded as she slipped back into oblivion.

# CHAPTER 5

At Northumbria Police Headquarters, Ryan continued to field questions about bureaucratic targets and chains of command from the confines of Conference Room A. The sun continued to blaze, more strongly than before as it climbed higher in the sky, and the blinds had been firmly drawn so as not to distract those present from the job in hand. Alongside an unreliable air conditioning system, the heat served to create a unique aroma that circled the room and, as Phillips would later comment, it was deserving of its own criminal code. Although largely desensitized to malodour, Ryan was spurred to move the general discussion on to what he considered to be the 'real' business of policing sooner rather than later.

"How come Major Crimes is taking the lead on this, then? Seems a job for Special Ops, if y'ask me," one bright spark was bound to ask.

Ryan was unfazed.

"The Chief Constable has asked Major Crimes—and me, in particular—to assume responsibility for leading this operation, not only because of the overwhelming increase in gang-related murders in the area, but because of the connection to several linked investigations on our books dating back to Moffa's day," he said, referring to the area's former gangland kingpin.

He flipped open a cardboard file on the desk at the front of the room and pulled out a single, blown-up photograph of a man, which he tacked onto the centre of the whiteboard.

"This is Paul Evershed, more commonly known by his street name, 'Ludo'."

Instantly, there were murmurs of recognition. The man known as 'Ludo'—thanks to an unfortunate predilection for Quaaludes back in the eighties—was infamous. He'd been the late Jimmy Moffa's right-hand man and, in addition to any number of less glamorous murders and grievous assaults, he'd been a key player in the high-profile escape of one of the nation's most notorious serial killers, The Hacker. Ludo had been on the run since then and remained one of the country's Top Ten Most Wanted Criminals. Every officer in the room knew that, if he was involved with the Smoggie gang, the stakes just got much higher.

"Our informants told us he was down on the Costa Brava," a man Ryan knew to be Detective Inspector Paul Coates called out. He was Gallagher's senior from the Drugs Squad, and generally known to be mild-mannered and approachable, having seen most things during his thirty years on the Force.

"If he was, he isn't any more," Ryan replied. "We have reason to believe Ludo has been involved in the murder of one or more known drug dealers right here, in the North East."

"Aye, I know the ones. But, surely, Evershed would be smart enough never to show his face around these parts again?" Coates remarked. "He's not exactly inconspicuous, is he? Any copper within a hundred-mile radius would know him on sight."

Ryan nodded. It was true that, at a muscular six feet five, with a weathered, pock-marked face, Paul Evershed was not easily forgotten.

"We don't know why Ludo's come back," he admitted. "But we have a number of witness sightings of somebody fitting his description, in connection with at least three murders."

Ryan sought out Lowerson, who was seated on the front row between MacKenzie and Phillips, Yates having chosen to sit in the row behind.

"Detective Constable Jack Lowerson from my team in Major Crimes has been Acting SIO on three of the most recent murders," he said. "Those murders now fall under the broader remit of OPERATION WATCHMAN, so it would be helpful for us to have a reminder of what his investigation uncovered before we move forward. Jack?"

Lowerson ran his fingers through his hair, then heaved himself up from an uncomfortable plastic tub chair to join Ryan at the front of the room.

"Thank you, sir."

He faced his friends and colleagues, who waited patiently for him to begin, and found himself momentarily lost for words. There was a constriction in his throat and, as his eyes skittered over the crowd to rest on Melanie Yates, it became painful.

"I—ah, thank you," he said again, and licked his lips. "Over the last week or so, myself and Acting Detective Constable Melanie Yates have led an investigation into three murders we believe to be connected. In each case, a man's body was found fully or partially nude, badly beaten and with all identifying traces removed, including fingertips. The bodies were recovered from various dump sites, none of which the forensic team believe to have been the same site where the victims were killed. Little or no DNA has been recovered—"

Yates was frowning at him, and he began to stammer.

"Ah, th-that said, we were able to identify each of the men given their previous involvement with the police over the years. For example, the most recent victim, Daniel "The Demon" Hepple, was already well-known to us. He had an extensive record for dealing and possession, aggravated assault and other violent crimes, so we were able to enter and search Hepple's home in Whitley Bay quite soon after his body was found. We believe that his assailant entered via the back door, which was smashed in, and that Hepple was attacked in his kitchen according to the blood spatter pattern identified by the forensics team."

"Any other DNA?" Ryan asked, but Lowerson shook his head.

"Unfortunately, our search did not yield DNA belonging to Paul Evershed, which we already have on file for comparison. However, door-to-door enquiries threw up several witness sightings of a man in the area matching Ludo's description, as well as some CCTV footage we were able to recover. We received similar witness statements with almost identical descriptions following the other murders, too. However, that's all circumstantial."

From her position in the audience, Yates waited for Lowerson to mention the ladies' knickers and burner mobile found at Hepple's home address, both of which were a vital link connecting Daniel Hepple to Bobby Singh, a wealthy businessman and philanthropist they strongly suspected as being a founding member, if not *the* founding member, of the Smoggies. They had already established that the burner mobile belonged to Singh's girlfriend, Rochelle, who had been conducting an affair with Hepple before he died. When they'd tracked the woman down only days ago, she'd been terrified that Singh had got wind of the affair and ordered Hepple's death, and, if that was the case, equally terrified of any further ramifications for herself. They'd hoped to convince Rochelle to become an informant for their team and it had seemed possible that she would agree.

Except, Rochelle hadn't been answering her phone, lately.

*Another thing to worry about.*

Yates said none of this, and was relieved when Ryan saved her the trouble. He was, of course, already fully briefed on their investigation but it was important to share any leads with the rest of the task force.

"Wasn't there a burner mobile found at the victim's home?"

Lowerson shifted his feet, feeling sweat begin to pool at the base of his spine.

"Yes, sir. There was a burner mobile found at Hepple's address, but the investigation is still ongoing—"

"The mobile belonged to a person of interest, sir," Yates interjected, still struggling to understand why Jack was being so evasive when the very success of the operation depended on transparency. "We also recovered personal items from Hepple's home, which we assume belong to the same individual, but we've been unable to confirm that without obtaining their consent to provide a DNA sample."

Ryan made a rumbling sound of agreement.

"Aside from not producing voluntary DNA, is this POI willing to co-operate?" he asked, looking between them both. "Are we talking about a suspect, or an informant?"

When Jack didn't answer, Yates picked up the baton again.

"Our working theory is that the individual is not a likely suspect, but may prove to be a useful asset to our investigation as an informant. For that reason, we're continuing to protect their name and any identifiable details, sir."

"Understood," Ryan said, flicking an interested glance between the pair of them. "Keep working on it, Yates."

"Yes, sir."

Ryan turned back to Lowerson, who looked positively unwell.

"What else can you tell us about Hepple's known associates? How can we be sure that Ludo is connected?"

Lowerson recovered himself.

"We've been working closely with colleagues in the Drugs Squad," he said, with a nod towards Gallagher and Coates, who were seated at the edge of the room, nearest the door. "As far as we know, Hepple is believed to have had a longstanding connection with the Moffa brothers. They are no longer active, and we assume they've been turfed out. If we further assume the Smoggies were responsible for that, it would be a safe bet that Hepple transferred his allegiance to them."

"In that case, why kill him?" somebody else asked. "If Hepple was a successful dealer, with a long track record of loyal service, he'd be a key player in the Smoggies. Why kill him, unless there was some kind of serious infraction?"

"Hepple died around the time the circus came back to town," Phillips put in, thinking of the travelling circus owned by Samantha's late father. "The return of the circus after eight years of being away would've opened up a new supply chain for anybody looking to expand their business," he explained, for any slow learners in the room.

"Or somebody who planned to set up shop on their own," Ryan surmised. "Defection wouldn't go down well with the ruling gang."

"Sir, we can't be sure that Hepple was planning to strike out on his own," Lowerson said, shifting his feet as pain radiated through his injured leg.

Ryan noticed the action and frowned, lifting a chin towards the chair he had vacated earlier.

"Have a seat," he murmured, but Lowerson gave a subtle shake of his head.

"Thank you, sir, but I'm fine standing."

"The kid's right," Gallagher intoned, his gravelly voice interrupting any further argument. "At this point, we don't know for sure that Ludo killed Hepple, and we don't know for sure it was because they were planning to set up on their own. It's all conjecture. Sounds like a dead-end, if y'ask me."

Ryan gave him another mild smile, then reached for his folder to draw out another photograph, this time of a much younger man somewhere in his thirties. He had the glossy good looks and grooming of a premiership footballer, and the dark, almost black eyes of a man who had seen things.

*Done things.*

"This is Balbir Singh, more commonly known as 'Bobby'," Ryan said, as he tacked the image onto the board next to Ludo. "He was born in Middlesbrough, where he spent his formative years in and out of juvenile detention. Nowadays, he's big into property development, construction, venture capital...everything. He has his fingers in a lot of pies, and spends a good chunk of time giving after-dinner speeches about the rehabilitation of child offenders, and how important it is never to give up on the so-called 'bad' apples."

"How touching," Phillips remarked, and began to unwrap the emergency Kit Kat he'd stashed inside his breast pocket.

"Indeed," Ryan drawled. "One cannot fail to be inspired. Except, of course, until you learn that Singh is suspected of dealing in various illegitimate business ventures, including drugs and prostitution, modern slavery and sex trafficking."

"We've only got rumours," one of the inspectors from the Vice Team chimed in. "We had a line on somebody who might've been willing to talk, a while back, but that went cold."

"How?"

"They buggered off," Prince shrugged. "Absconded, whatever you want to call it."

Ryan's lips fell into a hard line. Detective Inspector Terry Prince was as an officer of the 'Old World', and no amount of training in diversity or equality was going to make much of a dent. He was an imposing man of around fifty, who had been promoted thanks to a series of successful undercover operations in his formative years. Unfortunately, Ryan had to wonder whether the experience had jaded him too much, so that the ordinary level of compassion he demanded of all officers in his command was no longer present.

"Absconded, or went missing?" he asked, softly. "I'd say it's highly suspicious that a person who might have been able to provide you with useful intelligence has suddenly disappeared. I don't recall my team being made aware of this, either. In the spirit of sharing information, I presume I'll find a report on my desk by the end of the day?"

Conscious that the Chief Constable was still in the room, Prince folded his arms and gave a tight smile.

"Happy to," he lied.

Sensing the beginnings of dissent, Gallagher took the opportunity to throw in his tuppenceworth.

"If Lowerson's informant can confirm a link between the murders and Singh, then we'll be cookin' on gas," he said, drawing a couple of muffled laughs around the room. "But without it, all you've got is a lot of speculation. Yeah, there've been rumblings on the street about Singh, but that could be from his old days as much as anything else. He's always admitted to being a reformed youth."

"He's high profile," Coates added, with a sly note of caution for the Chief Constable's benefit. If they were going after someone like Bobby Singh, he wanted to be the first to register his concerns. "Singh is a patron of local charities, he builds low-cost housing for people in the region, and he's popular in all kinds of influential circles—"

"Exactly, and it could all be a front," Ryan cut in. "He wouldn't be the first to create a veneer of legitimacy."

He turned to the Fraud Squad again.

"Have you looked into Bobby Singh's financials? It would be helpful to know the source of his income."

DI Salam nodded, then pulled a face.

"It's like DI Coates has already said," she replied. "From what we've been able to find, Singh has legitimate business interests in large-scale property development companies, construction firms and the like. Mainly held off-shore," she added, sourly.

"Can't you drill down a bit more into the company structure?" Ryan asked.

"I'd love to," Salam said, with feeling. "Unfortunately, we can't go much further without a warrant, and that'll be hard to get without any direct link between Singh and any of these murders."

She sighed, and sent Ryan an apologetic look.

"Gallagher's right. We need a witness."

Ryan nodded, turning back to his team of murder detectives.

"If Singh is responsible for the Smoggie gang, he's a scourge on this region that we need to eliminate. But if we can't establish an evidential link, we can't start digging any deeper into his company structures or financial reports. We need a whistle-blower," he said, turning back to Lowerson. "We need that informant."

Lowerson nodded miserably and returned to his chair, his hope of being able to avoid the topic of Rochelle now abandoned.

"Yates? Continue to work on bringing that informant in," Ryan ordered. "If they're a link between Singh and an active murder, they need our full attention."

"Yes, sir."

Ryan stuck his hands in the back pockets of his jeans.

"The main priority is to find and apprehend Paul Evershed. He should be considered extremely dangerous, not only because of his previous offences but because he has nothing whatsoever to lose; you can only be given one life sentence, after all."

There were nods around the room, while people stared at the images on the whiteboard and committed them to memory.

"If Ludo is back and in the employment of Bobby Singh, that means Singh will be harbouring and protecting him," Ryan said. "I want a full list of Singh's known properties— ones he owns, and ones he is currently building or has built—as well as any vehicles registered to his name, any of his businesses, or any of his known associates."

He paused, then added, "I want to know about any vehicle Singh owns, but *doesn't have on the road.* Those ones would be easy to keep under the radar, if he changed the number plates."

"We can pull that information together from the data we already have," DI Salam assured him. "I know that Henderson—my sergeant—already has a list of Singh's known addresses, which we've already shared with the Drugs Squad."

Ryan thanked her.

More than two hours had passed since the briefing began, yet he was pleased to note that there had been no early exits or half-concealed yawns. Whether they admitted it or not, every person in the room wanted to be a part of something that was bigger and more important than themselves.

"While we're looking for Ludo, I want surveillance on Bobby Singh," he said, catching Chief Constable Morrison's eye. Whilst she didn't look overjoyed at the prospect of them putting a local philanthropist under surveillance, neither did she put up any protest.

*Good.*

"I'm tellin' you, mate, you're barking up the wrong tree," Gallagher argued. "He's too high profile to get himself tangled in drugs and that."

"Then he'll have nothing to hide," Ryan countered. "Will he?"

Gallagher slumped back in his chair, arms folded, while Ryan worked out the finer details of the surveillance operation.

"We need to liaise with local welfare organisations and healthcare centres, as well as schools and Social Services," Ryan told them. "I want a full and complete list of any reports of children demonstrating the key behavioural changes that would indicate they've been recruited by a gang. I want to know the addresses of highly vulnerable adults, too."

"That'll take forever and a day," Gallagher complained. "It'll be easier to have a word with a few junkies and see where the supply's coming from."

Ryan shook his head, battling frustration.

"This isn't about trading low-level intel from people who probably can't tell us anything new, even if they wanted to. We need to go out there and do this the old-fashioned way, with a bit of legwork. We need to stay ahead, not try and play catch up all the time."

He paused, holding up a hand to fend off any further comments.

"Listen to me: there's a killer out there, roaming the streets as if he owned them. He isn't afraid of us, and he's angry. We took away Ludo's lifestyle, his power and his employment. If we're right about this, he's back, and he has a new boss who's even more dangerous than the one before."

"Why? Why would he come back?" MacKenzie wondered aloud.

"He's an animal," Ryan breathed, turning to stare into Paul Evershed's dark, pixelated eyes. "A rabid dog we should've brought in long before now."

Ryan looked at the faces staring out at him from the wall, and thought they were a deadly combination. One, with all the brains and means; the other, with the muscle and cunning to kill.

"Find the dog, and you'll find his master," he said. "Ludo won't stray too far from the hand that feeds him."

# CHAPTER 6

Bobby Singh stood inside his large, tastefully designed orangery and looked out across the manicured lawn, which was crawling with workmen who were beginning to lay the paving around a new swimming pool. They'd worked tirelessly for five days now, digging and installing new pipework, foundations and concrete lining, but their progress was still too slow; he wanted them off his property, so he could enjoy looking out at the gleaming water without wondering whether one of them was a bloody pig.

"Sir? There's a gentleman here to see you."

Bobby cocked his head at the soft sound of his housekeeper's voice but didn't turn.

"Is he a big bastard?"

"Yes, sir."

He took a small sip of the iced water he held in his hand.

"Is he alone?"

"Yes, sir."

Bobby looked across the room to where a thin man with pale blue eyes and sharp features stood with his feet spread and his hands clasped. A tiny black ear-piece was just visible inside his left ear, and one side of his summer jacket bulged where his weapon was concealed beneath. The man nodded at his unspoken order and moved to the doorway to frisk the new arrival.

A few minutes later, heavy footsteps sounded on the marble floor.

"You carrying?" Singh's personal guard asked, and Ludo bared his teeth in what might have passed for a smile.

"Course I am," he growled. "You gonna take it off me, prick?"

Singh laughed, and turned away from the window.

"Give him the piece, Ludo," he said. "I haven't got time for a dog fight."

Paul Evershed reached inside his jacket and pulled out a handgun, which he set on one of the ornamental iron tables nearby. Then, he reached for the spare inside his other pocket, and for the knife inside the specially-made pouch of his boot.

"Didn't come with the full arsenal today," he explained, with a note of apology.

The guard patted him down, keeping a weather eye on Ludo's meaty hands, and then stepped away.

"Clear, sir."

Evershed waited until the guard had taken up a position a few feet away from Singh, then shook out another thin knife, which fell from one of his sleeves with a clatter on the floor.

"Oops," he said, lips peeling away from his teeth in another shark-like smile. "Miss something, did we?"

The guard felt the blood drain from his face, and small pearls of sweat broke out on his forehead as he shot a nervous glance towards his employer.

"I'm sorry, sir—"

Singh drained the last of his water and set the glass down, dabbed his lips with a cloth napkin and then turned to Robbo with a smile on his handsome face.

"C'mon, mate, it's an easy mistake to make."

The guard looked for any sign of a trap, and saw nothing but sincerity.

"Th-thank you, Mr Singh. I appreciate that, I—"

"Go and have a breather, son," Bobby suggested. "Here, take this glass back to the kitchen and have yourself a ham sandwich, alright?"

"Don't you want me to stay here?"

Singh gave him another smile, and jerked his head towards the door.

"Go on," he urged. "Take a breather."

Robbo felt their eyes watching him as he walked towards the door, expecting to feel a bullet tear through his flesh at any moment. When it didn't come, he lifted his shoulders and let out a soft sigh of relief. That was a lucky esc—

There was an explosion of pain as Ludo's fist connected with the back of his head, and he fell to the floor, where his nose broke with a sickening crunch against the marble.

Singh walked across to flick a switch on the wall and, moments later, bespoke blinds rolled down the windows in the orangery to block the view from any prying eyes.

"Make it quick," he told Ludo. "We've got things to discuss."

---

Ryan emerged from the briefing like a drowning man, and breathed deeply of the less stagnant air in the corridor outside the conference room. He was contemplating a quick sojourn to the vending machine for a coffee, when he was intercepted by the Chief Constable.

"Have you got a minute?"

It wasn't a request.

Banking down his frustration, Ryan followed Sandra Morrison into her large, corner office. It was a clinical room for the most part, with plain walls and furnishings, but was softened by the addition of several cluttered bookshelves that were brimming with paperbacks and policing manuals. Somewhat enviously, Ryan found himself wondering when on Earth she found the time to read them.

"Shut the door, would you?"

Morrison had a natural aptitude for both policing and politics, which was crucial for someone of her rank and entirely anathema to Ryan, who was contemptuous of the kind of political game-playing that brought resources and revenue into the constabulary. Whether he liked it or not, he was game enough to acknowledge that the world needed every type of person and, as far as bosses went, he'd definitely had a lot worse.

"Take a seat," she said.

"Thank you, ma'am."

Morrison waited until he settled himself in one of the visitor's chairs before flopping into her own desk chair and linking her hands on the top of her shiny beech wood desk.

"The meeting went well," she said, falling back on pleasantries. "Some resistance from Drugs and Vice, but no more than you'd expect. They're used to leading ops, not following."

Ryan lifted a shoulder.

"They'll come around," he said, and wondered if it was true. "The situation's getting out of hand, and we need to pull together. I've delegated a chunk of my caseload, so I can give Operation Watchman my full attention, ma'am."

Morrison shifted awkwardly.

"I'm afraid you'll need to make room for one more case on your roster," she said, and pulled open a desk drawer to retrieve a thin stack of papers which she pushed towards him. "Take a look at this."

Ryan raised a single, dark eyebrow, but fell back on good manners.

"What case?"

Morrison nodded towards the sheaf, which he began to skim-read.

"A house fire?" He was incredulous, and a little confused. Accidental deaths following ordinary house fires were sad, to be sure, but they were not a matter for CID.

"It's not that simple," she told him. "In the early hours of Friday morning, a house went up in flames with its elderly owners still inside. The occupants were Alan and Joan Watson, both eighty, both longstanding residents of Penshaw—"

"As in, Penshaw Monument?" he asked.

Morrison nodded, smiling slightly. Ryan had been a permanent resident in their neck of the world for so long, she sometimes forgot that he was not a native of the North East. He was a Devonshire lad, one who'd craved rugged coastlines and large, open spaces without any of the softer edges.

"Yes, Penshaw is the village at the foot of the monument," she said, referring to the large, neo-classical folly atop a hill overlooking the old mining village. "Most people think it's in County Durham, but the village falls within the borough of Sunderland, and therefore Tyne and Wear Area Command."

Ryan gave her a level look, knowing that she'd neatly covered off any potential arguments as to police jurisdiction, and tapped the papers in his hand.

"The summary says that Alan Watson was pronounced dead at the scene, after his wife tried to drag him out of the house. It's heroic, but I can't see that it's a matter for my team. There's no mention of arson, or fire-setting—"

Morrison shook her head.

"I had a call from Pinter," she explained, referring to the Senior Pathologist attached to the Constabulary. "He performed an autopsy on Alan Watson's body over the weekend and his preliminary report rules out the presence of any smoke in the dead man's lungs."

Despite his reservations, Ryan's interest was piqued. It would be normal to find large quantities of smoke inside the lungs of a regular victim of fire...unless, the victim was already dead before the fire began.

"You're thinking it's suspicious?" he asked. "I can ask one of the team to check it out—"

He trailed off as a thought struck him.

"Pinter doesn't usually report to you," he remarked. "And he doesn't do weekend overtime unless it's important. What's so special about Alan Watson?"

"It's not so much him, as his daughter," Morrison said. "Sally Emerson, née Watson, is head of the local council. She's very popular, and very influential."

"Let me guess," Ryan drawled. "She plays golf with the Commissioner and she's demanding the full service, all bells and whistles?"

"Assistant Commissioner," Morrison muttered, and then held her hands up. "Actually, Sally hasn't been making too much noise, but the AC wants to get ahead of it and be prepared in case that changes."

When Ryan continued to look unimpressed, she flushed.

"Look, I know you couldn't give a flying—"

"Fig?" he interrupted, helpfully.

"*Fig*," she agreed, testily. "But it's in all our interests to keep things running smoothly. We need to be seen to be taking steps, which means I need a senior officer—I need *you*—to get down there and do your thing."

Ryan glanced at the papers again and thought of an old man amidst the flames.

*It was no way to die.*

"Look, all you have to do is go down there and show your face. Palm it off onto Lowerson, or one of the others, once you've set things in motion," she added.

Ryan thought of the young man he'd mentored these past years, and felt a tension headache start in the base of his skull.

"I'll see to it," he said.

# CHAPTER 7

"It's nearly lunchtime."

Ryan overtook a slow-moving lorry on the motorway as they made their way to the village of Penshaw, then glanced across at his sergeant in the passenger seat.

"That's very observant of you, Frank."

Phillips pursed his lips as he watched the passing scenery, then tried again.

"All I'm saying is, there's a nice little farm shop at the bottom of the hill in Penshaw, near the monument."

"Good to know."

Since subtlety wasn't working, Phillips cut to the chase.

"Look, son, you don't get muscles like mine eating lettuce leaves," he said, without any irony whatsoever. "A man like me needs regular protein… besides, you like a bacon stottie just as much as I do."

Ryan laughed at that.

"Frank, I'm not sure there's a man alive who likes bacon stotties as much as you," he said. "But I wouldn't want you fainting on me, so we'll make a pit-stop on the way."

Phillips perked up immediately.

"You know it makes sense," he said, wisely, and then turned his mind to the task ahead. "Nice little village, Penshaw. Used to be, all the miners lived there and worked in the colliery nearby. That all changed after the strike, of course."

He fell quiet, thinking back to when he'd been a young police constable, and the job he'd been asked to do.

"—close?"

Phillips tuned back in, and realised he'd missed half of Ryan's question.

"What's that?"

"I said, from what I understand, many people who live in the village are ex-miners or the children of mining families," Ryan repeated. "When did the colliery close?"

"Must've been back in '85," Phillips murmured. "After the strike failed."

Ryan heard a note in his friend's voice and told himself to tread carefully. His had been a privileged upbringing, for which he was both grateful and embarrassed, in equal measure. He had never experienced the fear and uncertainty some families had lived. He had never worried about where his next meal would come from, so he would not pretend to know how difficult it would have been for thousands of men and their families to lose their livelihoods in such a way.

All he could do was use the opportunities and advantages he'd been given to be a decent person; or, at least, a better one than he was yesterday.

"I was only four or five at the time," he said, into the quiet car. "I learned about what happened, later."

*In a politics class, at his boarding school,* Ryan thought, with a measure of self-loathing.

"A lot of people are still feeling the effects of what happened back then," Phillips said. "You get these academic types talking about economic policy and how fossil fuels were on the way out..."

He gave an irritable shrug.

"All that might be true," he continued. "But, if changes needed to be made, they didn't have to happen the *way* they did. The *speed* they did. Now, all the old steel and mining towns have generations of families on the dole...there were some who bounced back and re-trained or moved on. Some people could do that, but plenty couldn't."

"It still hurts," Ryan said, softly.

"Yeah, lad," Phillips sighed. "It still hurts."

---

Melanie Yates watched Lowerson surreptitiously over the top of her desktop monitor at Police Headquarters. They worked from a bank of six desks, with his directly opposite her own, whilst MacKenzie was seated to Lowerson's right. He'd avoided speaking to her since the briefing and was, she suspected, relying on a certain amount of

British reserve in the hope she wouldn't raise anything too awkward in the company of their colleagues. Well, much as she would have preferred it to remain that way, she had a job to do.

Pushing back from her chair, she squared her shoulders and stood up.

"DC Lowerson? I'd like ten minutes to discuss our strategy in respect of the informant," she said, coolly.

Lowerson flushed, and shot an embarrassed glance towards MacKenzie, who was studying her monitor with sudden and complete intensity.

"Of course," he muttered, rising from his chair. "We can find an empty meeting room."

"Fine," she said.

As the pair of them stalked out of the room, MacKenzie risked lifting her head above the parapet, and gave an indulgent shake of her head. One week, they were Love's Young Dream, the next, it was a wasteland.

Ah, to be young again.

———

"Rochelle isn't answering any calls," Yates said, as soon as the meeting room door clicked shut. "The last time I tried, I got an automated message saying the number was no longer in use."

Lowerson walked over to the water fountain in the corner of the room, where he filled and re-filled three cups in quick succession.

"Did you hear what I said?" Yates demanded, watching him with narrowed eyes. "Something might have happened to her. She was worried Singh would find out about her relationship with Hepple, or that he'd find out she'd been talking to us. What if he did? What if he found out?"

"We don't know that," Lowerson said, crushing the paper cup in his hand.

Yates looked at him as though he was a stranger.

"What's the matter with you?" she demanded. "Don't tell me you haven't considered the prospect she might be missing, or worse."

Lowerson deposited the cup into the recycling bin, and composed himself.

"Have you considered the possibility that Rochelle doesn't want anything to do with us?" he said. "She never actually agreed to work with us, did she?"

Yates opened her mouth, then shut it again.

"Not in as many words," she admitted. "But why would she meet with us, if she wasn't open to the prospect? All we needed was another opportunity to talk, to convince her she'd be safe…"

Lowerson let out a mirthless laugh.

"Yeah? And how do you know we'd be able to keep her safe, Mel? Can we say for certain that he wouldn't be able to find her, and hurt her?" His eyes blazed across the room, and then he looked away, out of the window and across the car park.

"We have witness protection programmes," she said, a bit shaken by his tone. "We could have offered her immunity, in exchange for testifying against him, if she was willing. She was a link to Singh's inner circle, and now we've lost her."

Lowerson looked away again, feeling nauseous. He remembered, all too clearly, the impossible deal he'd offered Rochelle only a few days before.

"Has she turned up to work?" he asked, in a dull tone.

"I rang *Rochelle White Interiors* on Friday," Yates replied. "I posed as a potential customer looking to have my office re-designed, and asked to speak to the lady in charge. The receptionist said that she hadn't been in that day, but she'd return my call once she was back. I still haven't heard."

She paced the meeting room, thinking of what more could be done without arousing suspicion.

"Anything reported to Missing Persons?" Lowerson found himself asking, but Yates shook her head.

"Nothing," she said, curtly. "Although I haven't checked the alerts this morning."

Lowerson waited with a fatalistic, sinking feeling in his belly, while Melanie scrolled through the automatic e-mail alert she'd received from their colleagues in the Missing Persons team. Seconds ticked by, then he heard her sharp intake of breath.

"Rochelle White, reported missing first thing this morning. Last seen leaving the office last Wednesday afternoon."

Yates raised her eyes, and it was as though she looked straight through him.

"Who reported it?" he asked.

"Somebody from her office," Yates replied. "It wasn't Singh, which is unusual, considering she lives with him."

Lowerson blinked, seeing dark spots floating in his vision.

"It'll be one for our team," he said. "We need to discuss this with Ryan."

"He told me to investigate the asset and bring Rochelle in," Yates replied. "If she's been reported missing, I can go around, ask some questions—"

"*No!*" The word burst from his lips before he could prevent it. "I don't want you going in there alone."

There was an infinitesimal pause.

"Come with me, then," she said, and couldn't have known what she was asking of him. "We can go together, and find out why he hasn't reported his girlfriend missing."

"Anything to do with Bobby Singh falls under Operation Watchman, now," he insisted. "It isn't up to us to decide what action to take, and an officer of DI level or above needs to determine whether to treat her disappearance as suspicious, if she's disappeared at all."

Her jaw dropped.

"So, that's it? We just sit around here, twiddling our thumbs?"

"We've both got plenty to be getting on with," Lowerson said.

"Jack—"

"Mel, let me tell you something," he interrupted her. "I admire your dedication and your drive, but you have a lot to learn. You're a trainee detective constable, not the bloody superintendent. You can't just go barging into a volatile situation without getting the go-ahead from your superiors."

Yates could barely swallow the hypocrisy, and said as much.

"Really, Jack? You mean, like the time you went barging into a dangerous situation without waiting for back-up on Holy Island, and ended up in a coma for six months?"

"Mel—" he said, in a warning tone.

"Or, how about the time you jumped head-first into a relationship with your boss, who also happened to be a certified nut-job? You'd been promised a nice little promotion to detective sergeant, without having to put in the work…or, at least, not the same *kind* of work," she raged on, letting all the anger and hurt finally spill out. "Did you get the go-ahead from Ryan for that? No, you bloody didn't, so don't lecture me about police hierarchies and respect for authority, Jack. Not until you've taken a good, hard look at yourself in the mirror."

On that note, she scooped up her notepad and prepared to leave, but not without a final, parting shot.

"One last thing. Don't think I didn't notice how evasive you were at the briefing," she said, in a voice trembling with anger. "I don't know why you're behaving the way you are, but I'll find out, sooner or later. And, when I do, you'd better have a good reason. If I have to go around you, I will."

When the door slammed shut, Lowerson closed his eyes and leaned back against the wall, hoping for a miracle.

# CHAPTER 8

Penshaw village was bathed in sunshine by the time Ryan and Phillips polished off the last of a Lunchtime Special at the farm shop, which nestled at the foot of Penshaw Hill and boasted prime views of the monument at the top. An equestrian centre occupied the neighbouring plot of land, and horses grazed beneath its classical columns while daytime tourists climbed the steep pathway to enjoy panoramic views of Durham Cathedral, to the south-west; the coast to the east; Herrington County Park to the immediate west and, on a clear day, the Cheviot Hills on the far northern horizon.

"See the park over there?" Phillips nodded across the main road, where mature trees and parkland now grew. "That's where the colliery used to be."

Ryan followed his line of sight as they walked from the farm shop along the main road, towards the centre of the village.

"Looks lovely," he was bound to say. "I seem to recognise the name?"

"They have concerts at Herrington Park, and the Olympic torch passed through it back in 2012," Phillips replied.

"I'm glad they put the old site to good use."

Phillips nodded.

"There's a memorial in the park, dedicated to all the miners who lost their lives over the years," he said, and Ryan made a mental note to seek it out. "There's an amphitheatre, play park, and all that."

Ryan listened, and then frowned.

"There'll be a tight community around here, Frank. People who look out for one another, especially the elderly. Who would want to hurt Alan Watson, an old man of eighty?"

Phillips merely shook his head.

"You're always the first to tell me that age isn't a barrier to somebody being a wrong 'un," he said, matter-of-factly. "We've seen plenty of old thieves and vagabonds during our time. Plenty of wives who suffocate their husbands, or the other way around."

Ryan had to admit it was true.

"That line of thinking won't go down well with his daughter, Sally Emerson," he remarked. "Wouldn't look good for her next election campaign, for one thing."

"I never knew you were so cynical," Phillips joked.

"Really? Must've been living under a rock, all these years," Ryan grinned, and then sobered quickly as he spotted an incongruous black van parked up ahead.

"Faulkner's here," he said, referring to the Senior CSI in charge of the forensics unit. "Maybe he can give us a clue."

---

Alan and Joan Watson lived in a two-up, two-down, red-brick cottage at the end of a terrace on Penshaw Lane, a road running parallel to the farm shop and equestrian facility, with direct and unspoilt views of the monument. It ran from the former colliery site to the west, all the way to the epicentre of the old village to the east, with its quaint pubs and church, although Ryan and Phillips never made it that far.

"Hell's bells," the latter declared, as they spotted the charred exterior of the miner's cottage Alan Watson had lived in since he was a boy. "Must've been a real blaze."

Ryan made a small sound of agreement, while his eyes scanned the immediate vicinity. Behind them, the monument loomed over the village like a miniature Acropolis, a silent sentinel as the villagers went about the business of living and, in this case, dying. The cottage was almost at the junction to the main road, nearest the old colliery site, with an alleyway running behind it which gave access to the back yard.

In front of the house, two constables were stationed beside a police line, which had been set up to prevent a small but determined crowd of villagers from despoiling what may be a crime scene. A white forensic tent had been set up at the doorway, to afford a degree of privacy for the

CSIs who went about the business of sweeping the shell for evidence.

"It's accessible from the front or the rear, with plenty of scope to make a quick getaway," Ryan concluded. "The house is a ten-second walk from the main road heading north or south—less, if they were running."

"Surely, somebody would have seen them."

Ryan was doubtful.

"The fire started sometime in the early hours," he said. "It was a weekday, not a Saturday night, and this is hardly a party capital so most people would have been tucked up in bed. I doubt anybody would have seen anything amiss until it was too late, especially under cover of darkness."

"Fire spread to the neighbour's house, too," Phillips said, noting the empty windows and dark wash of smoke and char that stained the brickwork across the terraces.

"Hard to know if there was forced entry, since the doors are completely gone," Ryan muttered to himself.

"Eh? Nobody locks their doors around here, son. If somebody wanted inside, they could've walked straight in."

Ryan refrained from entering into a debate about home safety, and simply nodded. It was another mark of a good community, that people didn't feel the need to bar their doors, even at night. He wondered if they would feel the same way, after all was said and done.

"We can check with the family, when we speak to them," he said, raising a hand as Faulkner emerged from the tented entrance. "For now, let's see where it all started."

With a quick look in either direction, Ryan crossed the road to greet the CSI, who was dressed in his usual overalls and hair net. In deference to the sunshine, he'd removed the mask and hood, revealing a man with a shiny face and matted, mid-brown hair sticking to the temples.

"Good to see you, Tom."

"Ryan, Phillips," he smiled warmly. "Bit of a change to our usual grisly lot, isn't it? Quite nice, not having a body to deal with."

"Don't say I never do anything for you," Ryan quipped. "How's it looking in there?"

Faulkner scratched the top of his head, and blew out a breath.

"We've given it a good once-over, but there isn't much to play with; no leftover blood stains or anything like that, and the interior is still a bit soggy after being hosed down on Friday. The Fire Investigator's still in there, if you want to have a word with her, but I can tell you what she told me: the origin of the fire seems to have been in the living room," he dipped his head towards the blown-out window at the front of the house, now protected by plastic sheeting. "Apparently, the old feller was a lifelong smoker, and they found the remains of an ashtray on the floor, next to what's left of a sofa and a bottle of some kind. We'll test them both."

"Easy enough for someone to set a fire and make it look accidental," Phillips mused. "They could've lit a cigarette and let it catch on the sofa after bashing his head in, or many a thing."

"That's what I love about you, Frank—your optimistic outlook!" Faulkner grinned. "You'll be telling me it was the Russians, next."

Phillips started to deny it, then began to wonder whether the old boy had been mixed up in any espionage.

"Pinter will let us know whether there was a fracture to Alan's skull," Ryan cut across any wild theories his sergeant might have been concocting. "He's still looking at the body to get beyond the fire damage. In the meantime, I'd like to know how Joan Watson found her husband, and where he was lying."

"The son stopped by here, earlier," Faulkner told him. "Asking a lot of questions, wanting to know if we'd found anything suspicious."

"Was he, now? That would be..." Ryan paused to check the name of Alan's son. "Simon?"

But Faulkner frowned.

"No, not that one. He introduced himself as Mike."

"Mike Emerson," Ryan provided. "Alan's son-in-law."

"That's the one. He left pretty soon after, but he said he was visiting with his mother-in-law, who was getting out of hospital this morning. If you want to have a word with the widow, she's staying with the other son, Simon, who lives just up the street."

Ryan looked towards the village and nodded.

"Thanks, Tom."

———

A potent smell of smoke, char and burnt plastic clung to the material of their clothes when Ryan and Phillips emerged from the cottage some time later. It was a pitiful sight, to see an old couple's worldly possessions reduced to blackened sludge, and Ryan knew only too well the heartache of losing small, meaningful things; all the photographs and trinkets collected over the course of many years. It had been a couple of years since Anna's cottage in Durham had gone up in flames, but they had been devastated to lose what they had worked so hard to build.

*A home.*

"Apparently, the Watsons had lived in that house for nearly forty years," Ryan said, recalling the case summary as they made their way along Penshaw Lane towards the old village centre. "It's devastating, but the Fire Investigator hasn't found any of the usual evidence of fire-setting, or arson. At the moment, all we've got is the pathology."

"Maybe we'll have a bit more to work with, once we've had a chat with Joan," Phillips said, as they passed a couple of pubs and veered right, along a back road towards the edge of the village. "It's a hard knock, losing your husband and your home, all in one go."

Ryan thought of Anna again, and nodded.

"Doesn't bear thinking about," he murmured, slowing his pace as they came up alongside a tired-looking bungalow whose window frames were in dire need of re-painting. Parked on the short driveway was an old Volkswagen Beetle that had seen better days, and a black cat was stretched out next to its back wheel, shading itself from the sun.

"This is the place."

They passed the postman on the way up the short pathway to the front door, and exchanged pleasantries.

"Sometimes they know a bit about the people they deliver to," Phillips shrugged. "Pity he's new to the area."

"They can't all be gossip merchants," Ryan said, and rang the doorbell.

With a force of habit, both men stood up straight, arranged their faces into expressions of unthreatening neutrality, and retrieved their warrant cards ready for inspection.

"Yes?"

The woman who came to the door was somewhere around Phillips' age, in her mid to late fifties, with a mop of corkscrew curls cut artfully into a sweep around her face and dyed an improbable shade of red.

"We'd like to speak to Mrs Joan Watson, please."

"If you're from the papers, you can bugger off," she said, tartly. "She's been through enough heartache, without you vultures picking at her."

"We're not from the papers, Councillor Emerson," Ryan said, having recognised her from the image on her website. "My name is Detective Chief Inspector Ryan, and this is my colleague, Detective Sergeant Phillips. We're from Northumbria CID."

She peered at his warrant card, and seemed to relax a bit.

"Sorry about that," she said, stepping aside so they could enter the narrow hallway. "Not an awful lot happens around here, so, when it does, people can be a bit nosey. Did Gordon send you across?"

They knew she was referring to the Assistant Chief Commissioner, and it was a sticky question.

"We investigate all cases where the cause of death is not clear," Ryan replied, smooth as you like.

Sally gave him an appreciative look, and bent down to retrieve the stack of mail the postman had pushed through the letterbox.

"I see. Well, chief inspector, my mother is very unwell and still recovering. I'd rather she wasn't tired out or upset in any way."

"Of course, we understand," Ryan said. "We're very sorry for the loss to your family. We just want to ascertain the facts, and to understand the timeline of events on Friday morning."

Sally gave a weary shrug.

"It's hit us all pretty hard," she said. "Come through to the living room, and I'll see if she's up to it. This is my brother's house," she explained. "Simon's at work at the moment, but we're taking it in shifts to look after her. I was able to be here today."

"That's what family's for," Phillips said, with a smile. "Does your brother work around here?"

"Ah, yes, not far. Simon's one of the managers at the jobcentre in Sunderland," she explained, and led them into the living room.

It was a spartan affair, with a small PVC-leather sofa that had been torn at some stage, judging from the heavy-duty duct tape wound tightly across one arm. Net curtains blocked some of the sunlight but could not quite prevent it from illuminating the lack of personal mementos aside from a couple of dog-eared paperbacks strewn across a rickety coffee table.

"This is my husband, Mike," she said, as a man rose awkwardly from the sofa with an uncomfortable squeak of flesh. "They're from the police," she told him.

His eyebrows shot into his receding hairline, but he held out a friendly hand.

"Pleased t' meet you," he said, looking between them with open curiosity. "I thought the police had finished taking statements."

"We like to be thorough," Ryan said, and nodded as Sally excused herself to go and see if her mother was up to giving another one.

"I understand you and your wife live elsewhere?" Phillips began, in his easy way.

"Aye, we bought a place over in Shotley Bridge," he said, describing a scenic country town over the border in County Durham. We have a flat in Sunderland," he added quickly, presumably worried that they would question his wife's choice not to live permanently in the borough she represented.

"Very nice," Phillips replied. "Are you from Penshaw originally?"

"Born and raised," Mike replied. "Sally and I went to school together."

"Childhood sweethearts, eh?"

Emerson gave a half-hearted smile, and was saved from any further comment when his wife re-entered the room.

"Mum says she's happy to talk to you," Sally said. "Do you mind if I sit in?"

They heard the squeak of Mike Emerson's legs against the PVC-leather as they left the room.

# CHAPTER 9

Bobby Singh considered himself a very forgiving person.

As a youngster, when the kids at school had made fun of the colour of his skin, he hadn't lashed out in anger.

Oh, no.

He'd learned that the most effective way to enact retribution was to find a person's weakness, and exploit it accordingly. Depending on the gravity of the offence, he was always willing to consider mitigating circumstances and commute the sentence, accordingly.

Hadn't he been lenient with Vinny Bracken, when he'd learned that the fatso's mum had cancer?

He'd only taken one of his ears, and not both as he'd originally planned.

*Practically a saint.*

But he'd learned, very early on, that whilst violence was effective, emotional duress was even more so. Find their blind spot, find the person they loved more than themselves, and you were onto a winner. He'd seen every kind of hard man—and woman, come to that—and every one of them would have you believe they were a lone wolf, someone who didn't give two shits about anybody but themselves.

*Tough. Uncompromising.*

But, scratch under the surface a bit, and there was always some old nana who'd taken them to the park when they were a kid. Sometimes, it was animals. He'd never forget the time he'd seen a grown man and paid assassin cry his bleedin' eyes out because somebody broke his dog's legs.

*Pathetic.*

It paid to know a person's pressure points, to know exactly what made them tick, because violence was only part of the story. The rest came from the *fear* of violence; their own mind making up the shortfall and inevitably conjuring up much worse scenarios than even he might imagine.

Then again, he'd always been very imaginative.

For instance, he was presently occupied in a particularly vivid daydream, one which would result in the ultra-violent death of the two coppers sitting inside a supposedly unmarked vehicle at the end of his street. They were waiting for him to do something, or go somewhere but, when he did, all they would see is a man going about his legitimate business.

Singh had known they were coming, of course; he'd known since the phone call he'd received earlier that day, and had taken the appropriate steps to be prepared. He knew that one of the mugs in the car was on his bankroll, but the other wasn't ripe for turning, so it was as well to make sure that everything appeared above board.

But he wasn't really angry with the jokers in the black Mazda.

No, his anger was directed at another person, one who should have known better than to try to cross him. Apparently, the first lesson hadn't been hard enough.

It was time to continue their education.

———

While Bobby Singh planned his next move, Ryan and Phillips were admitted into Joan Watson's bedroom. There, they found a frail woman propped against a mountain of pillows, with a large bandage covering one side of her face and hair, and more bandages on her hands and arms. The rest of her body was tucked beneath a lacy bedspread and the room held a faint odour of antiseptic and floral perfume.

"Mrs Watson? Thank you for agreeing to see us," Ryan said. It was a cosy space, so he skirted carefully around the edge of the bed to make the introductions.

"I'll find a chair," Sally said, distractedly.

"Don't trouble yourself," Ryan replied. "We're fine standing."

"You boys are from the police?" Joan asked. "Sally said that you'd come from CID?"

Her voice sounded slightly slurred, and Ryan looked at her daughter with a question in his eyes.

"It's the medication they've got her on," Sally explained. "She gets a bit sleepy."

Ryan nodded, and turned back.

"We're very sorry for your loss, Mrs Watson."

"Thank you," she said, closing eyes which felt heavy all of a sudden. "Alan was…"

Her breathing hitched, as she battled fresh tears.

"Oh, Mum…" Sally reached across to squeeze her mother's hand.

"Can I—can I have some water?"

"Of course." Sally made a quick apology and hurried from the room. "I'll make some tea, too."

Once she had left, Joan turned to the pair of them with myopic eyes.

"I didn't want to say, not in front of Sally—he was her Da', after all…"

"Didn't want to say what, Joan?" Ryan asked.

"I didn't want to say that, really, it came as a bit of a relief."

"Alan's death?"

She nodded miserably, and a tear rolled down her bandaged cheek.

"I would never have divorced him," she said quietly. "Never in a million years. Not so long as I could remember how Alan *used* to be…rather than the man he became."

"How d' you mean, pet?" Phillips asked, forgetting the formalities.

"I knew him my whole life," Joan explained, pausing for a moment as they heard the kettle beginning to boil in the kitchen down the hall. "Alan was tall and good-looking, just like you."

She winked at Ryan, and Phillips barely held back a snort. It didn't matter whether the lass was eighteen or eighty, they were drawn like moths to the flame.

Just as well he liked the bloke so much.

"Anyhow, I loved him since I was twelve years old," Joan said. "By the time we were sixteen, we were courting, and he started work down the mine, so we could save up to get married."

Ryan smiled.

"He was hard-working, and he had his principles," she continued, remembering the man she had married on her twentieth birthday. "He worked hard and loved me and the children."

"But?" Ryan prompted, when she fell silent.

"The strike changed him," she said softly. "He was Deputy Chairman of the Mineworker's Union Lodge in Penshaw. He was a proud man, and not afraid to stand up and be heard. When they decided to strike, he did more than his share. We did our bit, too, setting up cafes and all that. Our Sally even got on the train by herself and went down south to pick up the money from the central Union to keep the families going. Scared to death, she was, of somebody stealing it, but it was all there when she came back. Even Mike…well, he tried his best. But, after that day when Tommy Coke got on the bus…"

Ryan had read about the buses the government had laid on, to entice striking miners to go back to work.

"There was a full-scale riot," Phillips said, in a distant voice.

Joan nodded, and another tear rolled down her face.

"It was awful. Like nothing we'd ever seen. The police—" She stopped herself, looking between their faces with mild embarrassment. "You two seem like nice lads, but it doesn't change how I remember that day. The police with their truncheons, and their riot shields, they treated us like the enemy. They knew the men would rise up, but it was as if they *wanted* it to happen."

Joan closed her eyes against a sudden jolt of pain that had nothing to do with burned skin.

"Later, after the mine closed, people started asking questions. They wondered how the police always seemed to know where the picket lines would be. Every morning, there'd be four or five police cars waiting for the flying picket, to break them up before they even started."

Phillips could remember, only too well.

"Well, Alan was one of the most senior in these parts, and somebody started a vicious rumour that it must have been him feeding information to the police, maybe even the government."

She shook her head, to clear away the bad memories.

"Alan would never have done something so underhand; it just wasn't in his nature," she said, tiredly. "But the rumours wouldn't stop. People even had a name for this... this mole, or spy, or whatever you want to call them. They called them 'The Worm.'"

"Like the Lambton Worm," Phillips said, and Joan nodded.
Ryan looked between them in confusion.

"Who or what is the Lambton Worm?" he asked.

"It's a kind of legend around these parts," Phillips replied. "John Lambton was heir to the Lambton Estate, and a wealthy landowner. The story goes that, as a boy, he went fishing one day in the River Wear, and pulled out a tiny worm. Thinking it looked a bit funny, Lambton chucked it down a well and forgot all about it. Years later, he joined the Crusades, and the worm grew bigger and bigger until it escaped from the well and coiled itself around a hill—"

"Penshaw Hill?" Ryan guessed.

"Exactly. The worm carried on terrorising local villages and killing the livestock on Lambton's estate. Brave knights tried to kill it, but nobody succeeded until John returned and slayed the worm in the River Wear."

Ryan had always thought one of the best things about his adoptive home was its folklore, myths and legends. At home, Anna would often tell him some of the Pagan legends she wrote about as a local historian.

"So, essentially, the worm grows fat off the land while Lambton's back is turned," Ryan said, and turned back to Joan.

"I think I understand why your husband would have been so insulted by the accusation."

"At one time, I thought he might...I thought he might have killed himself. He was out of a job and most of his friends and neighbours thought he'd betrayed them. I'll never forgive the person who started that rumour; it made Alan angry and bitter and, when he couldn't find a way to prove they were wrong, he picked up the bottle. It was a slow journey, after that."

"Do you think there's anybody who may still hold a grudge, or believe that he was The Worm?"

Joan didn't have time to answer before her daughter came bustling in with a tea tray.

"Sorry it took so long, I couldn't find where Simon keeps his tea bags."

"Thanks, love," Joan said, and smiled when her daughter leaned down to kiss her forehead. "You've been a tower of strength, these past few days. Your Da' would have been proud."

Sally gave a watery smile as she handed out cups of tea.

"I was telling these boys about how he...well, he changed a bit, over the years."

"He was a drunk, you mean."

"Sally..."

"Well, it's the truth," her daughter said, turning to the two detectives. "I'm sad that he died the way he did, of course I am. But he was an alcoholic, and gave my mother a difficult life."

"It was all the things they said," Joan protested. "Anybody would have been devastated, after all he'd done to fight for miners' rights."

Sally sighed and sank down on the edge of the bed.

"I know, Mum. I remember everything he did, to try to help."

"He just became obsessive," Joan said. "Every day, he'd try and think about what happened during those months in the strike, to see if he'd missed something...some important detail."

She shook her head, sadly.

"Did he keep any papers, Mrs Watson?"

"Yes, but they'll have gone up in the fire," she said. "Alan wasn't one for computers, really."

Ryan nodded, and then turned to the brief statement Joan had already given to the first responding officer, the previous Friday.

"Tell me, Mrs Watson, how did you find Alan when you went into the living room?"

"Lying there, on the sofa," she said, in a choked voice. "There was fire all around...on the carpet, and creeping up the sides of the sofa. It was burning my feet—"

"Was he lying face-up or face-down, Joan?"

Ryan deliberately kept his voice professional, to focus her mind on the facts rather than on the horror of what those facts meant.

"He was...he was face-up," she remembered. "One of his arms was hanging down, and it was burning. I could smell it..."

"And, was there anything covering his face, Joan?"

"No, I don't think so," she said. "I-I'm sorry, I hardly remember. The floor was on fire, and I didn't have any shoes on. I just ran across and grabbed both of his arms, then heaved him across the floor as fast as I could. I knew...I knew he was dead, but I had to try. I had to try."

She let out a sob, and Sally silently dabbed at the tears, flashing a warning glance at the two detectives.

"I think that's enough for one day," she said, and Ryan nodded.

"Just one last question, Mrs Watson, if you can manage it. Do you know of anyone who might have wanted to hurt Alan?"

Joan raised her hand as if to touch her face, then remembered the bandages and set it down again.

"If you'd asked me that thirty years ago, I'd have said there was a whole village full of people who wanted to hurt him," she said. "But now? I can't think of anybody. Why would they choose to hurt him now? He barely left the house, or spoke to anybody but me."

"Thank you, Mrs Watson, Mrs Emerson. We'll see ourselves out."

---

Ryan and Phillips spent another few minutes questioning Michael Emerson, and then bade him a polite farewell. Time was marching on, and Ryan still had a 'To Do' list as long as the Lambton Worm. All the same, he took a moment to stop and lean his forearms on the wooden fence overlooking the equestrian centre to watch the horses graze in the thick summer grass. Hazy afternoon sunshine bounced off the monument in the background.

"What'd you make of them?" Phillips asked, coming to rest beside him.

Ryan waited until a woman with a pram had walked past them, before answering.

"Undercurrents," he said, shortly. "Secrets and lies. The usual."

Phillips chuckled.

"For instance, it strikes me that Mike Emerson was cagey when we asked him his whereabouts in the early hours of Friday morning. According to him, he was working late."

Phillips guffawed.

"As the Head of Planning in a local council? Even the most dedicated wouldn't work past four or five in the afternoon," he said.

"I think we're more likely to find that Mr Emerson was 'working late' at his secretary's house, or something of that ilk," Ryan drawled. "He'll come out with it, when he realises that we don't tolerate lies."

"Aye, doesn't strike me as the brightest of sparks," Phillips said. "It's his wife who wears the trousers in that relationship."

"You sound like an Agony Aunt column," Ryan teased.

"Aye, and without my sound wisdom and guidance, you'd have found yourself in many a scrape, by now."

Ryan thought of the times he'd been stabbed—twice— thrown into a river, hunted, falsely accused and almost murdered on several occasions, but supposed it could have been worse.

"It's true, you've been a guiding light, these past years."

Phillips grinned.

"You're welcome," he said. "As for the Emersons, I'd say it's a classic case of two people who got married young and don't have much in common, anymore."

"Not forgetting, she's the local celebrity," Ryan put in. "Some men can't handle it, when their partner's more successful."

"Poor bastards," Phillips said, and scratched the side of his nose. "Truth be told, I bloody love the fact Denise is the one in the driving seat, as it were…"

*Words he could never un-hear*, Ryan thought.

"Ah, Frank—"

"Nothing like a woman in uniform," he continued, with a wicked chuckle.

When Phillips began to gaze off into the middle distance, Ryan judged it was time to make a speedy departure.

"Time to go," he declared, and set off at a brisk pace back to the car. "The widow couldn't tell us much more about the way she found Alan, except that he was lying on the sofa, face-up as you would expect."

"Aye, but it sounds as though everybody in the village knew what Alan Watson was like. Doesn't take much for people to learn that he's in the habit of staying up late at night, drinking himself daft. Sally Emerson confirmed what we already assumed—that her parents usually left the doors unlocked—so anybody could have snuck in and shoved a cushion over the old boy's face, while he snored."

Ryan could see it, all too easily.

Phillips waited a beat, then checked his watch. "What about that other business?"

"It's in hand," was all Ryan would say.

# CHAPTER 10

Lowerson was at his desk when the first photo message arrived.

He felt the burner mobile vibrate in his jacket pocket, and a sick feeling spread in his belly. As if she could sense his disquiet, Melanie Yates looked up from her computer screen and fixed him with a watchful stare.

"I'm going to make a cuppa," he said. "Anybody else want one?"

He rose unsteadily and waggled the cup in his hand.

MacKenzie smiled and shook her head, and Yates simply looked back at her computer.

"Back in a mo," he said, in a voice he hardly recognised as his own.

*Mo?* Any more ridiculous phrases like that, and the whole office would know something was wrong.

Instead of heading directly to the break room, Lowerson ducked into the gents toilets and, after a brief check beneath the stalls, shut himself inside the end cubicle. He put the seat down and sat on top of it, swiped a hand across his face and then reached for the mobile.

There were three messages.

The first was an extremely compromising image of himself, naked, on a bed with a woman lying on top of him in the throes of passion. His face was turned away from the camera, but his hands appeared to be wrapped around her waist, while her breasts brushed against his cheek.

The woman in the picture was Rochelle White.

The second picture message was similar, this time of the two of them sleeping side by side; she, naked at the front of the image while he lay behind with his arm draped around her naked waist.

The third message read:

YOU MADE AN AGREEMENT. ANY FURTHER FAILURE TO COMPLY WILL RESULT IN THESE IMAGES BEING SENT DIRECTLY TO THE POLICE STANDARDS DEPARTMENT. THIS IS YOUR LAST WARNING.

Lowerson knew who had sent them, and why.

He slid off the toilet seat onto the floor, only just managing to shove it up again before he was violently ill.

---

As MacKenzie shrugged on her jacket and prepared to leave the office to collect Samantha from school, she decided to take the opportunity to ask Yates the question that had been on the tip of her tongue all day. With Lowerson still out of the room, it seemed the ideal moment.

"Mel, are you alright?"

If it had been anybody else, Yates might have come up with a hundred different excuses, but she would not lie to MacKenzie.

"I've been better," she admitted, casting a quick glance over her shoulder towards the door.

"Has something happened between you and Jack?"

MacKenzie hoped not; it had taken long enough for the pair of them to finally admit their feelings for one another.

"I guess you could say, nothing's happened, and nothing will," Yates replied, swallowing the tears that lodged unexpectedly in her throat. "I thought we might have had something and, last week…well, it doesn't matter now. He told me this morning he'd rather stay as friends and work colleagues, so that's that."

She pretended to look at the words on her computer screen, but they swam before her eyes.

MacKenzie felt a wash of maternal feeling for the younger woman, and hardly knew what to say.

"I'm sorry to hear that," she said, and walked around to lay a supportive hand on the girl's shoulder. "Listen, it's almost three o'clock and I need to head off, but why don't you come over for dinner tonight?"

"Oh, no—I wouldn't like to impose."

"It's no imposition, Mel. We'd love to have you."

Yates almost refused, but then she thought of the solo journey home to her parents' house, which she was desperate to leave. The atmosphere was like a mortuary, and she couldn't face the prospect of another long, lonely night binge-watching the latest Netflix drama or picking up her sister's old case file.

"Alright," she said. "That would be lovely, thanks Denise."

MacKenzie turned to leave, then surprised herself again by reaching down to peck her friend's cheek.

"Chin up," she murmured.

---

Before they considered their duty discharged, Ryan and Phillips decided to take a detour on their way back to Police Headquarters, via the city of Sunderland. It lay between the cities of Durham and Newcastle, at the mouth of the River Wear. Like Newcastle, it had a long history of coal mining and shipbuilding but, following the decline of those industries, it had turned its hand to car manufacture and other high-tech ventures instead. Ryan had often thought that Northerners came from hardy and adaptable stock, able to turn their hands to almost any trade—and weather any storm, real or otherwise—and this was never truer than in Sunderland.

Despite the wealth of skills and a capable labour force, there was not a ready supply of jobs to meet the demand, and when Ryan pulled up beside the jobcentre in the centre of the town, they found a queue stretching along the pavement outside.

"Let's see if Simon Watson can spare us a moment of his time," he said, heading to the main entrance. "Did you run a quick check?"

"Is the Pope Catholic?" Phillips replied. "Course I did. He's got an interesting history, this one. Quite a few juvenile pops for shoplifting—nothing too serious, just a bag of sweets or a can of cider from the corner shop, that kind of thing. He narrowly escaped time in borstal for joyriding, back when he was fourteen. There was nothing else until his early twenties, when he was given a twelve-month ban for driving under the influence of drugs."

"What kind?" Ryan wondered.

"Class A—heroin," Phillips replied, and gave a long whistle. "Seems to have got himself back on the straight and narrow, if he's one of the managers here."

"Unless he didn't declare it on his application form," Ryan said. "How many workplaces always check the finer details?"

"Aye, that's true. I said I was six feet two and a professional stunt man for Robert Redford, before I joined the Force."

"Close enough," Ryan grinned.

---

They found Simon Watson engaged in an animated discussion on the telephone.

"What the hell do you mean, they won't endorse it? Get on to them again and tell them this is a point of principle!"

*A pause.*

"You're not listening," he said, to whoever was at the other end of the phone line. "Universal Credit is a bloody menace. I've got hardworking people coming in here every day—single parents who want to work rather than take from the state. I've got those parents tellin' me that they can't afford to eat during the long school holidays because they're on zero-hour contracts…yes, you know what that means. It means, they don't get paid bugger-all for the whole summer holidays because they can't get cover…aye, I know they can apply for Universal Credit but, the point is, that takes eight weeks to come through. The holidays are over by then!"

Watson spotted Ryan and Phillips, and held up one finger.

"Yep. Yep, well, listen, mate. I hope you never find yourself in the same position and, if you do, let's hope somebody gives a monkey's, eh?"

With that, he slammed the phone receiver back into its cradle.

"Sorry about that," he muttered. "Can I help you? I'm not sure if you're aware, but there's a ticketing system in place…"

"We're from Northumbria CID," Ryan interjected, reaching for his warrant card. "DCI Ryan and DS Phillips. We're looking into the circumstances around your father's unfortunate death, last week. Our sincere condolences."

Simon nodded mutely, and indicated the chairs arranged in front of his desk.

"We only need a few minutes of your time," Ryan assured him. "Perhaps there's somewhere more private?"

"Don't worry about that," Simon said. "You can barely hear yourself think in here, as it is."

Phillips could understand what he meant. The centre consisted mainly of one large, open-plan room the size of a community hall. There was a welcome counter at the front, and service desks were arranged at intervals, each with two visitors' chairs apiece. The entire place thrummed with noise, so it was difficult to make themselves heard without raising their voices above the usual level. It was also unlikely that anybody would be able to listen in to their conversation or pick out its content from the general chatter.

"We were hoping to ask you a couple of questions, if you have the time?"

"Now's as good a time as any," Simon replied. "Fire away."

Ryan smiled, wondering how best to approach the subject matter. From what he had seen, Joan Watson's children were very different in temperament and style. Sally was polished, whereas Simon was brash; Sally was well-dressed and groomed, whereas Simon was scruffy; and their overall manner was at odds with one another. Sally seemed to take a logical approach to her work whereas, from what they'd just heard, Simon preferred to shoot from the hip.

"To begin with, would you mind telling us a bit about your father? We're trying to build up a picture of his life."

Simon blew out a gusty breath and steepled his fingers against his chin.

"When we were kids, growing up, he was brilliant," he said. "He must've been knackered after a day down the pit, but he always found time for us. He was never too busy

93

to have a game of Monopoly, or a kick around with the football."

He cleared his throat, battling the wave of emotion that came with the old memories.

"He used to dance our mum around the kitchen," he recalled. "He'd turn the radio on, and waltz her across the lino squares."

Phillips smiled, thinking of his own parents, when they'd been alive.

"Sounds like a happy home," he said.

"Aye, it was. After the strike though…" Simon shook his head, and ran agitated fingers through his hair. "I was a part of it, too. Started working at Penshaw Colliery the year before the strike started. I was seventeen and Sally was twenty."

"You must remember quite a bit of it," Ryan said.

"I remember all of it," Simon said, in a low voice. "People were worried sick, wondering what would happen to life as they knew it. To us, it seemed like the government couldn't give a toss about what happened to us, after their bloody programme of closures."

"Anger still runs high, when you think of it?"

Simon gave a short nod.

"You asked about my Da'? I'll tell you what happened to him. He was a good man who worked hard, and the strike wrung him out. It changed him. But, even after it was all done with, he might have been able to pick himself up—he was talking about re-training as an engineer, going to night school. But then, the rumours started."

Ryan decided to play dumb.

"The rumours?"

Simon nodded again.

"You have to understand—people were hurt and angry. Half of them were in denial, even after the colliery gates closed for the last time. We kept thinking something would happen to reverse the decision. After all, the mine had been in profit before it closed…people couldn't understand. So, they started looking for reasons and ways to place blame."

"And they blamed your father?"

Simon nodded.

"Partly. He was big in the Union, back then. He went to all the high-level meetings, even met Scargill himself. When people heard the rumours about Silver Fox—that bloke who was feeding information to Thatcher's Head of PR—they started thinking about all the other moles who might've been helping her to break the strike."

"You don't really think all that was going on, do you?" Phillips put in.

"Doesn't matter what I think," Simon muttered. "The reasoning was, if somebody was helping the government, they'd need to be fairly senior in the Union to know what its plans were. People put two and two together and came up with ten."

Phillips made a quick, scribbled note in his pad about industrial spies, and put a question mark beside it.

"They called him The Worm," Simon said, and couldn't quite disguise the tremble in his voice. "They made it so he was ashamed to leave the house."

"That must have been very difficult," Ryan said.

"Difficult?" Simon laughed. "Try going to the pub and coming home with fresh bruises every night. Try getting served at the shop, or asking a girl out to the pictures. It wasn't just dad who got it in the neck; nobody wanted to have anything to do with us."

"Seems like your sister's done well, being head of the Council and all that?" Phillips offered.

"She could sell ice to an Inuit, that one," Simon said, without malice. "Always had the gift of the gab. To give her her dues, she did a lot to smooth things over for our mum. She couldn't work miracles, but people remembered that Sally had done her bit during the strike, too. She got her hands dirty, worked hard and mucked in."

*She wasn't shy to talk about it, either, if her last election campaign was anything to go by,* Phillips thought to himself.

"And, what about you, Simon?" Ryan asked, and then gestured around the office. "Seems like you've got yourself a solid place, here?"

"I have now," Simon admitted. "I won't lie, and you probably know it all, anyway. After the mine closure and all that stuff, I went through a bad patch. Ended up falling in with the wrong people and getting myself hooked on heroin."

They didn't pretend to be surprised.

"And now?"

"I've been clean for three years, now," Simon said, with a touch of pride. "It was the hardest thing I ever did, but I finished the programme. That's why they let me have a job, here. I worked my way up the ladder and now I'm a manager, and I've got some self-respect back. At least dad lived to see that."

"That must have made him proud," Phillips said.

Simon nodded, and looked away to hide the sheen of tears.

"Do you think somebody would have wanted to hurt your dad, after all these years?" Ryan asked. "Was he in any trouble?"

Simon shook his head slowly.

"It was years ago, and he kept himself to himself. If anybody wanted to hurt him, they'd have done it by now. Besides, he was eighty. What trouble could he get into?"

*That was the question*, Ryan thought.

"Look, you don't really…you don't really think somebody would've set the fire deliberately—do you?"

Simon looked between them with troubled eyes.

"We have to investigate every possibility, Mr Watson," Ryan said, and Phillips took his cue that it was time to leave.

# CHAPTER 11

It was almost seven by the time Ryan made it back to Elsdon.

He dropped Phillips off on the way, so that his sergeant could be home in time for dinner after Samantha's first day at her new school, and had politely declined an offer to join them. He'd been surprised to find Yates there too; but then, Frank and Denise had always been open-armed in their gestures of friendship. It was obvious to even the most casual observer that things were rocky between Yates and Lowerson, and he hoped it would be of short duration for both their sakes.

By the time he reached the top of the hill and turned into his driveway, Ryan's mind was pleasantly occupied with thoughts of an al fresco dinner with Anna on the patio, to make the most of what was shaping up to be a lovely sunlit evening. Unfortunately, he spotted two other cars parked on the driveway: one of them he recognised immediately as belonging to Chief Constable Morrison, but the other was anybody's guess.

"Shit," he muttered.

When the Chief Constable started paying house calls, it was time to ease off the pedal.

As he opened the front door, he heard the sound of polite conversation wafting down the hallway. It came from the direction of the large kitchen-dining room they'd built, with views across the valley. He might have liked a quick shot of whiskey to prepare him for whatever unexpected emergency had arisen, but office rules still applied when the Chief was on-deck, and he resigned himself to yet more coffee instead.

As he entered the room, his eyes were drawn to where Anna hovered with a jug of iced water, and then to the seating area, where Morrison lounged beside a man he'd never seen in his life before. He was around his own age, with a military-style buzz cut and the hard, muscular look of one who spent much of their time in the gym.

"There you are," Anna said, and crossed the room to greet him with an expression on her face he translated roughly as, 'Thank God you're back, and what the hell took you so long?'

"Sorry," he said, under his breath. "Have they been here a while?"

"Half an hour," she replied, in the same undertone. "I didn't realise you were expecting visitors?"

"Neither did I," he muttered, with a frown. "Thanks for holding the fort."

Anna smiled, and then excused herself to return to her own pressing work deadline in her study upstairs.

"Sorry to intrude on you at home," Morrison said, rising from the chair she occupied. "Your wife's taken very good care of us, considering we landed on her unexpectedly."

Ryan didn't bother to hide the fact that he was deeply unimpressed.

"A phone call would have been polite," he said, coolly, and then turned to the stranger who was making himself very much at home. "I don't believe we've met."

"We haven't," the man said, extending a hand. "DCI Andrew Blackett, Ghost Squad."

The 'Ghost Squad' was a slang term used to describe a secret Metropolitan police squad of anti-corruption officers, trusted former detectives, ex-MOD police and financial experts that was set up back in the nineties. Although it was now disbanded, the term had been taken up to describe any officer attached to the Anti-Corruption Unit of the Police Standards Department in their regional area.

Ryan's eyes flew to Morrison, who held up a hand.

"We're not here to make an accusation, Ryan, don't worry."

"Why are you here, then?"

The two exchanged a glance, and then Blackett gestured towards the door.

"Mind if we take a walk outside? It's a nice evening for it."

It was on the tip of Ryan's tongue to make some caustic remark about not really being in the mood for a romantic stroll, when it struck him that the man was clearly concerned his home may be bugged, or that Anna may overhear.

"This way," he said, and opened the patio doors.

Once outside, Blackett made a few polite comments about the beauty of the gardens and the views, but Ryan's day had been a long one and he was in no mood for small talk.

"Look, why don't you just come to the point?"

Blackett folded his arms and squinted in the early evening sunshine, watching a flock of birds rise up and float on the air.

"Alright. You've got a fox in the hen house, Ryan. Maybe more than one of them," he said. "We've monitored and analysed the outcomes following major operations across various units, including Drugs and Vice, and cross-checked against murder rates. For over a year now, the numbers have been going in the wrong direction. Nothing too big, nothing too obvious, you understand. But there've been too many times when a bust has gone wrong, or an operation has gone tits-up because there were no goods to seize or the person of interest had legged it. There's only one explanation."

"Somebody's tipping them off," Morrison finished for him, and Blackett gave a short nod.

"When Gregson was superintendent, the constabulary was a mess. Corruption was rife, and well organised; in fact, we're still unravelling the web he left behind. Still, after all that went down, we thought it would be too hot for coppers to think about going on the take, what with us watching their every move. As it turns out, maybe they were just waiting for things to calm down a bit before they returned to business as usual."

Ryan looked away, out across the garden. It had been two years since he'd put Arthur Gregson behind bars—the man he'd looked up to almost as a father when he'd first joined the constabulary. It had been hard, but he would do the same all over again.

"Are you sure of this?"

"As sure as we can be," Blackett replied.

"Why bring this to me?" Ryan turned on him. "You mentioned Drugs and Vice. What does this have to do with Major Crimes?"

Blackett and Morrison looked at him with twin expressions of pity.

"You can't possibly think someone in *my* team is bent?"

"We don't know anything for sure, yet, Ryan," Morrison said quietly, watching the emotions play over his face.

When Morrison had first learned that ACU would be conducting an undercover investigation into CID, she'd had much the same reaction.

"I don't want to believe it, either," she said. "But the facts speak for themselves, and it's worthy of further investigation."

"Ordinarily, I wouldn't make you aware of this at all," Blackett said. "I'm making an exception, on the recommendation of several parties, because you have an unimpeachable reputation. Added to which, we believe you'll be perfectly placed to help us since you're leading Operation Watchman."

Ryan's lips twisted, because he could see the sense of it.

"You're asking me to spy on my colleagues, some of whom are my friends," he said, very calmly. "I want to know the names of those you are looking at, in particular. Give me names."

"I can't—"

"Then I won't help you."

"Ryan—" Morrison began, but Blackett interrupted her.

"I can't give you specific names, Ryan. All I'm asking you to do is report back with any behaviour you deem unusual or that gives rise to suspicion. I should add that, with the exception of Chief Constable Morrison, you are the only other officer who is aware of the existence of our investigation. We have our own systems, our own databases, and operate as a separate force within a force."

The warning was clear: should anybody else happen to find out about their investigation, ACU would know who to blame.

"Well? Will you help us?"

The faces of his team passed before his eyes, every one of them dear to him.

"You're wrong about my team," Ryan said, quietly. "No man or woman amongst them would betray their badge."

He paused, battling with his internal moral compass, which never failed.

"Because I'm sure of that, right through to my very core, I'll agree to help you, if only to disprove your allegation."

Blackett smiled, and handed him a business card.

"I'll be in touch."

---

As Ryan showed Morrison and Blackett to the door, Simon Watson waved off the nurse, who'd taken over from his sister in looking after their mother while he was at work. A quick peek inside Joan's bedroom told him that she was fast asleep, and he topped up her water glass and replaced the straw, in case she woke up feeling thirsty. He left the door ajar, in case she called for him, and then made his way back to the kitchen to prepare a quick dinner for himself.

Looking around the bungalow, he could see his sister had given it a once-over, since the carpets looked considerably fresher than when he'd left them that morning, and the surfaces were sparkling clean. He had never been what you might call house-proud, and he couldn't stand trinkets or dust-collectors sitting around. He supposed it was a bit impersonal, though, and he made a note to himself to put some pictures on the walls and a few framed photographs around the place.

As he stirred boiling water into his Pot Noodle, Simon reflected that it was a surprise, really, that his mother had chosen to stay with him, rather than at Sally and Mike's much larger home in Shotley Bridge. He could guess the reason, although his mother would never admit it.

She was still worried about him.

Three years on, and she still worried that he would slip back into the old ways.

Simon wanted to feel angry about it, but he couldn't work up the feeling. He'd been an almighty pain in the arse, those years when he'd been addicted, and hadn't been able to see the wood for the trees. He knew, now, that he'd always be an addict, deep down. He might be in control of the urge, but he'd always have to be vigilant or risk taking a wrong turn. It wasn't easy; access to drugs was so simple, nowadays—they were practically giving them away. They'd give you a few grams and tell you it was alright to pay next time, and the debt would rack up until the dealer had something over you.

That's when they'd come for you.

*Just this one favour,* they'd say. *One favour, and we'll call it quits.*

But it was never just the once and, if you refused, they'd use muscle, or threaten your family.

He thought of his mother, lying asleep in the room next door, and set the noodles back on the countertop, his appetite having suddenly vanished.

That's when he spotted a stack of mail that Sally must have picked up and left for him to open. He reached for it and thumbed through the various circulars and junk post, weeding out the bills until he came to a thick brown envelope. It was addressed to his father, and Simon realised the postie must have decided to re-route the mail to Alan's widow.

*Were they allowed to do that?*

"Law unto themselves," he muttered, good-naturedly.

He wondered whether to wait until his mother was awake or open it on her behalf. He worried about its contents; what if his father had taken it upon himself to stir up trouble, or make some kind of ill-advised investment? It could be many a thing, none of which she was in a position to deal with at the moment.

He slid a nail beneath the seal and tore open the envelope.

Inside, there was a short stack of papers with a covering letter from the Freedom of Information Officer at GCHQ. Simon heaved a sigh, thinking that his father must have been sending off spurious demands for copies of official records again. He'd gone through a phase of trying to get hold of government memoranda a few years ago, but had been refused. Now, it seemed they'd decided to send him a few token bits.

Not expecting to find much of interest, Simon reached for his fork again and was about to take a mouthful of salty chicken noodles when his eye fell on something that would change the course of his life irrevocably.

The fork clattered onto the counter, splattering sauce onto his trousers and shirt, as Simon began to shake.

*Dear God.*

His father had been right all along.

There was an enemy within, after all.

Anna heard the front door close behind Morrison and Blackett but, when a few minutes passed by and Ryan hadn't come to find her, she shut down her computer to go in search of him.

She found Ryan standing on the patio outside, looking out across the mellow, sun-washed hills. He hadn't heard her approach, so she spent a moment admiring the long, straight line of his broad back, that seemed always to bend beneath the weight of whatever new drama came to his door.

Quite literally, in this case.

He was dressed casually in jeans and a white shirt rolled up to the elbows, and his hair brushed the back of his collar since he'd forgotten to have it cut for the past few weeks, softening the hard lines of his profile.

"Come and join me," he said, taking her by surprise.

*Bam,* she thought, as Ryan's bright, silver-blue eyes locked with her own and she experienced an outpouring of love that hit her like a fist to the belly. It had done so from the first time they'd met in a tiny pub on Holy Island, and would, she suspected, continue to do so until they were both old and grey.

Anna stepped out onto the patio beside him and, to her surprise, he reached for his smartphone and scrolled through a few songs until he found one of their favourites. He set it to play, put the phone on the table nearby, and then pulled her into his arms so they could sway together while Neil Diamond sang about a life lived forever in blue jeans.

It was like coming home, every time they touched. No matter what happened in the world outside, here was peace, pleasure, love and friendship. Here, there was no need to be anything other than themselves.

"I can't tell you why they came," Ryan said, rubbing his cheek against her soft hair. "It's confidential."

"I suspected as much." Her voice was muffled against the wall of his chest. "Just tell me you're alright."

"I'll be alright," he said, softly.

It wasn't quite the same thing, but it would suffice.

"Ryan?"

"Mm?"

"Whatever it is, please be careful."

He stopped moving and cupped her face in his hands, gently tipping it up so he could look at her and say what he needed to say.

"When you first met me, I was lost. I didn't know myself anymore. I was angry—"

"You were grieving," she said.

"Yes, that too." *He still was.* "The only thing I felt I had was work—it's how I coped, you see. If I could just save one more person; if I could just put one more killer behind bars...but, it never ends. Their faces...the faces of the dead—they haunt me."

*I know, love,* Anna thought. Sometimes, she was awakened by his thrashing on the bed, or she woke to find the bed empty beside her because he'd been unable to close his mind to the ghosts that crept in each night.

"The thing is, when it was only me, I didn't care what it took. I'd do whatever I needed to do, to get the job done. But, now...you've taught me caution, Anna, without ever meaning to. Just by existing, you've taught me to love something more than myself. If I wasn't careful before, I'm careful now because I can't stand the thought of losing what we have, and all that's to come."

"You're a smooth one," she said.

"I try," he said, and lowered his mouth to hers.

———

"Frank and Denise, sittin' in a tree, K-I-S-S-I-N-G!"

Samantha sang out the classic, tinkling rhyme and fell into giggles after catching her new foster parents in a quick smooch over a bubbling saucepan of meatballs marinara.

Phillips pretended to come after her with a tea towel, which sent her into even more wild giggles.

"Out of the kitchen, you two!" MacKenzie ordered. "Sam, go and lay the table in the dining room, please. Frank, why don't you see if Melanie would like a drink? I think she's in the lounge."

"How's she doing?" he asked, in a stage whisper.

"Hard to tell," MacKenzie replied, keeping an eye on the doorway so as not to give offence. Their gossip was well-intentioned, but it was still gossip, after all.

"Somethin' happened with Jack? I tell you, that lad's got no way with women," he grumbled. "Almost feel sorry for him."

"Aye, right enough, and I suppose you're a regular Casanova?" she teased. "It took you at least five years to ask me out on a date, as I recall."

Phillips adopted a haughty expression.

"All part of my strategy. Treat 'em mean, keep 'em keen, so they say. Here, I hope that isn't what Jack thinks he's doing. There's playing hard to get, and there's just being a wally."

MacKenzie huffed out a laugh.

"Whatever he's doing, it's not working," she decided, and picked up a wooden spoon to stir the sauce with an idle hand. "Come to think of it, he seemed out of sorts all day."

"How'd you mean, love?"

"I don't know," she said, gesturing with the spoon. "On edge, I suppose. Not quite himself."

"He was off work with that sickness bug," Phillips reminded her. "Maybe he's still hankering for it."

MacKenzie made a non-committal sound in her throat.

"He'd better not pass on his germs to me," Phillips said, and went to dip his finger into the sauce, before it was promptly slapped away with the back of the spoon.

"Go on and see if she's alright," his wife urged.

"Alright, alright. I'm going."

Presently, Samantha skipped back into the kitchen.

"I've put all the cutlery and napkins out," she said. "Do you want me to put bowls and plates out, too?"

"Thanks, sweetheart, but I'll just serve the pasta, here," MacKenzie said, and set a timer.

While it ticked away, she gave her full attention to the little girl.

"So? How was your first day?"

Samantha considered the question, thinking back over the course of the school day.

"Weird," she said eventually.

"I see," MacKenzie said, slowly. "Weird good? Or weird bad?"

"Good," Samantha said. "I just mean, everything is so regimented."

"That's a good word," MacKenzie said.

"Thanks, I learned it today. We're studying the Romans in history at the moment, and we're going to be visiting Hadrian's Wall in a few weeks."

MacKenzie thought immediately of the bodies they'd once found stuffed inside that wall, ones that were more recent than any Roman Centurion, but thought it probably fell under the category of, 'Things not to say to your child before bedtime.'

"That sounds like fun," she said, instead. "Did you meet any nice friends, today?"

Samantha nodded.

"There's a girl called Tallulah," she said. "She's really funny and smart, and she said I could sit next to her at lunchtimes."

"She sounds lovely," MacKenzie said. "We'll have to invite her around for tea, sometime."

The timer started to beep, and she reached for a colander.

"Denise?"

"Yes, sweetheart?"

"Thanks for letting me come and stay with you."

Before MacKenzie could respond, she felt the child's arms wrap tightly around her waist in a hard hug, before Samantha skipped off again to see what the others were up to.

In the residual quiet, MacKenzie found herself wondering how they'd ever imagined their life was complete without that little bundle of energy, with so much love to give.

---

Jack Lowerson sat at the bottom of the stairs in his maisonette, in an area of Newcastle known as 'Heaton'. It was near the city centre, but far enough from the office to preserve a healthy distance between work and home.

None of that seemed to matter, anymore.

Work had come into his home, and there it would stay.

He didn't know how long he sat there, staring at the front door, before the little burner mobile vibrated in his jacket pocket again, and his whole body jerked in shock. With trembling hands, he pulled it out and forced himself to look.

It was another text message, which consisted of one word only:

REPORT.

Jack let out a small sound of panic, and almost dropped the phone. He knew what they were doing; he should have seen it coming from the start. Singh, or Ludo, or both of them, planned to use those pictures of him and Rochelle to blackmail him into submission, or risk a professional standards board dismissing him for gross misconduct. They knew he had a dicey history, with his mum serving time, and he could not afford any more marks against his name.

Lowerson sat there a while longer, holding the mobile carefully, like an offering.

Or a set of scales.

Eventually, after night had fallen, he began to type a response:

SURVEILLANCE ONGOING. WILL UPDATE SOON.

After that, he let the phone clatter onto the floor at his feet.

# CHAPTER 12

*Tuesday, 11th June 2019*

Despite the company, Ryan had not slept well.

The new day dawned just as brightly as the last, blazing through the windscreen as he made his way to that most salubrious of destinations: the basement mortuary of the Royal Victoria Infirmary. Tiredness made his eyes water in the bold morning light, and he fumbled for a pair of sunglasses in the central compartment while he navigated the traffic. Rush hour in the morning was unpleasant, but he reminded himself that it wasn't half as bad as in the capital, where he'd lived for a number of years before deciding to migrate north. In London, every hour was rush hour, and it had been a stressful driving experience. Here, he could mostly sit back and enjoy the ri—

He let out an expletive as a man driving an enormous SUV careened around a mini roundabout, doing at least forty in a twenty zone. Ryan was tempted to flip on his blue light and chase the bloke down, if only to give him a fright, but there were more pressing matters on his mind.

After another tussle finding a parking space, he located Phillips in their usual meeting spot, beneath the canopy beside the service entrance to the mortuary, at the back of the hospital. To Ryan's great relief, he held two take-away coffee cups in his hands.

"Come here often?" Phillips asked, and handed his friend the stronger of the two.

"More often than I'd like," Ryan replied, polishing off the coffee in a few deep gulps. "Thanks, I needed that. C'mon, let's go and see if Pinter's been missing us."

Phillips couldn't imagine the pathologist missing anyone. Then again, Jeff Pinter was a first-rate clinician and, he supposed, an alright sort of bloke. They'd had their run-ins in the past, but he'd never let them down.

As they made their way down the flights of stairs towards the corridor that would take them to the mortuary, Phillips stole a nervous glance at his friend.

"What?" Ryan asked, dubiously.

"Nothing!" Phillips replied, a shade too quickly. "It's just that…well, you know how Samantha idolises you."

Ryan made a raspberry sound.

"I'd hardly say that, Frank. If anything, she idolises *you*, after all the kindness you've shown her."

Phillips glowed with pride.

"Well," he said gruffly. "There might be different kinds of admiration. And, when it comes to you, son, our Samantha definitely has the *other* kind."

Ryan was interested in his friend's life, but less concerned with his foster daughter's pre-teen hormones.

"Frank—"

"I'm getting to it," Phillips waved him away, and they reached the double doors at the end of the corridor, behind which lay their final destination. "The top and bottom of it is, Samantha's signed us up for a talk at the school, and she won't take no for an answer."

Ryan paused in the act of entering the security code for the doors.

"Come again?"

"The school were looking for some interesting speakers for their assembly, next week, and she's signed us both up."

"I—" Ryan wondered if it was possible to die from acute panic. "I've never done a school talk before."

"How bad can it be?" Phillips reasoned. "It's just a bunch of primary school kids. They'll probably want to know a bit about what we do."

Ryan looked meaningfully at the plaque on the door, then back at his sergeant.

"We don't want to give them nightmares," he pointed out.

"Aye, well, we don't need to go into any gory details, do we? Maybe show them our badges, remind them not to do drugs…that sort of thing."

"Frank, I've got a list as long as your arm of more important things to be doing," Ryan said. "There's a manhunt underway, in case you haven't noticed."

To illustrate the point, he nodded towards one of the posters of Ludo which had been tacked onto the wall, with a caption that simply read: HAVE YOU SEEN THIS MAN?

"I know, but it'd make her happy if we could manage it, and I think she wants to make a good first impression."

Ryan berated himself for being all kinds of soft touch, but found himself nodding dumbly.

"Alright, you win," he said, tugging open the mortuary door. "But that was dirty cricket, old man, telling me it'd make Samantha happy. You knew I wouldn't be able to say 'no.'"

Phillips let out a wicked laugh.

"Whatever it takes," he said, and preceded his friend into the mortuary.

The smile died on his lips as Ryan suddenly remembered DCI Blackett's house call the previous evening, and the man's suspicions about his team. If he was to be believed, there were men and women operating in CID without scruples to get what they wanted.

Just as quickly, he shoved the memory aside.

*Never in a million years,* he told himself.

He would not even think it.

———

They found the chief pathologist in excellent spirits.

Jeff Pinter jiggled his bony hips to the Kaiser Chiefs singing about a girl called Ruby while he checked the enormous immersion tank on the other side of the room, and waved to them with a begloved hand that dripped God-Only-Knew-What onto the floor.

"Be with you in a minute!" he called out.

The mortuary was quiet that day, with only one other technician in the large, open-plan space, and no cadavers occupied the examination tables lined up in the centre of the room.

"Been a quiet week, has it?" Phillips enquired, shrugging into an over-long visitor's lab coat that flapped around his ankles.

"Yes, it has," Pinter replied, washing his hands with surgical soap in a long metal sink at the back of the room. "Apart from the unfortunate gentleman you're here to see, we've only had the usual round of heart attacks and overdoses, as you would expect."

He dried his hands with a paper towel, then made his way across the room to greet them properly.

"Good morning, to the pair of you," he said, and beamed a smile so wide they feared it might crack his face.

"You're full of the joys of summer today," Ryan said, feeling slightly unnerved. "Had a bit of good news, lately?"

Pinter adjusted his glasses and gave them another dopey smile.

"You might say that. I met a very nice lady recently, and she... well, she decided to stay, last night."

Both detectives fell back on their training, and worked hard to ensure their faces betrayed none of their surprise. Pinter's love life had been a work in progress for as long as they could remember, and, frankly, they could hardly imagine the tall, gangly-legged man wooing anybody.

"Howay then, Jeff. Tell us a bit about this wondrous woman. We already know she's brave, takin' you on, but what's she like?"

Phillips' interest was sufficiently piqued that he almost forgot his surroundings.

*Almost.*

"Her name is Joanne," Pinter said. "She's forty-one, divorced, and has a little boy called Archie, who's nine. I haven't met him yet, but we're planning to take him to the cinema next weekend."

The other two goggled at him, wondering how their crusty friend would adapt to life as a stepfather, should the occasion arise. Somehow, it was hard to imagine this opera-loving, tweed-wearing doctor of pathology going on camping trips or watching football from the sidelines.

"That's great, Jeff. Really great," Ryan said, recovering himself. "So, ah, how did you two meet? Does she know what you do for a living?"

Telling prospective partners that he fished around in dead bodies all day hadn't always been a successful aphrodisiac for Pinter.

"That's the best thing about it," he exclaimed. "Joanne's a pathologist, too! She's based down near Richmond, which is a bit of a drive, but we'll make it work. We met at a convention in Durham, so I didn't need to tell her I was a personal trainer, or anything like that."

Again, both men fell back on innate politeness and professional training, to mask their dual expressions of shock at the idea of this bony man working as anything other than a living Reaper.

"Well, it all sounds hunky-dory, mate," Phillips said. "Just take my advice and don't wear yourself out. These younger lasses have a lot more energy…"

Ryan pulled a face as his imagination ran wild, again.

"Right. Well, on that delightful note, shall we have a look at Alan Watson?"

Pinter led them through the main mortuary space and down a separate corridor. A number of smaller examination rooms led off it, and he unlocked the one at the end.

"He's in here," Pinter said, and paused before entering. "Be prepared—it's not a pretty sight."

---

The pathologist had not been exaggerating when he'd told them that Alan Watson's fire-ravaged body was nothing to write home about. Ryan grieved each time he was faced with the shell of what had once been human, a person with thoughts, feelings and a lifetime of memories that made up the fabric of a life. He thought of their families or the loved ones they left behind, and of the pain their passing would bring. Anger usually followed, as he faced the possibility that their death had not been natural and was burdened with the task of bringing justice to those who remained.

In the case of Alan Watson, Ryan remembered all his family had told him about a proud, upstanding man who'd fought for what he believed to be right. He recalled their sadness at the loss of that man, a sadness he suspected had begun long before Alan passed away. For all he'd been a shadow of his former self, nobody deserved to be incinerated in their own home.

Not like that.

"Pinter stands by his preliminary report," Ryan said, as they made their way back outside into the morning sunshine. "No smoke in the lungs, so it seems clear that Alan died sometime before the fire began."

Phillips made a murmuring sound of agreement. "He's less sure about the cause of death," he said. "Seems fairly certain a heart attack might've done it, but a heart attack could've been brought on artificially by somebody shoving a cushion over his face."

Ryan nodded, and was glad there was somebody else in the world who conjured up grim scenarios like that as a matter of course.

All the same, he wondered if the job was making them jump at shadows.

"I don't know, Frank. There were no defensive wounds that Pinter could find, and we already know that Watson was a late-night drinker and a smoker. The Fire Investigator reckons it was a cigarette that started the blaze, and the toxicology tells its own tale about Alan's preference for Jamaican rum."

It all looked like an unfortunate accident.

And yet…

"Something still feels off," he muttered.

"Maybe it's all that hocus about 'The Worm'," Phillips said. "Puts you on edge, thinking about somebody being that underhand. Could've been one of their neighbours, if not Alan himself."

Ryan gave a half-hearted smile, thinking once more of Blackett's investigation and wishing he could speak openly without prejudicing it.

He wished he could tell Frank a lot of things.

He forced his mind away from problems close to home, and back to the image of Alan Watson lying there on the metal gurney, his life—and death—laid bare.

"It's a great leveller, isn't it, Frank?" Ryan said, as they watched the cars coming and going inside the hospital car park, and heard the distant wail of an ambulance approaching. "It comes to us all, in the end."

Phillips turned to him with a comical expression on his rounded face.

"What's brought all this on? Talk about one foot in the grave."

Ryan huffed out a laugh.

"Must be feeling my age," he said. "Seems sad to think that, no matter how much we do, no matter how hard we try to live a good life, in the end, it makes no difference."

Phillips shook his head.

"It makes a lot of difference to the people who'll remember us, when we're gone, lad. It means the difference between people talking of what a good man you were, or of how you were wasteful and threw away half your bacon stottie."

Ryan laughed.

"You're never going to let me forget that, are you, Frank?"

"Not in this lifetime, pal."

# CHAPTER 13

At Police Headquarters, a light rain had begun to fall, lending the sky a greyish hue that seemed to reflect the general mood of those harboured inside. Melanie Yates had spent much of the previous evening thinking back over the last few days, her treacherous mind dissecting every interaction between herself and Jack to try to pinpoint when things had taken such a drastic turn for the worse. Eventually, she'd fallen into a fitful sleep sometime after midnight and had woken with a throbbing headache and the feeling that she'd suffered uncomfortable dreams all through the night.

For his part, Lowerson looked as though he hadn't slept in days, which was probably because he hadn't. Although he'd taken a lot of trouble to make himself presentable, no amount of hair gel or snazzy ties could disguise the dark circles beneath his eyes that came from nights spent patrolling his own home.

"Morning," MacKenzie said brightly, making an effort to ignore the lingering atmosphere between the two younger detectives. "I just heard from Ryan. He and Phillips had to pay a visit to the mortuary, but they'll be back soon."

"Has there been another murder?" Yates asked, and thought of Rochelle White, who was still missing. "Do they have an ID?"

Lowerson lifted his head, breath lodged somewhere in his throat.

"They're not sure, yet," MacKenzie said. "It's an old man from Penshaw, who got caught in a house fire. They're trying to work out if it was accidental or not."

Lowerson lowered his head back to the file on his desk, feeling like every kind of lowlife. The unfortunate body lying on a slab at the mortuary might not have been Rochelle, but it was still worthy of his compassion.

"Ryan wants a progress report on Operation Watchman," MacKenzie told them. "He and Frank should be back soon. How're you getting along?"

Lowerson and Yates exchanged an awkward look.

"You go first," he told her.

"Thanks," she muttered. "There's been a setback. Our potential asset was reported missing, yesterday morning—"

"Who's been reported missing?"

With superlative timing, Ryan and Phillips entered the office at that moment, catching the tail end of Yates' sentence.

"Morning, sir," she said, not having broken the habit of formality despite Ryan telling her numerous times to call him by his given name. "I was just saying that we've had a setback. The asset I was telling you about at the briefing? She was reported missing, yesterday morning."

Ryan set his hands on the back of his desk chair.

"Now that her name's been made public and accessible via Missing Persons, we can dispense with the need for anonymity," he said. "I presume we're talking of Rochelle White—Bobby Singh's girlfriend? What efforts have been made to find her?"

"We wanted to seek your permission to take over this case, and to go ahead and question Bobby Singh on the whereabouts of his girlfriend. They lived together, yet he was not the one to make the report to Missing Persons. We'd like to ask him why."

Ryan glanced at Lowerson, who was noticeably quiet.

"Seems sensible," he agreed. "But when you question Singh, you don't go alone. You go as a pair and keep us fully appraised of your movements, at all times. Understood?"

Yates nodded and, after a moment, Lowerson did the same.

"What about Singh's properties, vehicles and so on? Has there been any progress on that score?"

"The Fraud Squad came through for us," Lowerson said. "DS Harry Tomlinson has been trying to unravel Singh's business ventures since we first came across him a while ago—back when you were staying at that cottage in Cragside."

Ryan nodded.

"I remember. There was some suspicion that Singh was seeking to launder money through the purchase of a large plot of land on the Cragside Estate."

"That's right. Unfortunately, the Fraud Squad haven't been able to mount a prosecution because there's no solid evidence, but they have a substantial file on Singh that we can use. DS Tomlinson's sent over a list of all the properties he believes are owned by Singh or one of his companies," Lowerson continued, tapping a printed spreadsheet lying on the desk in front of him. "He has well over a hundred residential properties that he runs more or less as a slum landlord."

"All in the city?" MacKenzie asked. "Or are they scattered around?"

"All over Northumberland and County Durham, predominantly," Lowerson replied.

"They would be ideal properties for somebody wanting to set up drugs dens over county lines," MacKenzie said.

Ryan nodded his agreement.

"Cross-check against any previous drugs busts," he said, and Lowerson made a note. "Drugs Squad should be able to help you with that."

"Right," Lowerson said, thinking pessimistically of the conversation that would entail with DS Gallagher and DCI Coates.

"If we can prove some of these properties have been, or *are* being, used as a base for drugs pushing, it would give us grounds for a warrant to dig deeper into Singh's affairs," Ryan said.

"Aye, but what if they're registered to his off-shore companies?" Phillips put in. "Hard to connect him, if it's the trust that owns those properties, not him as a private person."

"Tomlinson says they've traced the properties to Singh through a combination of tip-offs and forensic accounting, but they can't prove that he owns them," Lowerson agreed.

"How come?" Phillips asked, out of interest.

"The properties are all part of what's called a Nevada Trust."

When Phillips still looked none the wiser, Ryan helped him out.

"It used to be that people would set up off-shore companies in Saint Kitts and Nevis, maybe Guernsey or the Isle of Man," he said. "But the US and the UK systems are actually more corrupt, because we make it so easy to set up a company like that; even easier than on the islands, despite what people may think. Anyway, a Nevada Trust is the latest thing, because although the US requires all countries to provide them with their data, Nevada State Law doesn't allow the disclosure of trust beneficiaries to overseas investigators."

"In other words, they get to have their cake, and eat it too?"

"It's an ideal loophole," Ryan agreed. "And will make it almost impossible for us to find out whether Singh is the true beneficial owner of those off-shore trusts. Without that information, we'll need to rely on the witness statements and our own forensic accounting, like Jack says."

"Well, that's a bugger," Phillips declared, and then thought of something else. "If we're still pretty sure that

Singh's behind some or all of these, it's a fair bet that Ludo will be holed up in one of them.

"It would have to be one of the more remote addresses," MacKenzie said. "Ludo's got a memorable face, and there'd be less chance of him being recognised there than in the city."

The others nodded their agreement.

"Let's prioritise the rural addresses," Ryan said to Lowerson. "Send a couple of PCs out to each area to do a recce, but tell them under no circumstances to approach the address itself without our express authorisation. Paul Evershed is most likely armed, and is to be considered extremely dangerous."

Lowerson fell into a sudden coughing fit, and Phillips gave him a friendly thump on the back.

"Tea go down the wrong way, son? Here, have a slurp of water."

He handed Jack a bottle of water he found on the desk, and Lowerson didn't stop to worry about how long it might have been there before chugging down a few mouthfuls.

"Sorry," he wheezed.

Ryan gave him a long, considering look.

"Jack, are you sure you're ready to be back at work? You seem out of sorts."

Lowerson held back another nervous cough.

"I'm fine, sir."

Ryan sighed at the excessively formal tone.

"If you need more time off—"

"Thank you, but I said I'm fine."

There was an awkward lull in conversation, and then Ryan gave a curt nod and checked his watch.

*Eleven-fifteen.*

"Alright, what about the surveillance on Singh? Has it turned up anything of interest?"

MacKenzie shook her head.

"I spoke to the surveillance team last night, and again first thing this morning. Nothing out of the ordinary reported yet, but they'll keep on him for another couple of days."

"On whose order?" Ryan wondered.

"They've been reporting through Gallagher and Coates," MacKenzie replied, and Ryan frowned.

"Tell them they report to the head of Operation Watchman, in future. I want that man kept under surveillance for as long as I deem necessary."

MacKenzie smiled slowly.

"Funnily enough, I told them the same thing. I'll pass on the message again."

"What about leads on vulnerable persons?" he asked. "Have we had any data through from the outreach centres, schools—how about Social Services? I want to know if Singh's companies have a contract with the local councils to provide sheltered accommodation for vulnerable adults."

"They want to help, but they're run off their feet," Yates said. "I can chase them, sir, but I think it'll take a while before the data starts to come through."

Ryan had expected as much.

"Keep pressing them, Mel. If we can connect Singh to sheltered housing, which we know is often used by dealers as a base for their operations, it allows us to stay one step ahead of them. Let's keep the lines of communication open with the other units under the Watchman remit, too."

Even as he said the words, Blackett's warning about the other units in CID circled around Ryan's mind, and it was on the tip of his tongue to tell the rest of his team to be careful with the information they gave out.

But Ryan could not, and his hands were tied.

Besides, as he'd discovered long ago, the very best way to catch a liar in the act was to give him enough rope to hang himself.

# CHAPTER 14

"Joan? Wake up, Joan."

Her eyes were heavy with the pain medication, but she forced them open and groped around the bedside table for her glasses.

"Here, let me help you with those."

Mike Emerson hooked the glasses carefully around his mother-in-law's ears, and she patted his hand with her bandaged paw.

"Thanks, pet. Must've dozed off again, for a minute."

"You need your rest," he said. "But it's time for your next dose, and for something to eat."

She noticed the tea tray, laden with little sandwiches and biscuits for her to pick at.

"Ah, love. You didn't need to go to all this trouble. I know how busy you are—how busy you *all* are."

"It's no trouble for my favourite lady," Mike said, and she almost sighed. He couldn't seem to turn off the charm, which wasn't quite as charming as it had been when he was thirty years younger, and thirty pounds lighter. "I took a few days off work, to help out."

Joan was surprised. She'd known Mike ever since he was a boy, and—Lord forgive her—she'd never have accused him of putting others before himself, as a rule.

"That's very kind of you, love. Honestly, give me a few more days and I'll be as fit as a fiddle."

Mike knew that, beneath the bandages, her skin was still raw. The effort of trying to save Alan had physically exhausted her, and she'd suffered a very mild stroke on her way to the hospital. Not so bad as to affect her speech, but her right arm wasn't as strong as it used to be and would need physiotherapy once the burns had healed.

"You'll be right as rain in no time," was all he said, settling himself on the chair next to her bed. "How are you feeling, now?"

She looked up at the ceiling, trying to work out the answer.

"I think I feel a bit…numb. There were times when life was so hard with Alan—"

"I know," he muttered, looking down at his hands. He found himself thinking about whether, perhaps, he could've done more to help.

"I miss him so badly…" A fat tear worked its way down her cheek, and guilt lodged heavily in his chest.

"I should've come around more often," he said, and cast his memory back to when Alan had helped him get his first job down the mine. Those early years, when he and Sally were newly married, had been hard. Money had been tight, and tempers had run high.

And, of course, he'd slowly begun to realise that Sally didn't love him.

Or, perhaps, she'd fallen out of love with him, somewhere along the way?

It was hard to tell.

"You lead busy lives," Joan said, but it would have been nice to have had a little more support. "It wouldn't have changed things, anyway."

"I don't know," Mike said, running a hand over his chin. "I tried to speak to Alan a few times about all those rumours. You know, one time, he accused me of starting them?"

Joan tutted.

"He didn't know what he was saying…"

"I forgave him for that a long time ago," he said, magnanimously. "It was Sally who got the brunt of it."

Joan felt her chest contract as the years rolled back, and she remembered a particularly nasty episode in their front room; the one where Alan had died. After the mine closed and the men were put out to pasture, the younger ones went out and started to re-train, or get their GCE's so they could apply for the Civil Service. Plenty of the other women were happy to stay at home and bring up the children, clean and cook the meals.

But that had never been enough for Sally.

Being a part of the activism and helping to organise the cafes and the meetings, had given her a taste for something bigger. She wanted to do something useful with her life, and Joan had been proud to see her go back to school and get an education. Sally had always been bright, and so had Simon.

Alan hadn't understood.

If he had a failing, it had been that he was a traditional sort of man. He'd believed a woman's work was in the home, and that the strike belonged to the men, not the women. They could help out on the sidelines, but they hadn't been the ones to go down the pit every day and, so, what did they know about it?

Sally had understood. She'd grown up in a mining family and knew the challenges that faced them long after that industry had faded away. She was proud that her daughter managed to make something of herself and that she used her influence to try to make the world a better place for everyone, not just the wealthy.

Alan hadn't seen it that way.

*Strutting about on stage,* that's what he'd called it.

*Just like you,* Sally had thrown back, and that was true enough. There'd been plenty of times Alan Watson had given a speech down at the Club.

It had been a terrible row but, underneath it all, she'd known Alan wasn't angry with Sally; he was angry with all those who believed he had betrayed them, and had played judge, jury and executioner.

"Did you know, Alan kept all her cuttings?" Joan said, and Mike shook his head. "Oh, yes. He said a lot of things that he didn't mean, but he was proud of her. Deep down, he was proud."

Mike leaned his arms on his knees, looking down at the floor.

For a while, she thought he was about to say something else, but then they heard the doorbell ring.

"That'll be the nurse," he muttered, and the moment was lost.

---

"I want to know who's on your list."

As the rest of his team worked towards finding the whereabouts of Paul Evershed, Ryan drove a short distance across town to meet DCI Blackett. The café was small and packed with lunchtime customers looking for a baguette or a bowl of soup, hardly noticing the two serious-looking men occupying a small table in the corner.

"I've already told you, Ryan. I'm not able to share that with you."

"Bollocks," came the succinct reply. "You came to me because you think it's one of mine. I want to know who."

Blackett considered the man sitting across the table before answering. Maxwell Finley-Ryan was one of the most high-profile detectives on the Force. He'd earned a reputation for being able to keep a cool head, even in times of chaos. He had a string of commendations and, he happened to know, the brass had earmarked him for much greater things than being a lowly DCI.

But it seemed the man himself had other ideas.

He respected that.

Ryan was known to be a straight arrow; a man who kept to a code of conduct, not only by reference to the Police and Criminal Evidence Act but to his own standards of behaviour, which were probably higher. He was known to be high-handed, sometimes, but never without justification. On paper, his CV read like one of those privileged knobs Blackett had come across in Whitehall and at Scotland Yard; chinless wonders who wouldn't know how to police if their life depended upon it. Having now met the man, and taken the trouble to learn about the times when Ryan had indeed fought for his life and the lives of others, Blackett understood that appearances could be deceptive.

There might be privilege, but there was backbone, too.

"The truth is, Ryan, you already know who I'm looking at," he said, at length. "You know because, at some stage or another since our last discussion, you'll have thought about it and come to the same conclusions."

Ryan wasn't ready to talk about that.

Not yet.

"I don't know the Drugs Squad or Vice. We work together, on and off, but not daily. I wouldn't know about the internal dynamics, there."

Blackett took a sip of his tea, and thought about how much to share. It wasn't protocol, but, if it brought results…

"To be as successful as it has been in scuppering previous operations, and to have maintained such an extraordinary level of secrecy, we believe there has to be more than one senior officer who's turned."

"One in each unit, you mean?"

"At least. Most likely, several in each unit. Back in Gregson's day, when he worked in Vice, he had a fail-safe method of ensuring compliance from new members of a team. He'd arrange for some young idiot to go out on a 'date' with a girl who, it would later transpire, was a trafficked sex worker, probably underage. Once he had something on an officer, he held it over their heads to ensure ongoing loyalty."

Blackett gave a negligent shrug.

"It's the same story in Drugs. A senior officer would hand over something taken from a bust, usually drugs or money, and once the newbie had taken it, they were an accessory and a beneficiary of the proceeds of crime."

"And you think the same thing is happening now?"

"Undoubtedly," Blackett said. "Whether by that method, or something similar. You're no fool, Ryan. You're an idealist, but you're no fool."

"Thanks," Ryan muttered, with a generous measure of sarcasm.

"Look, none of us like what's happening. I know how hard you fought to get Gregson and his lot out, root and branch. You're like us, Ryan. You want law enforcement officers to do what they signed up to do—enforce the law, not exploit it."

Ryan nodded, and came back around to his original question.

"Who are you looking at, in the other units?"

Blackett decided to throw it all in. Sometimes, you had to take a punt and, if it turned out to be wrong, that would fall on Ryan's shoulders.

Win-win.

"Usually, to get a copper to turn, they have to start by finding their weakness; whether that be drugs, money, women, kids…" He took another gulp of tea, to wash the nasty taste of it from his mouth. "Whatever their weakness, there's an organisation who'll know about it, and want to use it."

"So, you do the same," Ryan realised. "You look for the weaknesses, to find out who are the most likely targets?"

Blackett raised his teacup in a toast.

"It's amazing, the things you find out. For instance, I wonder how many of your colleagues know that you're sitting on a personal fortune somewhere in the tens of millions, or that you set up a charitable foundation in your sister's name so you can give most of it away, every week?"

Ryan said nothing, but felt a wave of anger at the breach of privacy. He supposed it was the man's job but, in that moment, he felt just as exposed as Alan Watson laid out on Pinter's table.

"Nobody knows," he said, in a very controlled voice. *Nobody but Anna.* "I'd like to keep it that way."

Blackett held up his hands.

"You can count on my discretion," he said. "I'm only bringing it up to illustrate that, nobody really knows anybody else, Ryan. Not deep down. We all have our little secrets."

He took a quick glance around the café and leaned forward, hands linked on the table.

"As for the others," he said, very softly. "There's a potential whistle-blower on the Vice Squad, but he's scared. He's not whiter than white, himself, and he doesn't want his wife and kids to find out. We're working out a deal, but it all depends on what he can bring to the table."

Ryan thought immediately of DI Terry Prince, but it could just as easily be his sergeant, Stevie Cribbs. Both men had a reputation for long nights spent at the city's premier strip clubs and it wouldn't altogether surprise him that they'd found trouble there, or in the course of their so-called duty. Easy enough for the Smoggies to find out who they were, and whether they had any unusual or illegal predilections.

"And Drugs?"

"More than one of them had money problems, a couple of years back. Gallagher almost went bankrupt while he was still living down in London, but seemed to avoid it, at the last minute. He seemed to move up north on the spur of the moment, which rings alarm bells for me. He's living on credit, and it's a cycle that leaves him wide open to bribery. Same goes for Coates," he added. "His wife's paraplegic after a bad road accident a few years ago and needs constant care. The NHS doesn't cover all of that, not after all the cutbacks, and private healthcare is expensive."

As he listened, Ryan realised how easy it might be. If a person was desperate enough, or messed up enough, they might think it was a way to escape their problems.

Instead, they ended up creating an even bigger problem for themselves.

"There's a lot more we'll be looking at," Blackett said. "But they're the main ones."

Ryan looked him in the eye, and asked him the burning question.

"Alright. You've told me about the other units. Now, tell me about Major Crimes. Tell me who you're looking at, on my team."

"Like I said, Ryan. You already know."

# CHAPTER 15

As Ryan headed back to the car, his mobile phone rang out a tinny rendition of the theme tune from *Back to the Future,* which caused a couple of heads to turn nearby.

The caller ID told him it was Phillips.

"Frank?" he answered, whilst rummaging for his car keys. "What's up?"

"Where the heck've you been for the past hour? I've been running around the building lookin' for you, like a right muppet," Phillips burst out. "Listen, we've got a hot lead on a man matching Ludo's description. A couple of those PCs we sent out in the sticks have struck gold. Apparently, there's a feller who matches Paul Evershed to a tee, living in a holiday rental."

"Where?" Ryan demanded, as he slid into the driver's seat and switched to speakerphone.

"Biddlestone," Phillips replied. "It's a little place not too far from Rothbury—"

"I know where it is, Frank. It's a couple of miles away from my house in Elsdon."

There was a short, pregnant pause while they both considered what such close proximity could mean. Ludo had a lot to hold against Ryan, since he was the man who had demolished life as he knew it and had forced him to go on the run, keeping him away from his home and business connections—at least, until now. He was usually a paid assassin, but whether he also killed just for sport, they didn't know.

"How d'you want to play it?" Phillips asked.

"We need to bring him in; he's a danger to life. Get a team together," Ryan ordered. "We need a firearms unit, the full works, for deployment within the next half hour. Meet at Netherton—we can set up a control unit there, as it's only a couple of miles away from Biddlestone. I can be there in half an hour."

*If he stepped on it.*

"Ludo knows about Anna," Ryan added, and thought back to what Blackett had said about unscrupulous characters seeking out a person's weakness in order to exploit it.

If he had a weakness, it was certainly his wife.

"She's at the university in Durham, today," he said, with no small amount of relief. "I'll call her, but can you put a call through to Durham CID and ask them to send somebody round, just until we're finished in Biddlestone?"

It was unlikely Ludo would target Anna, but he wasn't taking any chances.

"Consider it done," Phillips said.

---

After putting a call through to Anna, Ryan floored it all the way along the A1 until the turn-off for Rothbury, where he followed the winding road through its Victorian streets until he reached the village of Netherton. He passed an inn on his left, and took the first right along a side road where a number of other police cars had assembled alongside two small vans carrying specialist firearms officers. Bringing the car to a jerky stop beside them, he moved directly around to the boot, where he kept his protective gear.

Pulling on the vest and tucking a helmet under his arm, he moved quickly to join the rest of his team in a huddle with the head of the firearms unit. Phillips wasn't present, as somebody was needed to collect Samantha from school, so it was MacKenzie who stood kitted out beside Lowerson, Yates and the others.

Before they had time to react, another car pulled up behind them, and DCI Coates and DS Gallagher spilled out, alongside a couple of constables.

Ryan turned to MacKenzie, who lifted a shoulder.

"Information sharing, remember?"

Ryan gritted his teeth, before diving in.

"Right, thanks for such a speedy response. We've got an eyewitness telling us that a man fitting Ludo's description is, at this very moment, in residence at a holiday let in Biddlestone, which is less than two miles north-west of here. According to the local police, there's a navy-blue, old-style Land Rover Defender parked on the driveway outside."

"Have you had the go-ahead from Morrison for this?" Coates asked, and Ryan gave him a cursory glance.

"Of course," he snapped, and turned quickly to planning their approach before any more precious time was wasted. "Alright, listen up. Our target is Paul Evershed, fifty-one years old. Most likely armed, and he may shoot to kill. Our primary objective is to contain and apprehend the target without bloodshed. However, we have been authorised to use lethal force if necessary."

He paused to let it sink in. No decent officer relished the prospect, or the responsibility, but the Force took a utilitarian approach. If it would serve to prevent more lives being lost, the taking of a single life was acceptable.

"Mac? Give us a bit of detail about the locale."

MacKenzie stepped forward.

"From what we understand, the holiday let is comprised of a farmhouse and two smaller outhouses a short distance from the main building," she said. "Biddlestone is largely rural, but there's still scope for the target to run to a neighbouring house, or make off across the fields. There's a quarry nearby, with some associated residential housing."

Ryan consulted his map.

"The farmhouse is located a quarter of a mile east of the quarry, and there's a mix of open fields and wooded areas.

To access, there's a B-road, from which a single-track lane leads to the farmhouse."

He looked up.

"Team A will consist of myself and Trainee DC Yates, alongside two firearms officers including DI Uzma Aziz, who will lead the firearms operation. Team B will consist of DI MacKenzie, DC Lowerson and two other firearms officers."

"Where are we in all this?" Gallagher demanded.

"You're not kitted out," Ryan said, eyeing their suits and ties. "We don't have time to wait while you sort yourselves out, so please remain here and advise us of any material changes that will affect the operation."

They weren't happy about it, Ryan thought, but they couldn't argue with the logic either.

"Team A to circle around and approach from the west," he said "Team B to approach from the east and take up a defensive position. Local police are under orders to set up a roadblock through Netherton and likewise to the west, towards Clennell. Is all that understood?"

There were nods around the small huddle of police staff.

"Helmets on," Ryan said, and slotted his radio to its holster. "Let's go."

---

There were two firearms vehicles, so Teams A and B split themselves between each van. Ryan and Yates were part of the team approaching from the west, which meant they needed to find a shortcut to help them circle around, before doubling back along the B-road towards the farmhouse. There was an eerie sense of calm, mingled with a healthy dose of fear—the kind that came with any situation that might lead to the discharge of a weapon.

Ryan, alongside MacKenzie and Phillips, had received additional firearms training, but had no desire to use those skills if he could help it. His police-issue Glock was a weapon of last resort he'd rarely been forced to use, especially not to kill, and he wanted things to stay that way.

"ETA one minute," Ryan spoke into his radio, and an acknowledgment crackled down the line from MacKenzie's team soon after.

They parked the van off-road, a quarter of a mile away from the turn-off to the farmhouse. Team A followed, half a mile in the other direction, and it was agreed that both teams would approach slowly on foot, taking cover in the outhouses that were located on the perimeter of the farm. Several local response teams were stationed in neighbouring villages and had already gone around the closest dwellings to evacuate any inhabitants, in the event that things went awry.

Ludo was not above taking hostages, as they had learned to their cost two years ago.

"Team B, approaching the south-westerly perimeter of the farmhouse," Ryan said, lowering his field glasses as he and Yates followed behind DI Aziz and her firearms partner. They held live weapons in their hands aimed at the patchy earth underfoot, and their heads moved this way and that, scanning the woodland as the driveway came into view.

On the other side of the driveway, Team A moved slowly across the far lawn as a couple of ramshackle outbuildings came into view. Ryan spoke again into his radio, and gave a hand signal across the lawn, which was received, and both teams made their way towards the huts.

The firearms team cleared them for entry, and they found an ancient, rusted ride-on lawnmower and some other garden tools inside, but not much else.

As both teams converged again behind the outhouses, Ryan radioed their position back to Control, and Gallagher's brash voice sounded out along the wires.

"No reports of anyone matching Ludo's description having made off on foot, or any sign of a Defender attempting to pass through the roadblocks," Ryan said. "But I can't see anything parked on the driveway up there, either."

It was true; there were no cars parked in front of the farmhouse, and no obvious signs of life.

"Could be around the back," MacKenzie suggested.

Ryan nodded.

"Alright, Team B will approach from the front; Team A take the rear, in case he tries to make a run for it."

They moved off again, keeping to the edges of the lawn under cover of the trees.

---

With every passing footstep, Ryan became more convinced that nobody was inside the farmhouse. He had no justification for the feeling; there was every possibility that Paul Evershed was inside and, at this very moment, preparing himself for their arrival. All the same, he could not shake the feeling that something was wrong.

They were too late.

As they drew nearer to the farmhouse, MacKenzie's team peeled away and went around the back, whilst Ryan kept to the front. The curtains were drawn in all the windows, so it was impossible to know whether anybody was at home.

They approached with extreme caution.

"On my mark," Ryan murmured into the radio, and readied himself for entry. "Three...two...one... ARMED POLICE! ARMED POLICE!"

He raised a small battering ram to the door and broke the lock, following which the firearms officers entered shouting the same warning. With other suspects, at other times, they might have taken a different, softer approach.

But not with Ludo—they could take no chances.

Ryan and Yates followed the firearms unit inside and heard the same warning echoed by their colleagues at the back door. They searched and cleared each room downstairs, while Ryan indicated that MacKenzie's team should take the upstairs, until they had searched every nook and cranny of the house.

"It's clear," one of the firearms officers said, as he traipsed downstairs again.

Ryan had been right; nobody was there. Nothing moved in the house—not even the stale, slightly garlicky air.

After making a brief report back to Control, who would relay the message to the Chief Constable, Ryan instructed his team to complete a search of the perimeter, to be completely sure they had covered the entire complex.

Once that was complete, he returned to the farmhouse and drew on a pair of nitrile gloves so he could take a more detailed survey. It was an old stone house, built sometime during the late nineteenth century, if he was to hazard a guess, although it had been renovated sometime fairly recently. There were new carpets on the floors and the furnishings, whilst basic, were also quite new.

"Look at this," MacKenzie said, drawing his attention to a laminated fire escape plan mounted on the wall of the kitchen, beside which was an extinguisher.

In one of the kitchen drawers, they found an old folder detailing how the various appliances worked and local areas of interest.

"Holiday let, or ex-holiday let?" Ryan said, and MacKenzie nodded.

"We can check the address against that list DS Tomlinson sent over, from the Fraud Squad."

Ryan nodded, and walked across to the built-in oven, where the smell of garlic was even stronger.

"Ludo was here," he said, laconically.

"We can't be sure it was him," MacKenzie replied.

Ryan simply opened the oven door to reveal a roasted chicken, still in its juices.

"We interrupted his lunch."

At that moment, Lowerson entered the kitchen, with Yates in tow.

"D'you think it was a wild goose chase, or maybe the witness got it wrong?"

Ryan closed the oven door again.

"No, I think Ludo was definitely here. In fact, he was here less than half an hour before we arrived."

"How could he have known we were coming?" Yates asked, of nobody in particular. "He must have been tipped off!"

"Yes," Ryan said. "That's what I was thinking, too."

There was a heavy silence in the kitchen, and then MacKenzie swore.

"Who'd do such a thing?"

"We can't prove there was a tip-off," Ryan muttered.

"It's the only explanation," Yates argued, and he smiled at her passion for the job. It would sustain her, in all the years to come.

And through all the disappointments.

"We'll investigate through the proper channels," he said. "For now, we've got an All Ports Warning out for Paul Evershed and his face has been plastered across every local and national news channel, as well as on posters in every newsagent, library and restaurant from here to Land's End. We've increased foot patrols by fifty percent, so there are officers on the streets. I want to keep the situation as calm as possible, for however long it takes to bring him in."

Ryan paused, shifting his helmet from one arm to the other.

"Until that time, we keep searching."

As they filed out, Ryan realised Jack Lowerson had been the only person not to utter a single word during their exchange.

# CHAPTER 16

Jack Lowerson felt the burner mobile vibrate four, five... six times in his pocket, on the journey back to Police Headquarters. Bile rose in his throat and he bore down against churning sickness as MacKenzie drove steadily along the dual carriageway, chatting to Yates who was seated beside her in the front passenger seat.

He rubbed a shaking hand through his hair.

"Do you mind if I put the window down?"

"Of course not," MacKenzie said, and gave him a concerned look in the rear-view mirror. "Not feeling a hundred percent? Would you like me to stop somewhere?"

"No, no. I'll be fine, thanks. Just needed some fresh air."

Lowerson raised his face to the wind, letting the air rush over his skin while the mobile burned a hole in his pocket.

"Alright, well, let me know if you change your mind. I really think Ryan was right, you know. Maybe you should take another couple of days off. There've been some nasty viruses flying around, lately," she said.

"Thanks," he managed.

"Bobby Singh's PA left a voicemail message, while we were up there," Yates said, with a deliberate lack of sympathy. "They say he'll be free anytime until five-thirty, if we want to go to his office in town."

Much as they would have liked to maintain the element of surprise, Singh's busy events schedule put paid to the possibility.

"There should be enough time to go along, if we hurry," Yates continued, consulting the clock on MacKenzie's dashboard.

*Half-past four.*

The thought of coming face to face with the man who was behind his present misery almost sent Lowerson over the edge.

"Great," he muttered.

Once MacKenzie turned the radio on to give them all a break from shoptalk, Lowerson risked bringing the burner mobile out of his pocket. He stole regular glances at the back of their heads, to check their eyes remained on the road ahead, and then he prepared himself for whatever fresh hell awaited him beyond the click of a button.

---

She was dead.

Lowerson could see that, very clearly, from the picture messages. He felt faint, as though his body was becoming weightless. He fumbled the phone back into his jacket pocket and turned his head towards the window, sucking in deep gulps of air.

The songstress on the radio sounded far away and distant, as though the music were wafting towards him beneath the weight of an ocean wave and he shook his head to clear the warped sound.

*Rochelle, lying naked on the bed, with blood all over the sheets.*

He propped his head on his hand and breathed through his teeth until the first wave of shock passed by.

*They had pictures.*

The images of Rochelle were imprinted on his mind's eye, never to be forgotten.

*Dead eyes.*

*Curled fingers.*

And his DNA all over her, and the bed.

There was a single message that came with the images, and it read:

YOUR WARNING CAME TOO LATE. NOW THERE IS A PRICE. DESTROY OR REPLACE ALL PHYSICAL EVIDENCE CONNECTING ROCHELLE TO THE DEMON BY TOMORROW NIGHT. DO IT, OR FACE CONSEQUENCES.

Unable to hold it in any longer, Lowerson threw up in the footwell of MacKenzie's car.

# CHAPTER 17

Simon Watson had spent a miserable day reading and re-reading the GCHQ paperwork he'd found inside his father's envelope, still unwilling to believe yet unable to ignore the truth it contained in stark black and white. He kept it with him at all times, in case anybody should discover its contents, while he thought about what to do for the best.

His first inclination had been to go to the police. In general, he wasn't a great fan of the boys in blue, but the two he'd met yesterday seemed decent enough.

Simon pulled the little white card DCI Ryan had given him out of his wallet and tapped it against the edge of his desk.

He sat there for a long time, staring at the usual stream coming in and out of the jobcentre and thought about all the different kinds of people in the world.

Good people, and bad people.

When he was young, it had seemed so simple; either you did good things or you did bad things, and that was the end of it. But growing older came at a price, and that price was disillusionment. The world was filled with people who occupied that murky grey area, somewhere in between. An uncomfortable purgatory filled with good intentions but no action. They sometimes did good for their fellow man but, mostly, people looked after Number One. They jogged merrily through life with very little care or understanding of what their misdeeds would cost the rest of the world, and slept soundly in their beds at night while others struggled to get through the day.

Simon thought of the jobcentre strike against Universal Credit he was organising, alongside all the other offices in the North East. Few of them agreed with the new benefits system the government had introduced, and even fewer enjoyed having to be the ones on the front lines implementing the complicated new rules that made it even harder for vulnerable people to get help from the state. The Department of Work and Pensions had chosen the North East to be the guinea pigs; the first area in the country to roll out the new system, as if its working poor didn't have enough to contend with.

Well, he had his father's blood in his veins, and Simon wasn't going to stand for that.

Thinking of his father reminded him of the envelope tucked inside his desk drawer, and he reached across to lock it inside overnight.

He needed more time.

Unexpectedly, the old urge reared up and Simon broke out in a sweat as his mind waged a battle between Simon and the Addict, with the latter whispering to him about where and from whom he could buy what he craved.

*Just a little bit, to pick you up a bit,* the Addict whispered.

*No!*

*NO!*

*It will make you feel better,* the Addict told him. *You won't feel any of the hurt or the pain anymore.*

*You're lying! It'll make me sick, angry—my family will hate me.*

*I'm the only one who knows you, the only one you can trust,* the Addict replied.

Simon made a grab for the phone and dialled a number he knew by heart.

———

While Ryan gave Chief Constable Morrison a progress report following the failed attempt to apprehend Paul Evershed, alias Ludo, Phillips busied himself in the kitchen making what he liked to call a 'Kids Special'.

Namely, chicken nuggets, chips and peas, slathered in tomato sauce.

"How was school today?"

Samantha was sitting at the kitchen table with a homework book in front of her, looking crestfallen.

"It was fine," she mumbled, pushing the book away. "The teacher will be happy when I tell her that you and Ryan can come in and give a talk at the assembly."

Phillips shook the chips on their oven tray and then wiped his hands on a tea towel.

"Aye, well, there's nothing we like more than giving school talks," he said, with as much sincerity as he could muster. Truth be told, he'd take being locked inside a room with a raving axe-murderer over a roomful of expectant children, any day of the week.

"Will we get to try out a stun gun?" she asked.

"No, pet. We don't tend to stun people, unless you count me stunning them with my dashing good looks."

Samantha chuckled, as he'd hoped she would.

"What about guns?" she asked. "Do we get to see any of those?"

Phillips shook his head.

"Bloodthirsty little thing, aren't you?" he joked, as he pulled the nuggets out of the oven. "We don't encourage the use of guns, especially not in schools. I don't think your teacher would appreciate that, do you?"

"S'pose not," she said, and thanked him when he set a heaped plate of food in front of her. "I know his face."

Phillips was confused.

"What's that, love? Whose face do you know?"

"His," Samantha replied, pointing her fork towards the tiny television they'd fitted to the wall. Usually, they kept it on the news channel with the sound muted.

Phillips turned around and saw that the local news was running a bulletin report about the manhunt that was underway for Paul Evershed. It hadn't stopped since he first went AWOL but, inevitably, the press preferred to sensationalise matters so that it appeared that a dangerous killer was suddenly on the loose…as if he hadn't been missing for almost two years, and a danger to society throughout that time.

"You know that man?" he asked, pointing at the mug shot of Ludo.

"Yeah, he worked for my Dad's circus when we were touring Wales," she said. "I remember him, because he had a scary-looking face and my dad told him he had to keep indoors or keep his clown make-up on."

"Ludo worked as a clown?" Phillips was agog.

"Who's Ludo?" Samantha wondered. "Did he use a different name, or something? He told me he was called Paul, and he told me he had a granddaughter my age."

"Oh, he did, eh?"

"Yeah, he said he hadn't seen her in a long time."

Phillips switched off the television set. He'd have a word with Ryan about what Samantha had disclosed, in the morning.

"Now then," he said, after she'd cleared her plate. "What about that maths homework, you don't seem too keen on? Anything I can do to help?"

When she showed him the lines of long division, Phillips wished he hadn't opened his big mouth.

"Ah… you know, I don't believe in giving kids all this homework. I reckon you've worked hard enough at school…"

But Samantha was determined.

"I don't mind maths, but I don't do it the way the teacher wants me to. I just do it my own way, but I want to be like everybody else."

Phillips smiled.

"Dance to your own rhythm, Sam. That'll be just fine with us."

She gave him a beautiful smile and set about answering two pages of long division sums correctly, in her own way.

---

When Ryan came out of a progress meeting with the Chief Constable and heads of the Drugs and Firearms Units, Jack Lowerson was nowhere to be seen.

"He went home," MacKenzie told him. "He was sick all over my car on the way back in, so I dropped him at home and told him under no circumstances to come back in to work tomorrow. He's obviously not well."

Ryan nodded, and told himself he'd give the man a call later on, after he'd answered a question that had been playing on his mind for hours.

"Mel? Can you send over a copy of that spreadsheet the Fraud Squad sent over—the list of Singh's properties and vehicles?"

"Sure thing," she said, and tapped a few keys while he settled himself at a computer.

A few moments later, he brought up the spreadsheet and ordered each of Singh's suspected properties alphabetically, before running a search for 'Biddles Farm'.

*Nothing.*

Next, Ryan brought up the spreadsheet containing the list of vehicles associated with Singh or his associates, and performed the same actions, this time running a search for 'LAND ROVER'.

*Nothing.*

Ryan's eyes turned a flinty shade of grey as he surveyed the people seated around him, every one a potential stranger.

"Have any changes been made to this spreadsheet since we came by it?" he asked.

"Not that I know of," MacKenzie said.

"We haven't had time to add in Biddles Farm," Yates added. "We're not even sure it's associated with Bobby Singh, so it seems prudent not to add it to Tomlinson's list."

"This was compiled by DS Tomlinson?" Ryan asked.

"Far as I know," Yates said. "Why? Is there something wrong with it?"

"No," Ryan muttered. "Just curious."

A moment later, he shut down the monitor and scooped up his mobile phone to go in search of Blackett. He needed to check the metadata on that spreadsheet, to find out who was the last person to make an alteration—such as deleting a significant address—but he couldn't use their own digital forensics team for that. Not without arousing suspicion.

"Any word on Rochelle White?" he asked, as he prepared to head off. "It's not too late for you to go and interview Singh."

He might have been inclined to go along to the interview with Yates, as a show of muscle, but that was his upbringing warring with the modern police officer inside him, who knew better. MacKenzie and Yates were more than capable of looking after themselves, and he had to let them.

The two women looked at one another and nodded.

"We'll let you know how it goes."

Ryan made it all the way to the door, before old-fashioned chivalry kicked in again.

"If you need me, just call. I'll be there."

"Thanks, Dad," Yates called out, and laughed when the air turned blue in the corridor outside.

# CHAPTER 18

Bobby Singh kept offices at a prestigious city-centre address. Ostensibly, they were held under the banner of Singh Properties Inc, an entity with legitimate tax returns dating back almost ten years, a robust Corporate Responsibility Programme and an even more successful PR machine, judging by the sponsorship deals and affiliations with local charities and much-beloved sports teams. Singh drew down his director's salary and paid his employees at the end of every month, in line with all the proper employment laws.

MacKenzie and Yates arrived outside the large, former Victorian warehouse just after five o'clock. It had been converted into luxury offices sometime in the last three years, if memory served them, and it now boasted jet-washed brick exteriors enhanced by acres of polished glass and engineered wood floors. The result was one of urban chic; a place inhabited by men sporting designer beards oiled to within an inch of their lives, and women in crop tops so short they would put the Spice Girls to shame.

"Trendy in here, isn't it?" Yates muttered, as they were buzzed inside the main foyer.

"Painfully so," MacKenzie agreed.

They were in Ouseburn, a former industrial area to the east of Newcastle, very near the river. It had seen a lot of regeneration over the past thirty years or more, and now boasted rows of smart new apartment buildings and quirky conversions, edgy music venues and a building devoted entirely to promoting literacy and reading for children.

Unfortunately, it was also where the Victoria Tunnel ended. The tunnel was a subterranean wagonway built to transport coal, which began on the other side of the city and finished at Ouseburn for onward transportation by sea. It had seen many uses since the 1800s, and had served as an air-raid shelter in the Second World War, but it was known amongst the staff of CID chiefly for having been the location for an epic chase between Ryan and The Hacker.

MacKenzie shivered involuntarily. She had her own memories of that man, and her own scars to contend with.

It came as a timely interruption when a girl of no more than twenty tottered over to greet them, wearing the most improbable high heels either woman had ever seen.

"She'll turn her ankle, on this shiny floor," Yates muttered.

"I'm Vogue, Mr Singh's personal assistant," she said, flicking her long hair to reveal an equally improbable chest. "Do you have an appointment?"

"Yes," Yates said, smiling politely. "I spoke with you on the phone earlier today? I'm Trainee Detective Constable

Yates and this is Detective Inspector MacKenzie. We're from Northumbria CID."

The girl didn't ask to see their identification, but they showed it to her anyway, for the sake of the many CCTV cameras dotted around the foyer.

"Oh, yes! I remember," Vogue said, with a little laugh. "Mr Singh is on a conference call at the moment. Do you want to wait?"

"We'll wait," Yates told her.

"Great! Can I get you some water? Coffee?"

"No, thank you," MacKenzie murmured. "Do you mind if we ask you a couple of questions, too?"

The girl looked nervous.

"Do I need a solicitor?" she asked.

MacKenzie gave her a motherly look, designed to put her at ease.

"Why would you need one, Vogue?"

"I dunno…That's what they say, on all the cop shows, don't they?"

She really was very young, they realised, and trod carefully.

"You can have a solicitor, if you like," MacKenzie told her. "But you're not in any trouble, and we're not arresting you for any crime, either. We just want to ask a couple of informal questions that might help our investigation, that's all. Would that be alright?"

"Yeah, I suppose so," the girl muttered, and noticed that the receptionist was putting a hasty call through to the boss.

"Great. I was just wondering how long you've been working for Mr Singh?"

"Um, about six months," Vogue replied, crossing her legs as she stood on six-inch heels, creating the impression of a flamingo balancing in a lagoon of marble.

"Working directly with Mr Singh, I guess you'll have met his girlfriend, Rochelle?"

Vogue's heavily made-up face turned a painful shade of red.

"Mm-hmm," she nodded. "She's…she's nice."

"When was the last time you saw her?"

"Um, Rochelle didn't really come into the office all that much," she replied. "I think it was a couple of weeks ago. She came in to meet Mr Singh for lunch."

"Right, thanks. And, how long have you and Mr Singh been seeing one another?"

Vogue went red, then white…and back to red again.

"What? Um, no…no, we're not. I don't know what you mean. You can't say we are!"

"Can't I? I thought we were just chatting, woman to woman," MacKenzie shrugged, while Yates watched this masterclass in witness handling with open admiration.

Vogue flapped her hands, which had been manicured with long, sharpened nails painted a deep burgundy shade.

"It was only a few times," she whispered. "Is it illegal?"

The two women looked at one another.

"No, it isn't illegal," Yates sighed, wondering if the woman could be any more of a walking cliché of their sex.

"Why are you here, then? He doesn't have a disease, does he?"

MacKenzie was almost relieved when any further conversation was forestalled by the arrival of the man himself.

---

"Thanks, Vogue. You can go home, now."

The girl nodded profusely, and mumbled a 'goodbye' to MacKenzie and Yates before hurrying across the lobby with a clatter of high heels.

"To what do I owe this pleasure?"

Singh wasn't hard to look at, they'd give him that much. He reminded them of one of those male models from a perfume ad in the nineties; all shiny-smooth skin and bright white teeth, with a pair of long-lashed eyes that seemed to peel away their skin.

They disliked him on sight.

It was hard to tell whether it was a basic, instinctive reaction to a predator, or whether it came from knowing— or, at least, suspecting—the things he had done.

"Mr Singh? My name is DI MacKenzie, this is my partner, Trainee DC Yates. Thank you for making time for us in your busy day."

"Anything to help," he said. "Why don't you come into my office, where we can talk more comfortably?"

Without waiting for an answer, he turned and made his way back to one of the lifts, which had a glass front and skeleton sides, so they could see the inner mechanism. As they moved across the lobby area, several security guards followed their progress and spoke softly into mics attached to their lapels.

One of the guards stepped inside the lift with them and operated the buttons. A moment later, the doors opened with a silent *whoosh* of glass to reveal Singh's office area, which consisted of the entire top floor to the building. It was an architectural dream, where wooden beams fused with concrete and glass, old and new working together in perfect harmony.

"Please, have a seat," he said, indicating a plush lounge area. "Can I offer you a drink?"

He was certainly the most affable criminal underboss, MacKenzie thought.

"No, thank you, Mr Singh. If it's alright with you, we'll come straight to the point."

Something flickered in his eyes, a warning that told her this man did not accept orders from anyone, especially not a woman and particularly not a *police* woman.

"As you wish," he said, sinking into one of the easy chairs. "Well, this all sounds very serious," he murmured. "Luckily, I happen to keep a legal department on site. Roger?"

A weaselly-looking man of around forty materialised from another part of the office, responding to his master's call like a whipped dog.

"These ladies are from CID—"

"Detectives, Mr Singh," MacKenzie put in, very sweetly. "We're only ladies when we're off duty."

He simply stared at her for an endless moment, and the sheer intensity of his gaze would have caused a lesser person to quiver.

Thankfully, MacKenzie did not fall into that category.

"We're here in connection with the disappearance of Rochelle White, aged twenty-five. We understand Ms White is your girlfriend, Mr Singh, and that you live together. Is that correct?"

"Just a minute," he said, affecting an air of surprise. "What do you mean, 'the disappearance'?"

"Precisely that, Mr Singh," Yates said. "Rochelle White was reported missing to the police yesterday morning."

Singh leaned forward urgently, and MacKenzie told herself to remain seated where she was and to fight the automatic urge to move away from him. Any sign of weakness would be ruthlessly exploited by this man, and she was determined to show none.

"This is all news to me," he was saying. "The last time I saw Rochelle, she was leaving for work, last Thursday morning."

"We understand Ms White was living with you—is that correct?"

He inclined his head.

"Didn't she return home, after work on Thursday?"

"I presume she did, but I wasn't there to see it," Singh said. "When I came back from a charity dinner, I found some of her things were missing and she'd left me a note. I still have it, if you wish to see it."

"We may well do," MacKenzie said, although what evidential value it might have, she didn't know. "Are you saying Rochelle moved out?"

Singh tried to look as he imagined a heart-broken man might look.

"It didn't come as too much of a surprise. I had a feeling she'd been seeing somebody else for a while," he said.

MacKenzie didn't bother to waste any time discussing the hypocrisy, given his relationship with his personal assistant. That wasn't her focus.

"Do you know the name of this...other person?"

"Not a clue," he said. "I thought he might have been one of yours, as it happens."

Both women looked up, at that.

"A police officer?" Yates said, and her stomach gave a funny little lurch. "What gave you that idea?"

Singh just shrugged.

"Just an impression," he said. "Little things she said. Do you think this man might have hurt her?"

Unbelievably, his eyes began to tear up, in what was either genuine concern, or a great piece of showmanship.

"I should have found out where she went," he muttered, rubbing the bridge of his nose between thumb and forefinger. "I'll never forgive myself, if something has happened to her."

They said nothing.

"Who reported Rochelle missing?" he asked, still looking tearful.

"We're not at liberty to divulge that information," MacKenzie replied, and saw it again. The little flash of anger mingled with something else, something darker, because she had crossed him again.

"Well," he said slowly. "Rochelle was a very...*special* lady, and I hope you find her. I wish I could be more helpful but, really, I don't know anything more than you do. I came home to find she had left me, to be with another man. I was hardly going to chase after the bird, once it had flown. I have my pride," he said.

They didn't believe a word of it.

"Just a few more questions, Mr Singh—"

He came to his feet, cutting Yates off, mid-sentence.

"No, I'm afraid that's all I have time for, today. I think you'll agree, I've been very helpful, and I'm a busy man. This evening, I'm hosting a charity event in aid of Alzheimer's and, I'm sure you'll agree, it's a cause we should all care more about. Good evening."

With that, he sauntered off, stepping through a glass door and into another part of his office, out of sight.

"I'll show you out," Roger said, and the looming security guard punched the button in preparation for their departure.

"How long have you worked for Mr Singh?" MacKenzie asked the solicitor, who gave her a reproachful stare.

"Really, inspector, you don't expect me to answer any of your questions, do you? To do so would be a breach of client confidentiality as well as my employment terms, which include a very strict clause on non-disclosure. I'm sure you understand, Mr Singh's business concerns can be market sensitive."

They stepped into the lift and, a moment later, it reached the ground floor.

"Thank you, Mr—?"

"Fentiman. Roger Fentiman. You'll find the name listed on the SRA website, as with all practitioners in good standing. Have a pleasant evening."

The foyer was quiet, now that most of the workers had left for home, but the eagle-eyed receptionist and the security staff remained.

"Where's Vogue?" Yates found herself asking.

"She's gone," the receptionist replied, with a malicious smile. "Good evening, do come again."

---

Outside, after they'd put a healthy distance between themselves and Singh's place of legitimate business, MacKenzie turned to Yates with a sad expression.

"Did you notice it, Mel?"

"Notice what, in particular? He's given us plenty to think about, as far as I can see."

MacKenzie smiled grimly.

"He referred to Rochelle in the past tense."

Yates swallowed, thinking of the elegant blonde woman she had met only once, and who was their best chance of providing a direct line into Singh's inner circle. If she was gone, their hopes on that score were gone too.

"He's lying about the policeman," she said, vehemently. "He's fabricating some old cock and bull story about Rochelle having run off with someone else so he can play the wounded party. Did you see those crocodile tears?"

"Chilling," MacKenzie agreed. "Unfortunately, a lot of people would fall for that. Maybe even a jury. Plus, he's good-looking."

"What difference does that make?"

"You know what difference it makes," MacKenzie replied. "Psychological studies have proven that people tend to ascribe positive characteristics to people they find attractive, and negative characteristics to those they find unattractive. If Bobby Singh turns on the tears and bats his big brown eyes at the female jurors, they'd acquit him on grounds of reasonable doubt."

"That's why the physical evidence is so important," Yates said. "We need more."

"We'll get it," MacKenzie said, with an admirable confidence she didn't altogether feel. He was smooth, that one. Charismatic and dangerous, well-organised and well-financed.

It was a lethal combination.

---

Much later, Simon Watson watched the night sky from the kitchen window in his bungalow, which looked out across Penshaw Monument. The moon was supernaturally bright and low in the sky, casting an ethereal white glow around its old walls, as if they had an aura or a soul. It was funny to think of the monument as a living thing, but he wondered if its vitality came from the people who had touched its stones or woven through its columns. Perhaps they left something of themselves behind, and the stones retained the memory of it. He wondered what secrets the monument might tell of all the men and women in the village, and the visitors from further afield. Times had changed, but the monument had not; it stood firm, everlasting and immovable on its mound of earth.

And so must he.

Simon moved away from the window and walked through to his mother's room, to check she was still sleeping soundly. He found Joan snoring peacefully, the medication having lulled her into a deep, dreamless slumber. He moved quietly beside her and, ever so gently, pressed a gentle kiss to her brow.

"Sleep well, Mum."

He tiptoed out again but left the door ajar, as always.

After that, Simon went back into the living room and settled himself on his favourite chair.

He was expecting a visitor.

# CHAPTER 19

It was after ten when Lowerson felt his eyelids begin to droop.

His body was in desperate need of sleep, the deficit now running so high he was almost hysterical, but his fear outweighed every other bodily need. Sleep could wait, when his own mortality was in question.

Images of Rochelle invaded his mind, playing like an endless showreel in a horror movie. In his mind, he imagined her skull shattering all over the bed, the life dying in her eyes as her fingers reached towards him for help. He wanted to spit out the awful taste in his mouth, the remaining bile he couldn't quite divest himself of.

He dragged himself off the sofa to do another round of checks; first, the doors, then all the windows. They were all locked but, by the time he returned to the living room, he felt the need to check them all over again. He stumbled to the fridge and sought out an energy drink, which he forced himself to swallow. He needed to think clearly and stay awake, just a little while longer.

The man sitting in a parked car across the street watched Lowerson's front door for almost thirty minutes before he finally got out of the car and crossed the street, wanting to be sure there was no surveillance detail. The road was badly lit, so it was hard to be sure, but he was reasonably certain nobody would see his approach.

He had a job to do.

Inside the house, Lowerson took up his usual position sitting in the hallway, and waited.

It took longer than he would have thought, but then he heard the soft tread of a man's footsteps on the path outside. His heart began to hammer against the wall of his chest as the man's body was silhouetted against the glow of the streetlamps, and his breathing stopped completely when the figure raised a hand to the front door handle.

It turned, left and right, but would not open.

Then came a soft tap.

Lowerson rose on shaking legs and made his way towards the door, breathing quickly, the air coming in short gasps through his open mouth.

"Open the door, Jack."

---

When Lowerson unlocked the front door, he found Ryan standing on the porch step, his face in shadow.

"Thanks for coming," he said, and Ryan gave a brief nod before stepping inside.

"You said it was urgent."

Lowerson nodded, and led the way through to the living room, where the curtains had already been drawn. He tried to pull himself together, to grasp at the threads of his sanity, before facing the man who had been his living idol as a younger man and remained the person he most admired.

Ryan was studying his face, searching it for clues.

"I'm here now, Jack. What's going on?"

Lowerson swallowed painfully, trying to find the words.

*I'm sorry.*

*I've let you down. I've let the team down, not to mention myself.*

"I'm out of my depth," he said, and was proud that his voice didn't waver too badly. "I've got myself into a situation I thought I could handle, but I can't. I need help."

Ryan frowned, and moved across to one of the chairs.

"You'd better sit down too, before you fall down," he muttered.

Lowerson complied, grateful to take the weight off his injured leg.

"What kind of situation?"

"The worst kind."

Ryan ran a hand over the stubble on his chin, looking at the man he'd trained, trusted and defended from foes within and without. If Jack had a failing, it was that he had a propensity to cut corners. He wanted to jump straight to the finish line, before running the race, which invariably meant making clumsy mistakes along the way.

But this was something else.

Something dark.

"What have you done, Jack?"

Lowerson's eyes fell away.

"I made a deal with the devil."

---

It was almost four o'clock in the morning by the time Ryan made it home.

The roads were empty at that time of night, which was lucky because he could not have vouched for the state of his driving skills at that particular moment. He drove on autopilot, keeping to a reasonable speed that was at least twenty miles per hour slower than his usual, and almost missed the turn-off for Elsdon while his mind was far away, consumed by other thoughts.

The house was in darkness except for the porch light, which had been left on by Anna and acted as a beacon, guiding him safely back into harbour. He questioned himself again, asking himself whether he had made the right decision.

*Did he do the right thing?*

All roads led back to the same question: where was Rochelle White?

Ryan locked and bolted the door behind him and, as Lowerson had done, made a thorough inspection of the other windows and doors around the house. Personal experience had taught him to be cautious, so there was a state-of-the-art security system at the touch of a button.

He activated the alarm and then went upstairs, in search of his wife.

Anna was curled up on his side of the bed, her arms wrapped around the pillow. A book lay open on the bedside table, some sort of tome on Northumbrian myths and legends, and it made him smile.

Almost swaying with exhaustion, he stripped off his clothes and climbed naked into the bed, too tired to care about pyjamas. He curved his long body around hers and breathed in the coconut scent to her hair, feeling his body begin to relax into sleep.

Just as he was drifting off, she stirred.

"I love you," she mumbled.

When he fell asleep, he was smiling.

# CHAPTER 20

*Wednesday, 12ᵗʰ June 2019*

Joan Watson awoke to the sound of birdsong outside her bedroom window and reached out an arm to the other side of the bed.

*Force of habit.*

Alan wasn't there, and hadn't been for a very long time.

As the chirping continued in the tree outside, her mind was caught somewhere between sleep and wakefulness as she caught snatches of the dream the birds had interrupted. In it, she was young again, and dressed in an outfit she'd worn in the late sixties, when she'd been a woman in her twenties. High boots and short skirts had been all the rage, along with a back-combed, beehive hairstyle, just like Nancy Sinatra.

*These boots are made for walkin'…*

She could even remember the feel of those old boots, and the way the right toe had rubbed a bit. Still, she'd worn them until they'd practically fallen apart and, in the dream, they were new again. There were no wrinkles on her face, no deep grooves or sagging skin she hardly recognised as her own. In the dream, she'd been Joanie, and they'd gone dancing.

Alan had always been a good dancer.

She remembered his touch, even the shape of his hands. Funny, the little things you remember.

Simon had the same hands; large and strong, with square nails.

Still groggy with sleep, she checked the time and realised it was still early; not yet seven o'clock. Simon would be up and about soon, so she would just sit and wait until he wakened naturally. He might have had a rocky start, but he'd put his life back on track and he worked hard, so he needed his sleep.

But when the clock slipped past seven-thirty, she began to worry he would be late for work.

"Simon?" she called out.

It wasn't a large house, so she didn't need to bellow for him to hear.

*No answer.*

She tried again.

"Simon!"

She waited, but there was no rustling in the bedroom next door, none of the usual clattering as he moved around, or the spray of the shower.

This time, she shouted.

"SIMON!"

There was no reply, and never would be again.

---

The call came through as Ryan was savouring the first hit of caffeine through his veins. He'd slept less than three hours, but it was better than nothing and he'd coped with much worse, in his time.

"Ryan."

"It's Morrison," said the Chief Constable. "I've just heard from Control. There's been another one."

Ryan paused; a fraction too long.

"Another what, ma'am?"

"Another death in Penshaw," she said, as if it were obvious.

Ryan was surprised.

"In Penshaw?"

She made an irritated sound at the other end of the line.

"Ryan, for goodness' sake, stop repeating everything I say. Yes, it happened *in Penshaw*, and that's not the worst of it. The DB is Simon Watson."

Ryan's face became shuttered. If he had been wavering as to whether Alan Watson's death had been an unfortunate accident or a suspicious death, he wasn't any longer. Two deaths in the same family, within a matter of days, was too much coincidence.

"Do you have any other details?" he asked.

"Just that the responding officer thinks it's looking like an accidental overdose," she replied. "The AC isn't going to like it."

"I'm sure Simon Watson likes it much less," Ryan said, with no small amount of sarcasm. *But how to investigate?*

He had urgent business to deal with today, and important calls to make.

"Ah, I could send MacKenzie over," he offered.

"You know how highly I think of Denise," Morrison said. "But I told you at the start, Ryan, the AC wants my most senior man on the job. Whether I happen to like it or not, that's you."

Ryan held off making any further remarks and resigned himself to a difficult day ahead.

"I'll be there within the hour," he said.

---

Word had already spread by the time Ryan and Phillips arrived back in the little village of Penshaw. Local people gathered at the end of Simon Watson's street, edging closer like zombies to the feast, until they were warned off by the two local bobbies tasked with guarding the scene.

"They don't mean anything by it," Phillips said, as he watched another nosy neighbour skirt around the side of a parked car, trying to get a better look. "They just can't help rubbernecking."

"I don't mind them taking an interest, if it helps the investigation," Ryan said, fairly. "But I've no time for people who come to pick over the bones of somebody else's misfortune."

In cases of accidental overdose, people could be quick to judge.

Once again, they spotted Faulkner's van parked a little further along the street, not far from an ambulance with its back door open in readiness to transport a patient. The reason soon became apparent when two paramedics wheeled Joan Watson out of her son's house on a stretcher, with her daughter hurrying alongside.

"You'll be fine, mum, don't worry. They'll take good care of you," she said, tearfully.

"There, now," her husband said, giving her an awkward pat.

"Mr and Mrs Emerson," Ryan greeted them, as they met on the pavement. "We're very sorry to hear of your loss."

Sally's eyes welled up, but she waved away any sympathy.

"Never mind us. Poor Mum—she found him like *that…*" Her breath caught in her throat as she battled the horrifying image of her brother sprawled on the floor, the last she would ever see of him.

"Is Joan going to be alright?" Phillips asked. "She's had two terrible blows, this week."

"I don't know, sergeant. I have no idea how she'll cope, or even *if* she'll cope. She suffered another mild stroke when she found Simon's body, and the hospital think there might have been a heart attack too, so they're going to run some more tests and keep her in overnight for observation. On top of all that, she's still healing from the burns."

"We'll need to stop by and have a word with Mrs Watson," Ryan said. "But we can wait a while, to give her a chance to recover."

"Thank you," Sally said, with feeling. "I really—we really must go now. I think the ambulance is leaving."

"Would it be alright to come and pay a visit at home, so we can understand the timeline of events, from your perspective?"

"Any time after three," Mike said, and, at her questioning look, went on to explain that he was due to be playing golf later that day.

"*Any time*," she corrected him. "We'll make ourselves available, chief inspector."

---

Jack Lowerson couldn't stay at home, even if he wanted to.

His every move was being catalogued, and he knew that Singh would find out very quickly if he hadn't shown up for work. Their bargain depended on him being at the office in order to feed information back, in exchange for Singh not revealing the images taken of him and Rochelle to the Ghost Squad.

As if they had read his mind, another message came through on the little burner mobile that stayed close to him at all times, like a doctor on call.

This time, the message was not what he expected:

MAKE SURE PENSHAW OVERDOSE NOT SUSPICIOUS. TELL RYAN ACCIDENTAL DEATH.

It took him only a matter of seconds to understand that Bobby's Singh's influence stretched much further than even he had imagined. He didn't know what the connection might be between a fifty-year-old manager from Penshaw, his eighty-year-old father, and a criminal underboss. All he knew was that, if he failed to follow the instruction, everything would fold.

***

After Sally and Mike Emerson left to follow the ambulance to the hospital, Ryan and Phillips retrieved their coveralls from the back of the car and readied themselves to enter the house. Once inside, they found the bungalow crawling with CSIs; androgynous figures whose faces were hidden beneath the masks they wore as they rustled through the remnants of a person's life.

"Faulkner?"

The Senior CSI looked up as they entered the living room, which appeared to be where the majority of the action had taken place. In line with emergency protocols, Simon Watson's body had been moved from its original position, so that the paramedics could attempt CPR. In this case, the emergency doctor had pronounced Simon dead soon after their arrival.

Now, he lay face-up in the middle of the floor, arms flung wide. His face was mottled and swollen, the veins in his right arm standing out like swollen black rivers against his deathly pale skin. Post-mortem lividity had caused the blood to settle in one half of his body—in this case, the front half, which was dark red.

"Looks like he was lying face-down when he died," Phillips said, after taking several deep breaths.

"Yes. The paramedics say he was lying over there, next to the coffee table, when they arrived."

"Had anybody touched him?" Ryan asked.

"Well, the paramedics say he looked obviously dead—his mother had tried to move him but couldn't quite manage it, because of the injuries to her hands."

Ryan looked across the room to where several small yellow markers had been set out beside a heavy-looking glass coffee table. On the extreme edge, there was a hairline crack encrusted with a small amount of blood and other fibres.

"Is there a head injury?" he asked.

"Yes, there's a deep cut on his left temple," Faulkner said, leaning down on his haunches to inspect the wound.

Phillips preferred to keep a safe distance.

"Usual drugs paraphernalia," he said, pointing to where a needle lay on the carpet beneath the coffee table, on top of which there was a spoon and a lighter.

"There was a tiny piece of needle protruding from his skin," Faulkner added. "I've bagged it for the lab. It seems obvious it's the piece missing from that needle over there, which we'll also bag for toxicology."

Ryan stood at the side of the room, noting the placement of each item and where it had fallen, trying to visualise what might have happened.

"So, he was sitting on the sofa when he took a hit from the needle, leading to a fatal overdose, and then, his body slumped forward, and he hit the side of his head on the coffee table when he went down. Is that it?"

"It's all pointing in that direction," Faulkner agreed. "We've only really just begun sweeping the place here, so I'll know more in a couple of days."

He paused.

"Something bothers me, about the coffee table," he said.

The other two waited for him to elaborate.

"If he fell right after he took the overdose, the blood would still be circulating," Faulkner said. "I'd expect to see more spatter on the coffee table, or on the floor."

Ryan nodded.

"There's something else that puzzles me," he said, walking carefully around the perimeter of the room until he reached the sofa, where he tested one of the cushions with a gloved hand.

"The sofa dips towards the back," he said. "It's also quite low to the ground. Common sense alone tells me that Simon Watson's recently deceased body wouldn't have had the upward thrust needed to fall out of the chair in the manner we're expected to believe."

"So what are you saying?" Phillips asked. "It was a set up? We already know Simon had his troubles with heroin, in the past."

"And everybody knew it," Ryan said.

"It's a risky business, with Joan in the house," Phillips remarked. "She might've heard something."

"Not under medication, late at night. Pinter should be able to give us a more accurate estimation of the time of death."

Phillips shook his head, sadly.

"It could be that the grief over Alan's death and all the stress of his mother being unwell sent him over the edge. As a recovering addict, he'd be more vulnerable in times of personal strife."

Ryan nodded.

"That might be true," he agreed. "He might've been perching on the edge of the sofa when he shot up, and that explains how he was able to fall forward."

He looked around the room again, then dropped down to look underneath the sofa. Then, with careful hands, he searched the dead man's pockets, gritting his teeth against the gassy odour that was beginning to emanate from the body.

"Has anything else been bagged, Tom?"

"Not yet," Faulkner replied. "We left things in situ so you could get a feel for the scene."

Ryan smiled grimly.

"In that case, I want to know what happened to the pouch."

Phillips gave him a quizzical look.

"How'd you mean?"

"The pouch where he kept the drugs, or the plastic bag the dealer gave him, with the residue inside. Where is it?"

All three men cast their eyes around the floor space, and even rolled the body to check it wasn't hidden beneath. For completeness, they checked the other rooms of the house, and used the forensic team's special wire camera to check that it had not been flushed down the toilet. It took extra time, but Ryan was not a man for half measures.

"Why would the dealer wait and take the bag away, afterwards? Unless they knew it was likely to be lethal…" Phillips said.

"Or, maybe, it was a tiny error on the part of Simon's killer," Ryan said. "There's no such thing as a perfect crime, and he's made a couple of slip-ups with this one. I wonder whether he—or she—was rushed into making mistakes."

Ryan looked upon the wasted body of Simon Watson with an expression caught somewhere between grief and fury. This man had turned his life around, had only just begun to live again, before it was all snatched away from him.

"The thing is, I can't see any motive," Phillips said. "It's the same as his father—who'd want to kill a frail old man, or a recovering addict?"

Ryan's phone signalled a new message, and he glanced over the contents before making a check of the time.

*If he was quick, he could make it.*

"That's what we need to find out, Frank," he murmured. "You stay here and see what else turns up; I need to get back to the office."

Phillips opened his mouth to ask what was so pressing, but Ryan had already gone.

# CHAPTER 21

Ryan did not go directly to Police Headquarters, but made a very short, very important detour to the pathologist's office.

"Jeff."

Pinter was munching on a ham sandwich, which was enough to turn Ryan's stomach, given the proximity of his office to the service area of the mortuary.

"Ryan! I didn't know you were coming," he said, and wiped his hands on some paper towelling. "Are you here about Simon Watson? He hasn't arrived yet, but I'm on standby—"

"I know, I've just come from the scene," Ryan said, and shut the office door behind him.

Pinter raised an eyebrow.

"Anything the matter, then?"

Ryan had thought carefully about what action to take following Lowerson's revelations the previous night. Subterfuge went against the grain but, he reasoned, it was all for the greater good.

"I need you to make two reports on Simon Watson. One report for the official file which states that everything points to an accidental overdose, and then another report with whatever your real conclusions are, for my eyes only."

Pinter was silent for long seconds.

"Is all this above board, Ryan? Why would you need two reports, and why is the real one 'for your eyes only'?"

"I'm sorry, Jeff, but I can't tell you that. I hope you'll trust me to act in the best interests of my team, and with the integrity required of my profession."

Pinter looked at the tall, raven-haired man he'd come to think of as a friend. Ryan was widely known to be incorruptible; a force for good in the world of law enforcement against which others might be measured and found wanting.

And yet, he'd asked him to falsify a report, and show the true report only to him.

There had to be a reason. He would not believe Ryan capable of wilful deception without having gone through the proper reporting channels, or having sought authority beforehand.

"Alright, Ryan," he said quietly. "I trust that you know what you're doing."

---

Ryan's next port of call was Police Headquarters but, instead of entering through the main doors as he usually would, he parked close to the rear exit which was mostly used when transporting suspects to court or detention elsewhere. He took out a small rucksack, which he slung over one shoulder, and made his way to the rear doors. There were two CCTV cameras, and he stopped to look up at them, before entering a key code to buzz himself in.

Once inside, there were no more cameras in the communal areas, and he made his way quickly to the Evidence Store. Before he rounded the corner, where he knew an attendant would be on duty keeping a log of all incoming and outgoing evidence, Ryan took out his smartphone and made a note of the time.

He was all smiles when he approached the desk sergeant, and her face lit up in response. She might have been a happily married mother of three, but she still had red blood in her veins, and the sight of DCI Maxwell Ryan—all six feet, four inches of him—was enough to brighten anybody's day.

"Hello, stranger," she said. "Haven't seen you in a little while."

"Hi, Kim," he flashed another winning smile. "I wanted to have a quick look at the murder weapon from one of my old cases, if you don't mind."

He reeled off the case number of a cold file, from a couple of years ago.

"We've had a spate of stabbings, and I wanted to see whether the weapon is similar to one we've seen before."

"I don't know how you find the time," she said, with admiration. "Just give us your autograph in the log, here, and help yourself. D'you need a pair of gloves?"

He took a fresh pair of nitrile gloves from the box she offered.

"You'll have to leave your bag here," she said, with a pained expression. "It's the rules."

"Of course," he said, scrambling for an alternative plan.

After he'd scrawled his name in the logbook, Kim unlocked the steel-caged doors leading to the Evidence Store and he stepped inside.

"Don't get lost in there!" she called out.

It was not altogether a joke, Ryan thought, as he surveyed row upon row of shelves, each containing boxes or larger items on their own, properly indexed.

He glanced behind him to find Kim still watching from her high desk chair.

"Wrong way!" she laughed. "It's in aisle seven, to your left."

Ryan pretended to slap his own head.

"Don't know my left from my right, this morning," he said, and duly turned around to make his way to the aisle she had indicated.

Unfortunately, it was nowhere near the aisle he *needed*. With lightning-swift movements, he scanned the shelves for a mobile phone and snatched up the first one he saw, inside a little plastic evidence bag. Peering through the gaps in the shelves, Ryan checked to see whether anybody else was coming, or whether Kim was looking in his direction, and then retrieved his own mobile from his back pocket, which he used to take a photograph of the random evidence bag. Then, he carried them both to the end of the aisle, furthest away from the desk, and hurried along the back wall towards the aisle he really needed.

The physical evidence pertaining to Dan "The Demon" Hepple's murder was being kept in aisle fourteen and, after a quick search, he found the two plastic evidence bags he was looking for. Ryan used his smartphone to take another photograph of the original tags on the burner mobile and ladies knickers belonging to Rochelle White, and then crouched to the floor while he made the swap. The fresh evidence bags he'd brought were still in his rucksack, and so he had to make do with what he had, conscious all the while that they could not be contaminated.

Rather than swapping the contents of each bag, he'd simply swap their codes.

Ryan always kept a biro in his pocket, which wasn't the same as the Sharpie permanent marker the forensics team used to label the bags, but it would have to do. With a steady hand, he altered the codes on each bag and took another photograph on his smartphone before setting the 'new' evidence back on the shelf. There was no ready replacement for the knickers belonging to Rochelle; the ones he'd brought to swap in for those were also in the rucksack.

He stuffed the small plastic bag inside his shirt, flattening it as best he could. They'd have to go missing, he thought.

His final task was to place Rochelle's old burner mobile on a shelf in aisle seven, because he was conscious that time was marching on. As he retraced his steps along the back wall, he heard the scrape of Kim's chair against the floor as she stood up and went in search of him.

Moving at breakneck speed, Ryan darted into aisle seven and searched frantically for an empty spot at the back of a high shelf, where only Ryan would know where to find it—although still technically in the Evidence Store, anyone else trying to find the mobile would be searching for a needle in a haystack.

By the time Kim stuck her head around the edge of the shelving unit, Ryan was holding up a clear bag containing an ornate knife, turning it this way and that.

"Everything alright?" she asked, cheerfully. "I was just about to go on my lunch."

"I'm finished here, anyway," Ryan said, making his way back out of the caged metal area. "Thanks, Kim."

He turned to leave.

"Ryan."

He froze, feeling the plastic bag rustle against his skin.

"Mm?"

"You forgot to sign out," she said.

After he'd scrawled his name again, Ryan didn't run but walked at a moderate pace, all the way out of the Evidence Store and around the corner of the basement corridor. He kept it up all the way to the lift, nodding to his colleagues who spilled out when the doors swished open.

Once he was alone and the doors closed softly behind him, Ryan leaned back against the mirrored wall and wondered what the hell he had got himself into.

# CHAPTER 22

Phillips spent half an hour surveying Simon Watson's home and, after a final word with Tom Faulkner and another fruitless hour completing door-to-door enquiries with one of the local constables, he decided to make his way over to the dead man's workplace. If Ryan's suspicions were correct and Watson's death was not as straightforward as it seemed, there had to be some reason why he was targeted by whichever unknown assassin entered his home. A quick look around that home had not helped matters; Simon Watson had been a frugal sort of man, not given to keeping trinkets or files of yellowing paperwork. Ordinarily, Phillips might have admired his restraint, but when it came to finding a motive for murder, it was mighty inconvenient.

Watson might not have been one for fancy technology or nights in watching Netflix, but one area in which he seemed to have been very committed was his work, and his activism, which must have been influenced by his father. Phillips reasoned that, if there was nothing to find at home, perhaps there might be something to find at the jobcentre in Sunderland.

And he was right.

The office was experiencing an early-afternoon rush when he stepped through the automatic doors, and it was a mission to find a member of staff who could spare a couple of minutes. He lingered beside the front desk, which he noticed was manned by a bored-looking security guard, and waited to cut in.

"Here! Can't you see there's a queue?"

Phillips turned to see a young woman pushing a wheelchair, on which sat an even younger woman, who was clearly very unwell.

"Sorry, pet, but I'm with the police. I just need someone to point me in the right direction, then I'll step aside and leave you to it."

She seemed mollified by that, and they stood patiently side by side until the manager at the desk finished with the customer she was seeing.

"Police, eh?" she continued, curiously. "Should we be worried?"

Phillips gave her a friendly smile.

"No, lass," he murmured, and decided he might as well make small talk. Sometimes, you learned the most helpful things, when you let people talk.

"What sort of job are you looking for, then?"

"I've already got one," she replied. "I'm here for Maisie. She's my sister."

Phillips smiled at the younger woman in the chair, who did not respond.

"Carer's benefit?"

She let out a mirthless laugh.

"Not quite," she muttered. "Apparently, Maisie's supposed to be applying for jobs, otherwise she's *lazy*. It doesn't matter that she was in a near-fatal car accident when she was only a baby, that left her with lifelong brain damage. She can't read or write—she can barely talk. She can smile," her sister said, reaching down to stroke the top of Maisie's head. "But they need her to check in, so that the government can be sure she's not leeching off the state."

Phillips was gobsmacked.

"You mean to tell me they're expecting her to apply for jobs?"

The woman nodded.

"It's soul-destroying. I'm all for disability rights, and looking at the whole person, but Maisie…she just isn't capable, and it's cruel to put her through this."

"*Next, please*?"

"Nice chattin' to you, love. All the best," he said, with another smile for Maisie. "I'll be as quick as I can."

---

"I can't believe it."

The duty manager was a woman called Moira, who became tearful almost as soon as Phillips imparted the bad news that Simon Watson would not be coming into work, ever again. "To think, I was cross at him this morning," she said, and blew her nose loudly. "I thought he hadn't turned up, and I tried to call him—"

*Mobile phone,* Phillips thought suddenly. *Had they found Simon's mobile?*

"It's a job share, you see. Simon does Monday to Wednesday, and I'm only supposed to do Thursdays and Fridays."

"Sorry to inconvenience you," Phillips said, with rigid politeness. "Did Simon have a locker or a desk?"

"We don't have lockers, but he has a permanent desk," Moira said. "I'll show you."

Phillips followed her to one of the wide desks set out at the back of the room, presumably situated so that Simon could keep an eye on the rest of the office.

Immediately, his eye landed on the locked drawer at the bottom and he remembered the keyring they'd found in Watson's bungalow, which was now bagged up with the rest of Simon's belongings.

"Do you have a master key for that?" he asked.

Moira bustled off to find it, leaving Phillips to discreetly draw on some nitrile gloves. Luckily, being at the back of the room meant there were fewer people to goggle at what he was doing—or question why he was wearing gloves.

The desk was clear and unfussy, which seemed to have been Simon's signature style. On his desk, there was a lamp, a pot containing some biros, a small bottle of antiseptic hand gel and some tissues. Phillips raised an eyebrow, and reasoned it would have been necessary to take precautions against illness, given the number of strangers the late Simon Watson might have met and shaken hands with, through the course of a day.

Presently, Moira returned brandishing the master key.

When she continued to linger, Phillips turned to her again.

"Sorry to be a hassle, but could I trouble you for a glass of water?"

"Of course!"

Left alone again, Phillips opened the locked drawers in Simon's desk and began to rifle through the first, which contained the usual assortment of stationery and notebooks he would expect to find. The second wasn't much better, seeming to hold a collection of policy documents for reference, as well as a number of files marked 'COMPLEX' or 'URGENT' and a stack of freshly printed leaflets advertising the forthcoming Jobcentre Strike against Universal Credit, and a rally to be held at Penshaw Monument that Friday.

But then, when he opened the bottom drawer, Phillips hit the jackpot.

Lying at the top of a stack of odds and ends was a medium-sized brown manila envelope addressed to Alan Watson, Simon's father. It was post-marked for the previous Saturday, and Phillips deduced that it couldn't have been delivered to Alan before the fire. Perhaps it had been delivered to Simon instead?

With careful hands, Phillips picked it up and peered inside the torn edge to see a small sheaf of papers and a covering letter bearing the government logo of 'GCHQ'. Spotting Moira as she crossed the room, he slid the envelope inside a plastic evidence bag and decided to assess its contents later, in the relative privacy of Police Headquarters.

"Thank you," he said, taking the proffered glass of water, which he duly sipped. "Tell me, Moira. Did you know Simon Watson well?"

The woman gave a half shrug.

"Not really," she said. "We were like ships in the night, working on different days. People liked him, though, and he was popular with the staff. He was organising that rally."

"You taking part?" Phillips asked, out of sheer curiosity.

"Of course," she said, as if it were a silly question. "Everybody in this office will be turning out. We might have to do the government's bidding, but it doesn't mean we agree with it, and it's about time we said as much. Simon's sister, Sally, is going to talk at the rally," she added, with a touch of admiration. "She's head of the local council, and every little helps."

Phillips nodded, and thought that, for all their misfortunes, the Watsons were a close-knit family who clearly supported one another. It reminded him of his own family, and the family he was still building.

"I hope it's a success," he said, thinking of Maisie and her sister, who were by now seated at another desk across the room speaking to a man who appeared to be shaking his head an awful lot.

He dragged his wayward thoughts back to the matter in hand.

"Do you know if Simon had been particularly worried about anything, or anyone?"

Moira pulled a face while she thought.

"No, I can't say that I do. He was very sad to hear what had happened to his father, of course. Dreadful thing, that."

"Mm, terrible," Phillips agreed.

Interviewing witnesses was like a dance, he thought. People needed a bit of back-and-forth, to help draw them out.

"He'd been preoccupied organising the rally ahead of the strike," she continued. "But, if anything, he was optimistic about it. I wouldn't say he was worried but, as I say, I didn't know him well. You might have more luck speaking to Sean—they were good friends, I think."

She pointed across the room to a young man.

"He's the one to speak to."

# CHAPTER 23

Sally and Mike Emerson left the hospital in Durham and didn't speak until they were safely inside their brand-new SUV. It was a bit of a risky purchase, given that Sally's reputation had been built largely on the presumption that she was 'one of the people.' The people in her borough liked to believe she was 'one of them'; a miner's daughter who understood what it meant to work—really work—as hard as you could, and still not be able to buy trainers for your kids' feet.

Sally had come to understand the power of persuasion very young in life.

Her father had been a classic idealist, and her mother wasn't much better. They both subscribed to the notion that there was no shame in being poor. They used to tell her that, so long as they had each other, they were rich.

She'd hated it.

She'd hated seeing pictures of pretty clothes in *Jackie* magazine that she'd never be able to buy. She'd hated seeing adverts for summer holidays on the telly, in far off places they'd never be able to visit. She hated seeing the Queen giving her ruddy speech from her golden palace, the likes of which she'd never know.

What made them so much better?

Soon enough, she'd realised that all those people she envied weren't better, they were just *smarter*. They'd educated themselves and taken whatever chances came their way, to get ahead in life. The problem was, she didn't even have GCEs.

That's when she'd enrolled in night school, and Simon had tagged along too.

*She'd always been the one to push him on,* she thought, with a sad little sigh.

"Looks like she's going to pull through," Mike said, interrupting her reverie.

Everything about her husband was an irritant, and had been since they were children knocking about in the playground. Michael Emerson had been a poser all his life; a flirt, a braggart, a man other men tolerated but did not necessarily like. Living with him had been a penance, and she'd paid it for long enough.

"I want a divorce," she said, very clearly.

She heard his shocked intake of breath, and he shifted in the driver's seat to look at her.

"*What?*" he blustered. "What are you talking about?"

"Oh, come on, Mike. You know there's nothing between us. There hasn't been for a long time."

*Ever.*

He sat in absolute silence for long, tense seconds as she stared out of the windscreen and watched a light drizzle coat the glass.

"You haven't thought this through," he said, but didn't bother to argue with the sentiment. His girlfriend had been asking for him to get a divorce for months, now, but he'd never actually planned to go through with it.

Their lives were too entwined. Too dependent.

"You need me," he said, simply. "It'll look bad for your next campaign."

Sally laughed.

"I need *you*?" she said bitterly, but stopped herself from launching into a tirade, not wanting to go too far.

"Listen, Mike. This can work for both of us," she said, in a placatory tone. "We can sell up and share the proceeds. We can still work together as business partners."

"Oh, aye," he said. "What about your new partner? What would he have to say about that?"

Sally said nothing.

"Well, he needs me too. You both do," Mike said, arrogantly, and turned the ignition. "Remember that, next time you think you can brush me off."

They both jumped when there came a sharp tap on the side window.

---

Phillips had been on his way to check on Joan Watson's status, but had spotted Sally and Mike Emerson seated inside their parked car and decided to kill two birds with one stone.

"Sorry to startle you," he said, when she lowered the passenger window. "I wondered if we could have a quick chat. Is this a good time?"

"Jump in," Mike said, and Sally shot him an angry glare that he chose to ignore.

Phillips settled himself in the back seat and took his time getting out his notebook and pencil, while he read the mood inside the leather-clad interior.

"Please accept our condolences again," he said, thinking of an ardent man who was now lost to the world. "How's Mrs Watson keeping?"

"The doctors say she's stabilised," Sally replied, speaking quietly. "My mother's always been the strongest person in our family."

"She seems a very fine woman," Phillips agreed.

When neither person offered any comment, he changed tack.

"Ah, well, I really need to ask you a few questions surrounding your brother's last movements," he said. "We're still a bit unclear about what happened last night."

"Seems obvious that he fell off the wagon again," Mike said, not unkindly. "It was hard to get him clean. Maybe he'd been struggling these last few days, and we just didn't notice."

"He seemed depressed, the last time we spoke," Sally said. "I didn't think too much of it, because I wasn't exactly feeling top of the bill, myself."

"That's to be expected, with the loss of your father," Phillips said, sympathetically. "When did you last speak to your brother, Mrs Emerson?"

"Sally," she corrected him. "Ah, it would have been yesterday afternoon. He rang to ask after mum, and to let me know what time he'd be back to take over. We had a sort of system in place, where either Mike or I would try to be there for mum during the day, to let the nurse in when she arrived and make her meals, then Simon took over the evening shift. He was ringing to let me know he'd be home a bit late."

"Did he say why he'd be late?"

"No—I asked him, but he told me it was just work stuff."

Phillips frowned. He happened to know that the jobcentre closed at a regular time each day, and the staff there didn't tend to work overtime due to the service nature of their roles.

"Did you sense anything strange about his general demeanour?" Phillips asked. "Did he seem anxious?"

"He was definitely out of sorts," she said. "He was being very philosophical about life, talking about whether any of it made any difference—the rally he was organising, for instance."

"Were you in fear for his safety?"

"You mean, did he seem suicidal?" Sally asked, and then blew out a shaky breath. "I—I don't know, sergeant. Now that I know he took an overdose, I've been thinking back over the conversation. Should I have said something different? Should I have known?"

Sally shook her head, battling tears.

"Simon was very unwell, trapped in a cycle for years," she said. "My mum and dad tried everything to get him off the drugs. I'd given up on him, for a while. We both had."

"He nicked off with a hundred quid out of my wallet, that time, and I said it was the last straw," Mike said, pensively. "But then, once he went through the programme and out the other end, he paid me back. Paid us back every last penny."

"Seems like, for all he had problems with addiction, your brother was a good man, Mrs Emerson."

Sally closed her eyes, trying not to remember the final image of her brother as a thousand images of them together washed through her memory. Fifty years of living, not all of them good ones, but they'd never been parted—until now.

"He was a good man, sergeant. Simon's problem was always that he never knew when to stop."

# CHAPTER 24

The two men stood behind one of the large, concrete pillars that supported an office block on the northern side of the River Tyne, directly overlooking a large roundabout that gave access to the bridge and the centre of town. In the middle of the roundabout, another tall concrete tower housed one of the area's local radio stations, as well as a couple of restaurants. Come Friday night, glamorous men and women would make their way down through the underpass and emerge to enjoy a haven of cocktails and Asian cuisine, as traffic passed them by.

Food was far from their minds as the two men spoke quietly beside the network of concrete walkways. Yards away, the site of a former Victorian soup kitchen took up a large plot on the other side of the road, where people could go and look around the old walls and talk about how sad it must have been in the nineteenth century while, in the tunnels beneath their feet, the city's present-day homeless set up their sleeping bags in preparation for another cold and hungry night.

"You're sure about this?" Blackett asked.

"I've documented everything," Ryan replied, while his eyes roamed the immediate vicinity, lingering on the shadowy corners.

"Hard to believe Lowerson would do it," Blackett said, thinking of the young detective constable he'd always viewed as more of a victim of circumstance than anything else.

"Yeah, well. It's always the quiet ones, isn't it?" Ryan muttered. "Are you happy to keep the status quo, for the moment, and see how it pans out?"

Blackett rubbed his chin, and then nodded.

"Yes, I think that's for the best," he said. "My officer on the inside reckons they're close to getting some of the others to come on the record. They need some more time."

Ryan frowned.

"On the inside?"

Blackett smiled.

"Did you think we've been sitting on our hands, these past twelve months? I've had somebody on the ground since last June."

Ryan ran through all the men and women assigned to Operation Watchman and tried to work out which of them it might be, knowing full well it would be a waste of breath to ask Blackett.

"You did the right thing, coming to me with this," Blackett assured him. "We'll take the appropriate steps, when the time comes."

Ryan thought of Jack, and stuck his hands in his pockets.

"Don't drag this out," he said. "I want this tied up, sooner rather than later."

"You don't get to make that call."

Ryan treated Blackett to an icy stare.

"And you don't get to play with people's lives, Andy. Remember that."

He turned and strode back through the concrete shadows, and out into the light.

---

It was past two o'clock by the time Ryan and his team convened in one of the smaller conference rooms at Northumbria Police Headquarters. As he watched them pulling out chairs and rustling through the summary sheets he always took the time to prepare, Ryan was struck forcibly by the uncomfortable sensation that he didn't really know any of them.

Not really, not deep down.

These were people he trusted and called friends, but he could never truly know them and all they were capable of. Nobody ever could; just as they would never know the deepest depths of his psyche, either. That hidden corner of his mind was the province of violence and rage, of hatred and guilt—all the emotions he kept rigidly at bay, or else be driven mad. There was an animal in each and every one of them that made it so that even 'good' people were capable of dark acts.

*And dark betrayals.*

The other people in the room were no exception. When the situation called for it, they were each capable of untold acts that went against their true nature.

The difficulty was in finding out *who* and *why*.

Ryan's gaze passed over the front row, where Phillips was seated on the end with a mug of tea in his hand. Emblazoned on the side was a faded picture of them both, their faces superimposed onto a picture of Batman and Robin that still made him smile. Next to him, MacKenzie balanced a file on her knees and was busy polishing off the remainder of a sandwich he presumed she hadn't found time to eat at lunchtime. Lowerson was seated on her other side, his skin appearing almost the same colour as his grey suit beneath the glare of the strip-lighting overhead. One hand rubbed his left thigh, while the other tapped his pencil in an incessant drumbeat rhythm against the notebook on his lap. Yates was seated behind Phillips on a separate row, indicating an emotional separation from at least one or all of the team, though Ryan would put his money on it being just one person in particular she wished to distance herself from.

Another thing to mourn, in all this.

"Right, now that we're all here, let's make a start," he said, and hitched himself up onto the desk at the front of the room. "Let's start with progress on Operation Watchman. Yates, MacKenzie? How did the interview go with Singh? Are we any further forward in understanding what happened to Rochelle?"

MacKenzie glanced behind to where Yates was seated and gave her a polite 'go ahead'.

"Ah, well, we paid a visit to Mr Singh's workplace last night," Yates told him. "He has high-level security in place at his offices, and a member of his private security staff was present at all times. Mr Singh had also arranged for his solicitor to be present, so the interview was conducted with him in attendance."

Ryan nodded.

"Go on."

"We questioned Mr Singh about the nature of his relationship with Ms White, first of all. He told us that, whilst they had formerly been in a cohabiting relationship, this ceased to be the case sometime during the course of last Wednesday. He states that Ms White left the home they shared to go to work on Wednesday morning but that's the last time he clapped eyes on her. He claims that he returned home to find a number of her possessions, including a bag, had gone missing."

"And he didn't think to report it?"

"Mr Singh says he had suspicions that Rochelle had been seeing somebody else on the side. Given the physical evidence we have linking Rochelle to Dan 'The Demon' Hepple, we anticipated his name would arise but, in fact, Mr Singh claims that Rochelle was seeing a police officer."

Lowerson leaned forward, resting his forearms on his knees, and looked down at the floor. It was a necessary action, to encourage more blood to flow to his brain, which seemed ready to go into meltdown.

"Does he have any basis for thinking that? Did he give any names?" Ryan asked, and didn't so much as glance in Lowerson's direction.

"No, sir—he had no names or any real basis that we could see," MacKenzie replied.

"So, it could easily be a fabricated story designed to detract from his own misdeeds," Ryan concluded. "How original."

"No way of proving that, either," Phillips pointed out, with his usual precision. "Does he say why he never reported her missing?"

"He cites a broken heart," MacKenzie said, her voice dripping with sarcasm. "Apparently, Mr Singh felt there was no need to report a relationship breakdown, so as not to waste police time."

"So thoughtful," Ryan cooed.

"Mr Singh says he knows nothing about her disappearance and has nothing to add," Yates continued. "He wouldn't budge on that, sir, and is sticking to his story that he came home to find her gone."

"Does he have CCTV at his house? If he's hot on security, it seems likely," Ryan said.

"He's unlikely to offer it voluntarily," MacKenzie said. "He'll make us get a warrant, and that comes back around to the same problem as before: we don't have enough on him to prove reasonable grounds."

"He'll have wiped it by now," Ryan said, and tried another approach. "What about Rochelle's work colleagues—the woman who reported her missing? Any family?"

"No family to speak of," Yates supplied. "Mother and father both in Canada, no siblings or grandparents. She seemed not to have many friends, either."

"Classic move," MacKenzie muttered. "Target a vulnerable woman and then isolate her from anybody who matters. I'm surprised he let her work."

"It seems to have been more of a hobby than a professional enterprise," Yates said. "We've already spoken of the possibility her design business was being used to launder the proceeds of crime, and the number of projects and footfall through her place of business would suggest that's the real source of income."

"At least they cared enough to call the police," Ryan said. "Who was it who made the call?"

"A woman called Ella rang it in when Rochelle didn't turn up for work on Monday morning. She hadn't been into work the previous Thursday or Friday, either, but she was sometimes in the habit of going off for days at a time, without much warning."

"What made this time different?"

"We had a chat with Ella this morning and she says Rochelle was distracted and seemed anxious the previous week. I had the impression she was worried about Singh having something to do with that, but didn't like to say as much," Yates replied.

"When did she last see Rochelle?"

"Ella Marks says that Rochelle came to work on Wednesday morning, then left for lunch and never came back. At first, they assumed she'd taken the afternoon off, or had set up a meeting somewhere."

Lowerson was, by now, almost swaying in his chair. He fiddled with his pencil, running it between his fingers like a stress toy.

*Back and forth.*

*Back and forth.*

*Rochelle's dead eyes, staring across the room at a camera lens, empty and glassy like a porcelain doll.*

They'd never find her, now. Not so long as Singh believed she was the best way to keep him at heel. Rochelle was their ace in the hole, and those pictures the perfect leverage.

He only hoped he could pull off a miracle, or he'd be up on a charge for murder.

# CHAPTER 25

"Okay, here's what we're going to do," Ryan said.

"Yates, try to get your hands on any video footage from Singh's workplace and home on a voluntary basis. We have an expectation that he won't provide either, but we have to try. Remind him that, since he says he has nothing to do with her disappearance, he should have nothing to hide."

"Will do."

"Mac? I want a warrant to enter Singh's property. Get Morrison involved, even the Commissioner, if necessary, because Singh's bound to have some of the magistrates in his pocket. Let's give ourselves a fighting chance."

"Right," MacKenzie said. "And what about pushing Rochelle's picture out to the press?"

Ryan was in a quandary. Normally, he would have suggested the same thing, but there were significant extenuating circumstances in this case.

But there was no question of not doing what was right.

There never was.

"Yes, get it out to the press—let's see if the public can help us out here."

"Right enough."

"Lowerson?"

Ryan spoke the name deliberately, and it sounded clipped and formal, betraying the edge to his voice.

Jack looked up.

"Sir?"

"I'd like an update, please. What progress has been made in locating Paul Evershed, alias 'Ludo'?"

Lowerson cleared his throat.

"Ah, I'm afraid very little," he said. "There've been no sightings of Paul Evershed fleeing Biddlestone. Officers have been stationed at the farmhouse on the off-chance he will return but there's been no movement, at all."

"Must have been tipped off," Phillips said. "There's nowt else for it."

Ryan trod carefully. There were other forces at work, here, and if he allowed too much chatter about tip-offs and kickbacks, it might drive the guilty ones to ground.

"It's a strong possibility," was all he said, and it was the truth. "What happened to the Defender? What about his vehicle?"

"Again, no sightings, sir. However, I've been in touch with the DV*A to obtain a list of current and previous vehicle registrations. A red Land Rover Defender with '02 plates was registered to *Frankly Flowers*, which is owned by its parent company, *Rest Easy Inc.*, a subsidiary of *Mainland International*, one of the off-shore trust corporations we believe to be owned and operated by Singh."

The others sat up, suddenly energised.

"There you go," Phillips said. "We knew Singh would have a hand in this, somewhere."

"Good work, Jack," Ryan said.

In truth, he had already known. The metadata analysis of the spreadsheet of known addresses and vehicles associated with Singh, compiled by the Fraud Team, had come back to show that a Land Rover Defender had originally been listed on that spreadsheet, right up until Monday afternoon, when somebody had deleted the entry. They had also taken the trouble to delete the address entry listed as 'Biddles Farm'.

The tracking analysis had enabled him to find out the name of the person who had made the changes, the name of whom Ryan had passed immediately to DCI Blackett. In line with proper protocol, he had not told another person, and that included his friends in the room, the Chief Constable or even his own wife.

DCI Blackett's team of undercover data analysts were now in the process of unravelling what other alterations had been made to police intelligence, some of which may prove useful in finding Paul Evershed's present location.

In the meantime, there was the surface investigation to deal with.

"What car does Rochelle drive?" Ryan asked.

"White Range Rover," Yates said, and reeled off the registration plates. "There's been no sign of it. I've requested all the ANPR footage from Highways England, but it's a big ask considering Rochelle could have gone anywhere after leaving work. I'll concentrate on the area immediately around there, and see if we get lucky with the footage."

Ryan nodded his approval. It was good, solid work, and it gave him no pleasure to know that they were hunting for a woman who was already dead. The decision to help Jack Lowerson was more of a burden with every passing hour, one he would rather not bear.

That was the price of leadership; sometimes, decisions had to be made that would test the strength of longstanding friendships. He wondered if all the people in the room would be prepared to forgive the omissions he was making, once it was all over and done with.

He pushed away from the desk and paced around a bit, before moving on to the next matter on his agenda.

"Let's turn to other active cases," he said. "Frank and I have been dealing with the suspicious death of an eighty-year-old man, Alan Watson. Control came through this morning to tell us his son, fifty-two-year-old Simon Watson, took an overdose sometime during the night."

"Awful for the rest of the family," Yates said, and there were murmurs of agreement.

"How did it go at Simon Watson's bungalow—have the CSIs finished up there?"

Ryan turned to Phillips, who took a slurp of his tea.

"Well, they were still going when I left them," he said. "I had a snoop around the bungalow to see what's what, but the bloke lived like a puritan; no junk anywhere and no sign of any other drugs knocking around, either."

Ryan could see the direction of his sergeant's thoughts, and wondered how he was ever going to manage to convince him that Simon Watson's death was accidental, especially when he, himself, had been the one to question the supposed overdose in the first place.

That was before he'd received a message from Lowerson telling him of the latest threat he'd received, which strongly suggested Singh was somehow involved in one or both deaths. Ryan had taken the decision to help Lowerson and that meant pulling the wool over everybody's eyes, or risk Jack being thrown to the wolves.

*Oh, the tangled webs we weave…*

"It's sometimes the case that, when a former addict hasn't touched anything for a while, their body reacts extremely badly when they pick up the habit again, because they take the same dose they'd been used to back when their body had built up a kind of immunity," he said. "So, it's not surprising there weren't any other drugs stashed away in Watson's cupboard."

Phillips nodded.

"That's a fair point," he conceded. "It still doesn't solve the issue of how he fell, or what happened to the drugs pouch."

Ryan opened his mouth, but could think of no plausible reason for either of those discrepancies, so snapped it shut again.

"Anyhow," Phillips carried on, "I had a quick chat with one or two of his neighbours, who had plenty of nice things to say about him. Nobody remembered anybody unusual or suspicious turning up, which isn't surprising since Simon died sometime after dark."

"Anything else?"

"Well, I stopped by the jobcentre on my way back to the office, just to see if there was anything lying about, and I found a few bits and bobs including an envelope addressed to Simon's dad."

Ryan hadn't been expecting that and, by the look on Lowerson's face, neither had he.

"Alan?" he queried. "Why did Simon have one of Alan's old envelopes at his office?"

Phillips shook his head.

"The envelope wasn't old," he said. "It had a recent postmark and must've arrived sometime in the last couple of days, but not before the fire. I've been trying to get a hold of the local postie, to see if he'll confirm dropping that envelope off at Simon's house."

"You think he took the redirection into his own hands?" MacKenzie asked, and Phillips nodded.

"Had to be," he said. "There were other letters addressed to his mum or dad, and they were all redirected. Faulkner found a stack of them on the kitchen counter, and a bunch of circulars in the recycling."

"But this was the only envelope Simon took into work with him," Ryan said. "The only one Simon locked away for safety. What was the content?"

"It was an FOI response," Phillips replied.

Yates was momentarily confused.

"FOI?" she queried.

"It stands for 'Freedom of Information,'" Lowerson muttered, shifting in his chair to face her. "People are allowed to make 'FOI requests' to public bodies for accessible information."

She nodded, her eyes lingering for a second too long.

*Damn him.*

"Which public body had he applied to?" Ryan asked.

"GCHQ," Phillips replied, taking them all by surprise again.

"Why on Earth was Alan Watson pestering GCHQ?" MacKenzie demanded. "I'd have thought most of their information was protected, anyhow."

"It was, for quite a while," Phillips agreed. "But they finally coughed up a bit of information Alan had been asking about for thirty-odd years. He wanted to know about the government strategic operations behind the 1984-85 Miners' Strike and, in particular, whether there was a government mole operating around the village of Penshaw at the time."

"You mean, 'The Worm,'" Ryan said, and explained the relevance for those who had not been privy to their investigation so far.

"Aye, that's it. Seems like old Alan had the bit between his teeth and wouldn't let go. He wanted answers."

"And? Does the paperwork from GCHQ give any names or anything that would tell us who it was?"

"It all reads like a spy novel, to me," Phillips complained. "I can't make head nor tail of it, with all the redactions of 'sensitive material', but you're welcome to have a go. I sent the original over to the lab, but Faulkner's made a copy of its contents."

Ryan nodded, his mind kicking into over-drive.

Suppose the hapless, well-meaning Simon Watson had come home to find the post intended for his father, and had decided to open it—never knowing what he might find inside. Suppose that he read the contents from GCHQ and recognised the person known as 'The Worm'. What then? Would he come to the police or try to confront them himself?

Ryan feared he already knew the answer.

"Joan Watson's being kept in hospital," Phillips continued. "She can hardly stand another shock, with her husband and son both going in the space of a week. Any word from the pathologist?"

Ryan kept his tone light, and thought back to the unprecedented conversation he'd had with Dr Jeffrey Pinter.

"He's sent through his preliminary findings," he said, referring to the report that was available for those with police access to view under the case file number on their intranet. "The general opinion is that Simon Watson passed away sometime between midnight and three o'clock. He wasn't found until nearly eight o'clock the following morning, which means he'd been dead for up to eight hours by then."

"Any suggestion of foul play that he can see?" Phillips asked.

Ryan opened his mouth, then his eyes flicked back to where Lowerson was seated, eyes almost wild with fear of discovery.

"Ah…no. No, not yet."

Phillips made a tutting noise.

"It's fishy, that's for sure. Something isn't right about all this. Everybody I've spoken to seems so sure that Simon wouldn't have taken an overdose—deliberately, or otherwise."

"What about his sister, and brother-in-law?" Ryan asked. "Do they agree?"

Phillips frowned.

"They seemed a bit more open to the possibility, but both seemed genuine. We really need to speak to Joan."

After an action plan was agreed and MacKenzie left to collect Samantha from school, since it was her turn, Phillips intercepted Ryan as he made for the door.

"Where'd you rush off to, earlier?" he asked.

Ryan swore inwardly.

"I had a couple of meetings to go to," he said. "Why? Is there anything urgent?"

Phillips had a sudden thought.

"Here, they're not trying to talk you into taking that superintendent's job again, are they? The last two supers have been duffers, so they need a decent officer to take it on—but it's a poisoned chalice that, lad."

Ryan looked at his friend with sudden emotion and made a silent promise this would all be over by the end of the week, whichever way the hammer fell.

"Don't worry, Frank. I would never abandon the team."

He put a hand on his friend's shoulder and then moved off, leaving Phillips to stare after him.

# CHAPTER 26

"The police say it was an accidental overdose."

Mike Emerson spoke softly to his mother-in-law, who lay on the hospital bed looking so different from the woman he'd known the week before. Joan Watson had always been a second mother to him; the one who'd cooked his meals and listened to his triumphs and disasters as if he was her own son. When he'd plucked up the courage to ask Sally to marry him, she'd been the first one to welcome him into their family.

Not even Alan had gone quite so far.

Oh, he'd been friendly enough—always including him in a few after-work jars down at the pub. He'd even introduced Mike as his future son-in-law, which had been nice.

But he knew Alan had never liked him.

He'd never been good enough for Sally, according to Alan. He'd never said it, in so many words, but it had been as plain as the nose on his face. When all the rumours had started about Alan being 'The Worm', Mike could have done more to stop them from spreading.

But he didn't.

Now, with Sally shooting daggers at him across the width of her mother's bed, Mike wished he hadn't wasted his time with any of them.

"Nuh," Joan was saying. "Nuh. Don' blve 't."

The second stroke had taken it out of her, he thought. The first had knocked her, but this one had robbed her of the use of some of her muscles, so the left side of her face drooped like a melting ice-cream.

"I know, it's hard, Mum."

Joan was getting frustrated, her bandaged hands slapping against the hospital bed.

"P'leez," she was saying. "P'leez."

"Please, what?" Sally wondered. "What can I get for you?"

She looked at the pillows, the bedspread and the water bottle, trying to interpret her mother's request.

"*P'LEEZ!*" Joan cried out, catching the attention of the nurse.

"There, now, Mrs Watson. Don't get too upset, it's not good for your blood pressure."

Trapped inside her own head, Joan thought of the handsome police detective and his sergeant, who'd called around the day before. She wanted to send up a flare or call 999.

People talked, you see.

They forgot themselves and talked, while they thought you were asleep, or unable to reply.

*And she heard.*
She'd heard it all.

***

Ryan needed air.

He was tired of looking up and seeing Lowerson's ashen face or Phillips' confusion. He didn't want to see Yates' heartbreak, either. It was only four-thirty, but he couldn't stomach another minute wondering whether somebody from the Evidence Store would turn up to ask why he'd taken it upon himself to alter the forensic records. Never before had he been called upon to interfere with the course of an investigation, and it turned his stomach.

"I'm taking an hour's personal," he announced, and Phillips looked up in surprise.

"I thought we could have a swift one, down at *The Shipbuilder*?" he objected, checking the time on his watch. "I could finish up here—"

"Thanks, Frank—another night."

Ryan grabbed a printed copy of the GCHQ response Alan Watson had received in the post, and then made for the door. In another few minutes, he was inside his car, reversing out of the staff car park with swift, precise movements, and on his way to the only place he knew would make a difference.

*Home.*

***

'Home' was not the bricks-and-mortar house Ryan and Anna shared in Elsdon, but the feeling they shared when they were together. Therefore, he did not take the A1 northbound after leaving Police Headquarters but, instead, turned south towards the city of Durham. It was a cool thirty-minute drive, but he'd have driven twice that distance, if only to be with her.

Ryan crossed the River Tyne and glanced briefly to his left to see the perfect harmony of seven different bridges spanning the water, each with its own history. Never again would he look at those bridges without remembering the fear and mayhem one sick person had reaped upon the city, not so long ago.

*What right had one person to terrorise another?* he wondered.

Their world was a shared one, and there needed to be rules so they could all get along in relative peace. As a younger man, he'd never understood what drove one person to maim or to murder; to steal or to cheat. He supposed that's what had driven him to work in law enforcement: a desire to restore order, and balance.

But the world wasn't built that way, and neither were people. They didn't conform to laws made by their fellow men, not even when their liberty was removed or, in other countries, when it cost them their own life in exchange.

Life experience had taught him a lot since those early, idealistic days. It had taught him temperance, and fortitude. He'd lost much along the way, including his sister, but he'd gained a skinful of wisdom, too. It would never be an equal exchange, but it was something to cling on to.

Ryan passed the turn-off that would lead him to Penshaw, and thought again of the people who lived in that quiet village. What connection could there possibly be, between Bobby Singh and the Watson family?

He didn't know yet, but he would find out.

He owed it to a man who'd lived for thirty-five years with the shame of being called 'traitor'. Alan Watson died having lost the respect of his friends and family, without ever knowing who was the worm who turned.

---

Inside the History Faculty building in Durham, Dr Anna Taylor-Ryan moved her presentation on to the final slide of the day, then turned back to the full auditorium of master's level history students, all of whom were taking her course, 'Early Pagan History in Northumberland' as part of their degree.

"As you know, 'paganism' comes from the Latin *paganus,* meaning 'rural' or 'rustic'," she said. "It was a largely pejorative, derogatory term first coined by early Christians during the fourth century, to describe people in the Roman Empire who were polytheistic. In other words, it became known as a religion for the peasants."

At the very back of the auditorium, the door opened and Ryan slipped inside. The movement caught her eye, and she smiled across the rows of eager faces.

"If history teaches us anything, it's that human behaviour moves in cycles," she said. "Back in the Bronze

Age, early pagans tried to make sense of their natural surroundings and began to worship gods they assigned to various elements of the natural world, much like the early Egyptians. With the advent of Christianity came conflict, much like the divisiveness that can come from differing religious beliefs today. So, the essay question for this week is a reflective one," she said, moving behind the lectern to shut down the presentation. "Please tell me, in an essay of no more than five thousand words, what is the most important lesson that can be learned from the parallels between early Pagan Northumberland and modern Northumberland?"

She paused, while they scribbled the question on scraps of paper, or typed it onto their laptops.

"I'll be around for five minutes at the end, if anybody has a burning question to ask. Otherwise, I'll see you all next week."

Soon after, the students began to file out of the lecture theatre, in a cloud of cheap aftershave that barely masked the smell of yesterday's pants. Ryan waited for them to leave and then jogged down the wide auditorium steps to greet his wife.

"This is a nice surprise," she said, feeling oddly vulnerable. It had been a while since Ryan had paid a visit to her workplace. "Did you have business in Durham?"

There was always work to be done, and his colleagues in Durham CID would, no doubt, have news to share with him regarding Operation Watchman. However, it wasn't the reason he was there.

"I wanted to see you," he said simply, and watched the smile blossom on her face.

"Really? Well, in that case, why don't we go for a walk along the riverbank, like old times?"

Anna used to own a little stone cottage by the banks of the River Wear, in the shadow of the mighty cathedral which loomed over the rest of the city like an elven castle, too beautiful to be real. Before that cottage was lost at the hands of a madman, he and Anna had spent many a happy day and night within its cosy walls, watching the river roll by.

"Sounds good," he agreed. "So long as I can carry your books."

She chuckled, and rose up on her tiptoes to give him a kiss.

"I can carry my own books, but you can carry the laptop."

"It's a deal."

# CHAPTER 27

Denise MacKenzie had always considered herself a fast learner, and the art of parenting was no exception. In many ways, the affection and love for her new—she hesitated to say, her new *daughter*—came as naturally as breathing. It was no hardship to love the wiry little girl with a mop of wild auburn hair not unlike her own. If they had ever been blessed with their own biological offspring, he or she could not have been a more perfect fusion of her and Frank. Sassy and smart, loving and loyal, the little girl was everything they could have hoped for, with a dash of cheek and a dollop of humour thrown in, for good measure.

She smiled as she stood at the fence overlooking the low pasture, where Samantha was cantering across the grass on Pegasus, the horse left to her by her family, who were all gone now.

"Hi, Mac!"

Samantha waved as she passed, holding the reins with ease, yet still managing to cause MacKenzie's heart to skip a beat. The girl had grown up with horses, as she had, and knew almost all there was to know about the beasts, but it didn't prevent the maternal worry that she would take an unexpected fall.

"Eyes forward!" she called out, and the manager of the livery in Elsdon laughed across the yard.

"You've got a fine horsewoman, there!" she said.

"Aye, well, I wish she'd keep her eyes on the road," MacKenzie quipped, but it was true that watching Samantha on the horse was like poetry in motion. They had a unique connection, this girl and the white stallion, and she was grateful to Ryan for coming to a favourable arrangement with the livery so they were able to keep him. She suspected the arrangement was being subsidised by their friend, but he refused to admit as much, and anybody she tried to ask fell back on what was obviously an agreed party line.

So, she was content to be grateful, for herself and on Samantha's behalf.

Presently, girl and horse slowed to a trot, then a walk as they approached the fence. Samantha dismounted in a smooth motion, and took the reins in her hand.

"C'mon boy," she said, rubbing his neck with her gentle hand. "Let's go and rub you down."

Rather than go to school, Samantha's family had entrusted her with the upkeep of the horses as soon as she was old enough, so MacKenzie had no need to ask whether the girl knew what she was doing. Instead, she walked back to the stables alongside, their feet keeping time with the *clip-clop* of Pegasus' shoes.

"I forgot to ask you, how was school today?"

Samantha bowed her head.

"It was fine," she mumbled.

"Doesn't sound fine," MacKenzie replied, peering beneath Pegasus' chin. "Want to tell me about it?"

"Doesn't matter," Samantha said gruffly. "I don't care what they say."

"What who says?"

"The girls at school."

MacKenzie sighed. It had barely been two days, and already the meanness had started. Would things never change?

"What did they say?"

Samantha led Pegasus into his stall and reached for a bucket of feed, which she set in front of him while she began to unfasten his bridle.

"Just stuff."

MacKenzie fell back on her interview training, and used it to draw the girl out.

"Unkind stuff?" she queried.

Samantha nodded, reaching down to unstrap the horse's saddle while Pegasus stood calmly, waiting for her to finish.

"One of them said I was a dirty gyppo," she whispered. "The other one said I wasn't to be trusted because everybody knows my dad was a criminal."

MacKenzie felt white-hot rage rush through her veins and, in that moment, she wanted to hurt those who had hurt her little girl.

"Thank you for telling me," she said, wanting to reinforce the fact it was always the right thing to do. "It was very wrong of those girls to say those things, and it was very hurtful."

Samantha began to brush Pegasus' hair, in long, smooth strokes.

"Did the teacher hear this?" MacKenzie asked.

"No, they said it at break time, when they knew nobody would hear."

*Sneaky little…*MacKenzie thought.

"Okay. Did you tell the teacher?"

Samantha shook her head.

"They'd tell everyone I'm a snitch," she said, with a resigned shrug. "Besides, their parents are rich, and the teacher thinks they're great, so nothing will happen."

*We'll see about that,* MacKenzie thought.

*We'll just see about that.*

"Maybe it's a one-off," she said, working hard to remain optimistic for the girl's sake. It had been a big step for Samantha to start school, let alone begin to enjoy it, and she'd be damned if she'd let a couple of ill-bred brats ruin all that.

MacKenzie wondered what Frank would make of it all, and the very thought brought a smile to her face. When Phillips found out, he was liable to go around and arrest the pair of them.

Once Samantha had finished and said goodbye to her horse, MacKenzie slung an arm around the girl's shoulders and pulled her in for a hug.

"You don't have to manage alone, Sam. We're going to be here for you, now, remember?"

The girl turned her face into MacKenzie's stomach and clung on tightly, breathing in the scent of something she'd never had.

# CHAPTER 28

"Something's troubling you," Anna said.

She and Ryan walked hand in hand along the riverbank in Durham towards Prebends Bridge, enjoying the warm breeze rippling through the rushes while rowers moved across the water with barely a ripple, the muscles in their arms glistening in the late afternoon sun.

"I know you told me you couldn't say," she continued, in the same quiet tone. "But I need to know that you're alright."

Ryan spotted a bench up ahead, where they could sit and enjoy the lazy flow of the river as it made its slow journey to the sea.

"Come on, let's sit for a while."

Anna was happy to sit beside him on that pretty patch of earth, listening to birds rustling in the long grass while the world went by. Their lives rarely allowed for this sort of indulgence; there was always something more pressing to do. It wasn't just Ryan's job that cut into their personal lives, either; her career had always been her solace, and she was unwilling to sacrifice all she had earned and all she enjoyed, for the sake of expedience—nor would Ryan expect her to.

But it did take a bit of juggling.

"I still can't give you specifics, but I'll give you some hypotheticals. How would that be?"

Anna gave him a long, knowing look.

"That'd be just fine. Consider me bound by a doctor's oath of confidentiality."

"You're not a medical doctor," he reminded her.

"Same principle," she said, with a wink.

Ryan blew out a long breath and settled back against the seat, holding her hand between both of his own. She watched his profile as he looked out across the river and thought it was little wonder he grew so frustrated by the number of people who saw only his exterior, which he considered to be a transient, fickle thing. Beauty was in the eye of the beholder, after all, and was subject to change.

But to this beholder, he was beautiful, and always would be.

"Let's say there's a young, ambitious detective who wants to make his mark on the world," Ryan began, as if he were telling her a bedtime story. "His heart is always in the right place, but he tends to rush things and take short-cuts, rather than putting in the time necessary to achieve his goals."

"I've a very clear picture in my mind," Anna said, thinking of Jack Lowerson. "Go on."

"This young detective has had a spate of bad luck," Ryan continued. "Some things he could never have foreseen and other things…he could have prevented with better decision-making."

Anna nodded, thinking it was only the truth.

"Let's say this detective finally seems to be getting things back on track, when he sees an opportunity to fast-track again."

"Uh-oh," Anna murmured, wondering what Jack had gone and done now.

"Indeed," Ryan said. "Instead of seeking the help of his team, this young detective walks into a situation where he is at the mercy of some very bad men."

Anna was worried.

"Does he escape?" she asked.

"Yes, he does," Ryan said, in the same smooth, story-telling voice. "He's allowed to survive, but he's now beholden to these men because they have some evidence against him that would look very, very bad for him if they were to send it to his seniors, or to the Professional Standards Department."

Anna looked across at her husband.

"How bad?" she asked. "Bad enough to be sacked?"

"Worse," Ryan replied, shortly. "Bad enough to go to prison."

Anna put her elbow on the edge of the bench and rested her head in her hand, while her mind spiralled with ideas about what Jack Lowerson might have done.

"Now, let's say this young detective has a good friend who happens to be his boss," Ryan said, and thought it was an odd sort of exercise describing himself in this hypothetical tale. "This man notices that his protégé hasn't been himself, lately, but puts it down to illness or something else. He's had his ups and downs, after all. But then, the young detective contacts him and asks him to come over, late at night, and to be careful that he isn't seen."

Anna thought of the night Ryan had been very late coming home, and was glad to know why.

"This older detective is concerned, so he goes to see his young friend," Ryan said, thinking of how bad Lowerson had looked when he'd first walked through the man's front door. "He learns about the corner this friend finds himself backed into, and begins to understand why the young man is too worried to sleep, or eat."

"Poor Jack," Anna muttered, and Ryan didn't bother to correct the slip.

"The older detective is faced with a new problem. Unbeknown to anybody, the Professional Standards Department have separately approached him with their theory about there being several moles operating across the different command divisions—"

"Including—" Anna started to say, and Ryan nodded.

"Yes, including Major Crimes."

There was a moment's pause, while Anna went through similar emotions to those Ryan had experienced when he'd first heard the words from DCI Blackett.

"This older detective is already concerned about whether there might be a mole operating in his team, working with nefarious criminals, when this young friend tells him that's precisely what he's been doing."

Anna gave him a searching look, and squeezed his hand.

"How did you react?"

"I can tell you how this *man* reacted," Ryan said, pausing to brush his lips against hers. "He was shocked and disappointed. He felt all the emotions, and he wanted to know what leverage these people had over his young friend. The leverage was bad—I won't tell you how bad, Anna. But it would have been enough for him to walk out of the door again and report the young man, there and then."

"What stopped...him?"

"This young man isn't capable of doing what he's being framed for," Ryan said. "So, together, they concoct a plan, but it requires total secrecy."

"Not telling their other friends, or their family?" Anna finished for him.

"Exactly. It also requires some doctoring of files and evidence, in the short-term, to make things appear authentic for anybody who happens to be watching."

Anna didn't know what to say.

"Both of them are worried about whether their plan will work, and if the rest of their team will forgive them for the subterfuge," Ryan said.

Anna nodded.

"What about their safety?" she asked. "Are they both safe?"

Ryan raised her hand to his lips and pressed a kiss to her palm.

"I don't know, Anna. We're going as fast as we can to put it behind us."

There was a lot she might have said, words she could have used, but she simply leaned her head against his chest and listened to the strong *thud* of his heartbeat.

"You're not alone," she said. "I'll always be your friend, Ryan, and the others will too. You know why? Because you're a good man, and they know that as well as I do."

To his embarrassment, a lump rose in his throat.

"Thank you," he said, huskily.

# CHAPTER 29

"They said *what*? I'll kill the little toe-rags!"

MacKenzie put a finger to her lips and then pointed upstairs, to where Samantha had recently fallen asleep.

"*Shh*, Frank! Do you want to wake the whole neighbourhood?"

"D' you think I care about waking up old Albert at Number 22, when my girl's had to listen to that awful nonsense, all day? They ought to be ashamed…"

"It's the parents, as much as anything," MacKenzie murmured. "You might want to tone down the death threats, what with us both being murder detectives. It looks bad."

His lips twitched at that, and then his face fell back into angry lines, reminding her of a bull preparing to charge.

"It also means I know how to cover one up," he muttered, darkly, and held up a hand when she would have told him off again. "I know, I know. They're only kids, too. But there's no call for that kind of thing."

"I agree, especially as it's a very sensitive time in her life," MacKenzie said, keeping her voice low. "I was going to suggest having a word with her teacher, so she can be aware."

Phillips took a couple of deep breaths and couldn't help thinking that, when he was a lad, a couple of short jabs was usually enough to stop any nonsense from a school bully.

"I'm really hoping this was just a one-off," MacKenzie said, in worried tones. "She's been through enough…"

Phillips set aside his own anger to comfort his wife.

"There, love. Come and have a sit down," he said, as they settled on the sofa. "We can't protect her from all the nasty people in the world, even if we wanted to. It's a part of living."

"I know, you're right. But you hear about young kids who've been bullied for years, and end up taking their own life. It's the stuff of nightmares."

"It'll never come to that," he assured her, and thought he'd sooner go around to the parents' house and give them a good thump, before it ever got that bad.

MacKenzie sighed.

"She loved visiting Pegasus today," she said. "I think it really cheered her up. We called in to see Anna and Ryan, since they're next to the livery, but nobody was home."

Phillips reached across to start rubbing her feet, which usually ached at the end of the day.

"Ryan's been a funny bugger today," he said, with his usual eloquence. "Hardly saw him all day and, when I did, he was cagey. It isn't like him."

"I wonder if something's wrong," she said. "Is everything alright between him and Anna?"

"Oh, aye, never better," Phillips said. He'd always had a soft spot for Ryan's wife, who he'd had the honour of walking down the aisle when she married his friend. "I don't think it's that."

"Something at work, then? He's got a lot on his plate, managing Operation Watchman, plus this Penshaw case Morrison threw on the pair of you, at the last minute."

A shadow crossed Phillips' face.

"I don't know if that's what's been bothering Ryan, but I can tell you the Penshaw case has raked up a few old memories for me."

She leaned over, to rub his arm.

"What memories, Frank?"

"Alan Watson was a Union man, during the '84 Miners' Strike," he told her. "Well, back then, I was just getting started on the Force and, over the summer of '84, almost every constable in the district was sent in to put on a show of muscle. The brass told us it was about keeping the peace but, I swear, Denise, when we got there, it was peaceful enough."

She continued to rub his arm in soothing circles.

"There were some rowdier than others, some loudmouths, but there was no need to send in a bloody army of us. I've never felt more uncomfortable," he said. "It made me question whether I'd done the right thing, joining the police."

"What kept you going?"

"It made my Da' proud," he admitted. "And then, later, I was transferred to Major Crimes and I started getting a taste for the job."

"D'you think Ryan's having a bit of a crisis like that?" she wondered. "He's weathered a lot of storms, for a man his age. He's got a lot of responsibility on his shoulders. Do you think he's feeling it?"

Phillips considered the question, and couldn't rule out the possibility that she was right.

"I don't know what it is, love. He's not talking about it, and I don't want to keep asking."

"He'll tell us when he's ready," she said. "When he does, we'll be there to listen."

"You're a good woman, Denise MacKenzie."

"Too good for the likes of you, Frank Phillips," she shot back, with a smile.

"Never a truer word spoken, my love."

With that, he stood up from the sofa and held out a hand to pull her up with him.

"Bedtime?" he said, and wiggled his preposterous eyebrows.

***

Jack Lowerson checked into a hotel beside the airport, which he'd selected chiefly for its anonymity and distance from the centre of town. He didn't kid himself that Ludo or another of Singh's goons couldn't find him with a little research, but he could no longer sit inside his own flat and watch the door, night after night.

He needed sleep.

Lowerson passed at least three couples on the way to his room, all of whom carried little or no luggage and appeared to have just finished work, judging by the suits and high heels. He didn't feel particularly judgemental—how they chose to spend their time was no concern of his—but he would have preferred to know there were other people spending a full night on the same floor, rather than a quick, two-hour romp.

He let himself into a soulless room with beige walls and a stained, maroon headboard that hung halfway from the wall. The carpet had a number of old cigarette burns and a musty odour somewhere between tobacco smoke and mildew. The bed let out a plaintive whine as he perched on the end, its metal springs clearly on their last legs.

It would do.

Anything would do, so long as he could sleep for more than thirty minutes at a time.

He locked the door to his room and pulled up the desk chair, wedging it beneath the handle. He'd requested a room on one of the upper floors to make it harder for anybody to access from the outside, and he was reasonably certain nobody would find him, since the room had been booked and paid for under Ryan's name, for an added layer of protection. His friend had suggested coming to stay with him for a while, but it was too dangerous, and might arouse suspicion. Ryan had suggested putting him up in a hotel much nicer than the one he was presently enjoying, but fancier places drew fancier crowds, like dealers with money to burn in the hotel bars.

No—here would do him just fine.

Lowerson had a long shower, trying and failing to scrub away the grimy layer of guilt that stuck to his skin, and then checked all the windows again. He sank down on the bed with a towel still wrapped around his waist and geared up the courage to complete the final task of the day.

Sure enough, when he checked the burner mobile, another message popped up:

TIME TO REPORT.

Lowerson typed a carefully considered reply:

DEMON EVIDENCE TAKEN CARE OF. PENSHAW CASE LOOKING ACCIDENTAL. JOB DONE.

There was a ten-second delay, and then another message landed:

JOB IS NEVER DONE. REPORT AGAIN TOMORROW.

Jack gave in to frustration and lobbed the plastic phone across the room, where it made a small dent in the wall and then dropped to the floor. Immediately concerned that he'd damaged his only line of communication, he hurried to check it wasn't broken.

The cheap burner phone was still intact. Much like a cockroach, it could survive most things.

No longer able to contemplate sleep, Lowerson took out his laptop. There was work to be done, the kind that was better taken care of out of the office and away from prying eyes. Since the text had arrived asking him to downplay the death of Simon Watson in Penshaw, he'd been trying to understand what possible connection there could be between Watson and Bobby Singh. There was the fact that the former was a recovering addict, and Singh made much of his income from men and women like that, but Singh was unlikely to sully himself with petty deals.

No, there had to be something else.

As part of his routine enquiries, Phillips had requested the CCTV footage from the main road and surrounding businesses within a radius of Watson's bungalow, and Lowerson saw that a response had come through already from a local convenience store and service station. There was also some ANPR footage of the motorway within a few miles of Penshaw, all accessible with his passcode. Jack's eyes were dry, and his vision blurred, but sleep would not come, so he clicked on the first file.

And, unbelievably, managed to hit lucky.

The only camera footage to come through from Penshaw village was taken from the local convenience store, the owner of which had invested in a high spec camera which was positioned to capture the till area, with a second external camera situated outside the door. Both cameras had captured a man Lowerson recognised instantly as Ludo entering the shop at ten fifty-five. He moved directly to the till area, where he was picked up by the other camera, and purchased two packets of cigarettes, a lighter and a chocolate bar. He wore dark jeans and a dark sweatshirt and, when his face turned slightly and Lowerson froze the screen, he could see that Ludo had begun to grow a beard. At first, Lowerson was incredulous at the audacity of the man allowing himself to be captured on CCTV on his way to commit murder, but then he realised that Ludo really had nothing to lose, since he was already wanted for so many other equally serious crimes.

After an exchange lasting no more than a minute, Ludo exited the shop at ten fifty-six and turned right, where Lowerson happened to know there was space on the kerb for parked cars. Two minutes later, long enough for a quick fag, Lowerson caught sight of the bottom half of a Land Rover Defender passing quickly along the top of the image. He paused the video and went back frame by frame until the number plate was clearly visible. It didn't match the plate they had on file for the Defender last seen outside the farmhouse at Biddlestone, so Lowerson ran it through the DVLA database. The licence plate was registered to an address in Cornwall but had only shown up on Automatic Number Plate Recognition cameras in the local area in the last couple of days. That could only mean one thing: *Ludo was using false plates*.

His pulse quickening, Lowerson searched the ANPR database and found a cluster of matches around Washington Services. None of the footage from the main roads immediately surrounding the village was available, but there were at least five CCTV cameras dotted around

Washington Service Station, a major site spread across the A1 motorway in both directions, connected by a high walkway, with food and drink retailers on both sides. If a person planned to drive from Penshaw northbound towards Newcastle or Northumberland, or in the reverse direction, it was a safe bet they would pass those services.

To reach the service station from that direction, a car would have to pass beneath the flyover before entering the car park or the petrol station on either side, and there was an ANPR camera covering both directions of traffic. Lowerson clicked open the file provided to them by Highways England showing the southbound approach into the service station, which started to play automatically from around seven-thirty in the morning. He decided to fast forward, concentrating his efforts on the times flagged up by the ANPR system, when he caught sight of a Land Rover Defender passing beneath the camera.

It was gone in a flash at around seven-thirty-six a.m., but Lowerson rewound the footage and watched it over again, fiddling with the screen so he could try to zoom in on the number plate or the driver's face.

Instead, Lowerson found the rolling footage from the service station on the southbound side, and concentrated his efforts on the time Ludo would have been likely to drive in or out after passing beneath the ANPR camera. There was no sign of him entering the car park or the service station, and he was afraid Ludo might have driven past the services to continue his journey on the motorway.

Then, he spotted the edge of the Defender.

It was in the background of camera footage capturing the entrance to the car park, nearest to the service station hotel.

In the footage, Ludo entered the car park and parked in the first available slot, nearest the exit rather than nearest the entrance to the service station and restaurants. The footage was extremely grainy but, after then, it appeared Ludo walked away from the service station and towards a pedestrian pathway, after which he soon dropped out of sight.

Lowerson froze the screen again and leaned back against the sticky maroon headboard to consider what this meant. There were quicker, safer ways to access Washington, a small town located not far from Sunderland and Penshaw, than parking at the service station and entering the area on foot, so why would Ludo choose that route, or that method?

There was always the possibility he was seeking to approach Penshaw via a circuitous method, having left his car at the service station car park, it would be too far to walk from there to Penshaw, and Ludo would have no means of making a quick getaway.

Then, there was the timing.

If Simon Watson died late at night, and the convenience store put Ludo in the vicinity around eleven o'clock, why then was he captured on the ANPR and service station cameras driving past hours earlier, just after seven-thirty in the morning?

It didn't make sense.

Lowerson brought up a map of the area to give himself a better understanding of where the pedestrian pathway would lead, if that's the direction Ludo had taken. Tracing the pathway with the tip of his finger, Jack saw that it passed through a housing estate until it connected with another main road, on the other side of which was a primary school.

He frowned, wondering if Ludo was staying in one of those houses.

It seemed highly unlikely that he would be visiting the school.

But, as he moved into the tiny hotel bathroom to brush his teeth, the thought percolated in his mind and he began to wonder.

What had happened to Paul Evershed's family?

Before drugs and crime had ruined him, he'd been a salesman, with a wife and children who subsequently left him. Perhaps one of those children had since made him a grandfather?

Spitting toothpaste into the sink, Lowerson hurried back into the room and brought up the other files the service station had supplied, covering the last five days, three of which were weekdays and, consequently, school days, too.

He chewed his lower lip as he clicked on Monday's file, and began the recording at seven-fifteen. It was a tense wait as he watched lorries and cars passing through, and he was by now so tired he could barely see in a straight line.

Then, his index finger tapped the button to freeze the screen.

At around the same time, seven-thirty, a Land Rover Defender turned into the car park and slid into one of the empty parking spaces nearest the pathway. A moment later, a tall, broad-shouldered hulk of a man unfolded himself and walked away from the camera, in the same direction as before.

Jack went through the same process for the previous Friday, and found the same outcome. Every day, at the same time, Paul Evershed parked his car and made his way to a destination that lay somewhere through those houses.

He needed to find out where, because, if Ryan had taught him anything, it was to look for patterns of behaviour. Once you found the pattern, you found the man.

# CHAPTER 30

*Thursday, 13th June 2019*

The following morning, the weather took a turn for the worse.

Gone were the balmy blue skies of the day before; they gave way to deep grey rain clouds that rolled in from the North Sea and hovered overhead like an ominous threat, ready to give out at any moment. When the heavens finally opened, Melanie Yates watched it patter against the windows inside the Chief Constable's office.

Sandra Morrison had a lot of time for Yates, in whom she saw a lot of herself as a younger woman. However, it was no longer her job description to deal with Human Resources matters. She was a busy woman, and said as much.

"I do apologise for bothering you with trivial things, ma'am," Yates replied. "However, as DCI Ryan is handling several more urgent matters at the moment, I felt you were the only other person who would be able to sanction my transfer request."

The truth was, she didn't want Ryan to talk her out of it, as she knew he could. It had been hard enough to make the decision to transfer, without having to go through it all again.

"Why do you believe a transfer is necessary?" Morrison asked. "I understood you were happy in Ryan's team. Is there anything I should be aware of?"

Now that it came down to it, Yates didn't know what to say. After a moment, she decided that the truth was always best.

"Ma'am, the relationship between myself and DC Lowerson has become strained," she said. "I take responsibility for my share in letting that happen—we embarked on the very early stages of a romantic relationship which has, predictably, gone south."

"Well, this isn't *Love Island*, Yates!" Morrison burst out. "If you get into romantic entanglements with your work colleagues, you have to be prepared for things when they don't work out. You can't expect to run to your boss and have them parachute you out of an awkward situation—"

"I realise that, ma'am," Yates said, in a firm tone that took Morrison by surprise. "My decision to transfer isn't based solely on that. I no longer have confidence in DC Lowerson's ability to train me, which has the capacity to affect my career pathway and personal goals I've been striving towards for a number of years."

"Somebody else within the team could take over," Morrison suggested. "Phillips was originally assigned to train you, I recall."

"That's correct, ma'am. The fact is, I believe that the tensions that now exist both personally and professionally may impact on the wider team, which is something I'm seeing already and want to prevent getting worse. I believe this is the best way."

Morrison looked out at the rain and sighed.

"You seem to have your heart set on it," she said.

Yates felt her stomach quiver, but she ignored whatever reservations she might have had, and answered clearly.

"Yes, ma'am. I do."

Morrison nodded.

"In that case, leave it with me. You say you want to stay in Major Crimes? That'll mean a transfer to another command division, since Ryan's team covers such a broad area, up here. I'll see if there's room for you in Durham CID."

Yates nodded, feeling somehow deflated.

"Thank you, ma'am."

"Dismissed."

Ryan had spent much of the previous evening reading through the GCHQ papers that had been provided to Alan Watson, in an effort to understand whether they were relevant, or another one of those red herrings that could lead an investigation down the wrong track. It was far from clear, given that the content of what appeared to be government memoranda was at least thirty years old. However, it did confirm one thing: there had been a local person who had fed information back to the government, which had allowed the police to know in advance where flying pickets would be set up, as well as various other sensitive details pertaining to the strike. It was perfectly possible that, without the actions of this mole and others like them, there would have been less violence and less unrest, though Ryan couldn't say whether the strike would ultimately have succeeded.

Now, seated at his desk at Police Headquarters, Ryan picked up the papers again. The government codename for the Penshaw mole was not "The Worm"—that had been coined by the locals. GCHQ had kept things simple and used, "P", which could relate to their given name but was more likely "P" for Penshaw. Ryan imagined other people living in other towns might be assigned "E" for Easington, and so forth. There were long passages detailing the methods by which P could be contacted, and the location which was, fittingly, Penshaw Monument. It seemed that P's handler was a man called Jasper Ogilvy, who conducted any of the face-to-face meetings or other direct communications. The paperwork contained heavily redacted passages giving the content of each meeting, but it was the contents of the appendix that interested Ryan the most. It read:

*"Ogilvy has been reprimanded for misconduct relating to his handling of this matter and has been reassigned as of 1.1.1985."*

Ryan ran a quick Google search and found that Jasper Ogilvy had subsequently been knighted in the 1990s, but at the time of the strikes had been a junior civil servant seconded to the National Coal Board. Unfortunately, Ogilvy died over ten years earlier, so would be unavailable for him to question.

Ryan was beginning to wonder whether the secret of P's identity had died with him.

# CHAPTER 31

Lowerson had been up with the larks.

His first stop had been to pick up a rental car from the airport across the road, since his own vehicle might be recognised. After collecting a nippy little three-door Corsa, he checked the time and drove towards the A1, turning southbound along the route that would take him to Washington Services. There was some morning traffic but, by seven o'clock, he was in position in the service station car park, with a good view of the entrance. He'd thought carefully about whether to tell Ryan, or any of the others, but there was little time to spare and he wanted to avoid Ludo being tipped off.

Time ticked by, and Lowerson kept his eyes trained on the entrance, waiting.

*Tick-tock, tick-tock.*

At seven twenty-five, a different car turned into the car park and, to begin with, Lowerson was thrown. He was expecting to see a Land Rover Defender, but Ludo had obviously acquired a new vehicle which was, he supposed, the smart thing to do.

The dark green Nissan parked in the usual spot, near the entrance and a short distance from where Lowerson hunkered down inside the rental car. He watched Paul Evershed step out of the vehicle and take a quick glance around, his eyes lingering on the other cars in the car park. Luckily, the service station was always a busy one, and Lowerson's Corsa didn't stand out any more than the rest.

Evershed turned onto the pathway, the back of his head disappearing behind the hedgerows, and Lowerson judged it the right moment to follow.

He stepped out of the car, and moved swiftly across the tarmac.

***

While Lowerson tailed one of the country's most wanted men, Phillips and MacKenzie bickered light-heartedly about whether the ending to the recent *Game of Thrones* television series was to their taste.

"Jon Snow should've been the one to kill the Night King," Phillips was saying. "That was his fight, and he was robbed."

"Aye, but Arya was a hero," MacKenzie said. "She had the skills, and she used them."

"Should've saved them for that one with the white-blond hair," Phillips complained. "You know? The one with the dragons."

"Fun night at the MacKenzie-Phillips household, I take it?" Ryan chimed in.

"You have no idea," MacKenzie replied. "I've never heard the end of it."

"Fancy a bacon sarnie?" he asked. "The canteen's open."

"S'pose that'll have to do," Phillips complained. "The bloke from the Pie Van's off on holiday, this week. He's got no idea how much we hardworking officers of the law depend on him to sustain us, through the long hours of the day."

"You should've auditioned for Jon Snow," Ryan quipped, drawing a chuckle from MacKenzie. "With speeches like that, you could've been the King in the North."

"Aye, well this old king needs a stottie cake, or he's at risk of fainting from a lack of bacon in his diet."

"Lead the way, my liege."

---

Lowerson kept a safe distance from his target, blinking through the rain which was now falling steadily. Ludo was a giant of a man, who walked with a loping gait about a hundred yards ahead of him, the toes of his boots scuffing against the pathway as he wound his way through the housing estate that bordered the Washington Service Station. His hands were tucked inside a navy-blue, all-weather bomber jacket that looked expensive, for a man who was supposedly on the run.

Paul Evershed was the sort of man who kept to his own course, and did not waver for man, woman or child. Consequently, he did not move aside for a mother pushing a pram, or an old woman out walking her dog. They were forced to move awkwardly around his colossal frame, the wheels of the pram running into the muddy grass by the side of the pavement.

Ludo continued along the pathway, which was flanked by semi-detached houses on either side, until he came to the main road at the end. Lowerson, who was only just turning onto the pathway at the other end, kept him in sight and jogged lightly to catch up, moving politely aside for the lady with the pram, and stepping around the old woman with the dog.

It was just how normal people behaved.

When he reached the end of the path where it met the main road, he slowed down considerably and stuck his head around the corner, half expecting Ludo to lunge for him.

But he didn't.

Evershed, he could see, was otherwise occupied standing on the other side of the main road, peering through a gap in the fence behind which, Lowerson knew, was a school playground.

He might have assumed the worst and, given Ludo's other character traits, it would not necessarily have been a surprise. However, he had already done a check on Evershed's family, to see where they were now, and had found that Ludo's daughter lived only a few streets away and her two young children attended the primary school.

Ludo was visiting his grandchildren, the only way he could.

It turned out, Singh was right: there was always a weakness, if you knew where to look for it.

---

In the staff canteen, the three detectives were about to tuck into some inferior bacon stotties, when Ryan noticed something on the local news, which was playing on a flatscreen television with the subtitles turned on.

"That's the park near Penshaw, isn't it?" he asked Phillips, pointing to the screen.

His sergeant turned around to glance at the screen.

"Aye, that's the one. Are they hosting an event there? If it looks any good, maybe we could take the little'un," he said to Denise.

"Not an event," Ryan said slowly, his eyes tracking the subtitles as they appeared on the big screen. "The local planning office has given the go-ahead to build three hundred houses there."

"*What*?" Phillips said. "That doesn't seem likely. The locals love that park. It's basically a memorial to the colliery that was there before. There's no way the local council would allow all those houses to be built there."

"I know—but look, Frank," Ryan said, and called out for someone to turn the sound back on.

"*The project, which is in line with the government's sustainable housing initiative, is designed to provide affordable housing to people in the local area,*" the newsreader said. "*The development has earned the backing* of the head of the local council, Councillor Sally Emerson, who had this to say…"

Ryan watched with hard eyes, while Emerson gave a short speech about investing in the region's future.

"*I grew up in Penshaw, and my father was a miner. I know what the area's history means to a lot of people, but I also know it's important for the children of today to have adequate housing. I firmly believe this project will be a success, and we are proud to work with the Priory Development Group to make this happen.*"

"She's a smooth one," Phillips remarked.

"This kind of project would need high-level planning permission," Ryan said, turning to the other two with the light of battle in his eyes. "Who's the Head of the Planning Office in that area?" he asked, rhetorically.

"Mike Emerson," Phillips said, with disgust.

"He won't have his name anywhere on the paperwork," MacKenzie thought aloud. "They'd want to avoid the suggestion of there being any collusion."

Ryan nodded.

"I want to look into the Priory Development Group," he said. "I don't remember seeing it on the list the Fraud Team sent over."

"I'll check it out, right away," MacKenzie said. "Are you thinking there's a connection between this and the deaths in Penshaw?"

Ryan looked at his friends and thought of the warning Blackett had given him, and what would happen if the undercover investigation were jeopardised.

"I don't know yet," he said, not having seen the CCTV footage of Ludo placing him in Penshaw on the night Simon Watson had died. "But I know Singh had a hand in this, somewhere. I can feel it."

# CHAPTER 32

Jack Lowerson watched Ludo from the corner of the street for fifteen minutes, during which time a number of families with young children passed him on their way to the morning drop-off at the primary school across the road. Ludo didn't react to any of them, until a young woman crossed the zebra crossing beside the school gates, holding a spotted umbrella in one hand and a four-year-old boy in the other.

Evershed's body straightened up and he kept to the edge of the fence, trying to make himself invisible, then moved back to his gap in the trees where he could watch their progress for a while longer until they disappeared inside the school building.

When he began to step away, Lowerson turned and beat a very hasty retreat, sprinting full pelt on his bad leg to reach the other end of the pathway before Evershed could cross the road and see him, up ahead.

Lowerson almost made it.

When Evershed turned back on to the path that would take him to the car park at the service station, he caught the tail end of a man's running figure at the far end of the path. He couldn't make out a face, or even much of his build, but he was immediately on full alert.

As he rounded the corner, there was nobody there.

He continued walking back to the car park at a steady pace, but reached for the piece he kept in his inside pocket, moving it to the side pocket of his jacket for easier access if he should need to act quickly.

Nobody was waiting for him when he entered the car park, and his eyes searched behind the windscreen of every car, peering through the rain to see if he'd been marked.

Eventually, having satisfied himself that all was well, Ludo slid back inside his Nissan. He'd barely strapped on a seatbelt, when the headlights of a Vauxhall Corsa came on, indicating somebody had started the car.

The only problem with that was, there had been nobody in the car when he'd checked.

There had been nobody crossing the car park to get inside it, either, which could mean only one thing.

*Police.*

It couldn't be one of theirs, he thought. It had to be some 'Have a Go Hero' who'd spotted him and decided they'd try to bag themselves a big name, in time for the commendations dinner.

They'd have to catch him, first.

When Ryan returned to his desk, he found the pathologist had sent over a private report concerning the death of Simon Watson to his personal e-mail account, as requested.

Jeff Pinter had come through for him.

He began to read its contents, which confirmed what he already expected. Although there were no defensive wounds to indicate Simon Watson had fought for his life, there was something far more revealing to be found in tandem with the forensics report. What they had believed to be one head wound was, in fact, two wounds; the second layered on top of the first, possibly to hide it. Pinter theorised that the first wound would have led to the blood spatter Tom Faulkner had remarked upon but not found anywhere in the living room where Watson fell, and the second wound would have left little or no spatter at all.

Pinter's explanation for the lack of blood spatter when Watson fell from the sofa to the coffee table—if he fell at all—was simple. Watson was already dead by that point, which meant the blood was not pumping through his veins in order to spill out following a blunt force trauma. This, alone, would not have been conclusive. After all, if Simon died following a drugs overdose, he would also have been dead before he fell, leading to the same clinical outcome.

That's where the first wound became significant.

During the course of their sweep, Faulkner's team isolated a large area of bleach on the wall and floor of the hallway beside the front door of Watson's bungalow, which was a highly suspect but unexplained anomaly.

Now that Pinter was of the firm belief that Simon Watson had suffered an earlier head wound, it was possible this occurred when he opened the front door and his assailant attacked him immediately, in order to disable him. If this assailant went to considerable trouble to stage Watson's death as a drugs overdose, it was certainly possible they took the trouble to clean any blood from the wall or floor before they left.

Finally, early toxicology results had come back to show that Simon Watson had died following a massive cardiac arrest occasioned by the noxious blend of heroin cut with fentanyl, which was widely agreed to be one of the most lethal drugs combinations available.

No pouch had ever been found, and no fingerprints had been found on the syringe, either.

Not even Simon's.

———

At the service station in Washington, Lowerson watched Paul Evershed slip inside his green Nissan. Rather than moving at a snail's pace, as was customary, the car pulled out of its space at high speed, taking Lowerson by surprise.

He put his rental car into gear and hurried to follow, desperate not to lose the man they'd all been searching for, and surged out of his own parking space.

It was obvious something had spooked Evershed, because he didn't slow down. In a 10-mph zone, Ludo was pushing thirty or forty, taking the narrow, winding corners at dangerous speed as he prepared to join the A1 and accelerate into the rain.

Lowerson was not far behind and had the advantage of some advanced driving training, albeit he'd seldom needed to use it.

Now was one such time.

The tyres squealed as he rounded the corner, following the bumper of the dark green Nissan. Up ahead, there was a short slip road to join the A1, which was by now filled with cars and lorries grappling with rush hour traffic.

Lowerson saw the danger in the nick of time, but Ludo did not.

With a fierce, tigerish smile, he watched the Corsa brake on the slip road behind him, sending a spray of rainwater up into the air. He assumed the pussy had lost his nerve, whoever he was, and accelerated wildly to celebrate. A lorry was taking up the slow lane, so Evershed reasoned that he could speed up and nip into the gap ahead of it, before moving across to the fast lane without so much as a pause.

But he hadn't seen the second lorry, which was filling the space in the fast lane, effectively blocking his path.

Lowerson punched his hazard warning lights seconds before the collision happened, bringing his car to a standstill on the hard shoulder. He'd had a prescient notion of what was to come and, with detachment, he watched the dark green Nissan outrun the first lorry, then heard an ominous screeching of metal as it smacked into the second lorry in the fast lane.

A small cloud of food produce rose up from where the first lorry had spun across the road, trying not to become embroiled in the collision.

Traffic came to a standstill and, in the seconds that followed, Lowerson moved quickly.

Wishing he had his blue light with him, he pulled across the front of the incident, forming a barrier with the side of his car. On the motorway, cars had come to a stop, and he held up his warrant card to reassure them somebody was in charge.

He found a couple of tiny orange cones in the boot of the rental car and thought they were better than nothing, so he set them out to form a makeshift barrier.

Having secured the traffic as best he could, Lowerson knew it wouldn't be long before the local police arrived to deal with the pile-up, and he put an urgent call through to the emergency services.

He ran around the edge of the fallen lorry to where the green Nissan now lay upside down, its windows completely shattered, and its metal frame squashed like a can of Coke. One of the lorry drivers was helping the other one, who had suffered injuries, and Lowerson understood immediately why he hadn't wasted any time on the driver of the Nissan.

Ludo's head had been completely severed, the force of the impact having caused the upper metal sheet of the car's bonnet to break through the windscreen and disconnect Evershed's head from his body. It was a grotesque sight, something he had rarely seen before, but Lowerson told himself he'd deal with the image later.

There wasn't much time.

He hurried across to the open window, with its jagged glass edges, and forced himself to reach inside Evershed's pockets until he found what he'd been searching for.

Wallet and phone.

The phone was activated by a fingerprint, which acted as a passcode, and he gritted his teeth, took the dead man's index finger, and used it to unlock the phone. In the seconds that followed, he went into the settings and changed the access mode, so he would no longer need to use Ludo's fingerprint.

He left the gun lying on the underside of the fallen roof—it had slipped from the passenger seat where Ludo had placed it when he'd pulled out of the car park.

Just then, Lowerson heard the long wail of approaching sirens, and prepared himself to lie again.

One last time.

# CHAPTER 33

"Detective Lowerson? Thanks for making things safe until we got here."

The traffic sergeant shook his hand, and then jerked a thumb over her shoulder, to where three ambulances and four police cars were now on the scene, as well as specialist road sweepers who were clearing a path so that standing traffic could move slowly around the edge.

"What exactly happened here?"

Lowerson had already prepared what he would say.

"I saw the whole thing," he said. "I happened to be coming out of the service station, right behind that green Nissan, and the driver flew out of the slip road like a maniac. He wanted to get ahead of that blue lorry, which was in the slow lane, and cross over two lanes to get to the overtaking lane. Unfortunately, he hadn't seen the other lorry, that was already sitting in the overtaking lane. I think he hoped to get past the first one and go straight into the outer lane so he could be on his way, but ended up hitting it straight on."

"What kind of speed was he doing?" the woman asked.

"At least sixty," Lowerson replied, and that was true enough. "He was doing forty as he left the service station."

"I see," she said, and tutted. "They never learn."

It was an odd thing to say, Lowerson thought, especially since the man was dead. However, he had no time to dwell on social niceties.

"I set out a couple of cones, called it in, then checked the driver's status. I'm afraid he was clearly dead."

The traffic cop nodded, looking a bit green around the gills.

"Yes, I saw," she muttered. "There's nothing you could have done."

"I guess not," Lowerson sighed. "I had a quick look for any ID, but couldn't find anything, so I ran the number plates, in case it's helpful. The bloke was called...Steven Marshall, D.O.B. 13th March 1961."

He wondered whether it should concern him, how easily he was able to lie.

"Thanks, that saves us a job."

*And will buy me twenty-four hours,* Lowerson thought. Until some observant so-and-so at the mortuary realised who they were dealing with, he had some time to play with.

"Look, I'm late getting into the office, but feel free to call me if you need a statement."

"Right, we'll do that. Thanks again."

Lowerson walked swiftly back to the rental car and re-joined the slow-moving traffic as it skirted around the edge of the crash site. Only when he was free and clear did he let out the pent-up breath in his lungs.

Paul Evershed might be dead and gone, but he had left behind a gift—one Jack fully intended to use.

---

Sally Emerson shut the door to her office in City Hall, and made two phone calls.

The first was to the hospital, to check how her mother was doing. She and Mike had taken all the time off work they reasonably could, but it was a wrench to leave her alone when she was still so frail. It was hardly surprising, since she'd lost her husband, her son and her home—all in the space of a week.

The ward sister told her that her mother was doing very well, and had managed to eat a good bit of breakfast, which was a positive sign. She kept trying to talk, working desperately hard to make herself understood, and had been asking for a chalkboard or pen and paper to be able to write down her thoughts, since she could not speak them aloud.

Sally agreed to stop into the hospital gift shop and pick something up, later on.

The next phone call she made was to the family liaison officer at the police station, who had been their main point of contact during the investigation into Alan and Simon's deaths. This time, though, she was transferred straight through to DCI Ryan.

"Good morning, Mrs Emerson," he said, in his smooth, southern voice. "I understand you had some queries about what progress had been made in the investigation?"

"Yes, thank you for taking my call," she said. "The last time I spoke to the family liaison officer, I was told that my brother's death was being treated as an accidental overdose, and that the autopsy had been completed. However, when my husband rang the mortuary to request Simon's body for cremation earlier this morning, he was told that they're not quite ready to release his body. Naturally, I'm concerned. Is there some sort of problem?"

Ryan shifted the phone to his other ear and wrote, 'CREMATION' on a pad of paper, which he then held up for Phillips to see.

That was a tenner his sergeant owed him.

"I see," he said. "Well, I shouldn't worry, Mrs Emerson. The mortuary often has a few last-minute checks to do, before they can release a body. I assure you, it's completely normal."

"Oh, I see. Do you have any idea how long it'll be, before we can hold our funeral service?"

"I'm sure it'll all be resolved in a day or two," Ryan said.

There was a slight pause, as Sally considered what her husband had said to her, after another blazing row about her wanting a divorce, the night before.

"Chief inspector, do you think there's any reason for us to worry about my mother's safety? She was in the house both times, when my father and my brother died."

"Since both deaths have been determined 'accidental', there's really no need to worry," Ryan said. "Incidentally, I caught the news segment this morning, Mrs Emerson. I thought you gave a very nice interview."

Despite herself, Sally blushed at the other end of the line. "Thank you."

"It's a great project you're backing," Ryan continued, once more setting his personal views to one side for the sake of the greater good. "Our part of the world is crying out for more affordable housing. Your father must have been proud to know the land was being put to good use."

"Ah, yes—yes he was. It was mostly Mike he spoke to about it…" she found herself saying, and instantly regretted it. As the head of planning, Mike's name wasn't to be associated with the development, or they'd both risk allegations of corruption.

"Thanks again, chief inspector, I must be getting back to work."

Ryan returned the polite farewell, and replaced the desktop receiver. Across the bank of desks, Phillips sent a paper aeroplane across to him made from a ten-pound note, which he caught one-handed.

"D'you know? Sally Emerson rang to query why her brother's body hadn't been released, but didn't ask about her father. That's rather strange, isn't it?"

"Perhaps they weren't close," MacKenzie said. "Or, it could be the grief. It can make people disorganised."

Ryan said nothing.

"I know Pinter seems to think it's all cut and dry," MacKenzie remarked, having only seen the 'official' pathology report into Simon Watson's death. "But I can't help thinking about the surrounding circumstances. Something doesn't sit right."

Again, Ryan said nothing, trapped between his duty not to divulge the undercover elements of an operation, and his duty to be open and honest with his colleagues.

"I had a look at the CCTV footage that came through from some of the businesses around Penshaw," Phillips said. "The funny thing is, Jack seems to have beaten me to it. He must've had a late one, last night."

Ryan set the little aeroplane down on his desk, with exaggerated care.

"Really?"

"The system says the CCTV files were downloaded around ten o'clock, last night. Must be why he's slept in, this morning," Phillips joked.

Ryan was immediately concerned about Lowerson's whereabouts.

"Was there anything on the footage?" he asked. "Anything to help us?"

"I haven't had a chance to go through all of it, yet, but there's clear footage of Paul Evershed buying cigarettes and chocolate from the convenience shop in Penshaw, just before eleven on the night Simon Watson died."

Ryan was faced with a decision. He could no longer pretend to his friends and colleagues that Watson's death was an accident, when the evidence was stacking up to suggest pre-meditated murder. However, DCI Blackett had issued a clear warning about the consequences he would face if he was responsible for jeopardising the undercover anti-corruption investigation.

Before he was forced to decide, his mobile phone began to ring.

*Lowerson.*

Rising from his desk, Ryan hurried from the room to take the call, leaving Phillips and MacKenzie to look at one another in confusion.

"Here, I hope he's not having an affair, or 'owt like that," Phillips muttered. "I'll have a few words to say to him, if he is…"

"Don't be daft, Frank. He's probably dealing with some sort of top-secret, undercover operation that he can't share with us, and it's making him act out of character."

Phillips considered that possibility, then pulled a disbelieving face.

"Nah. Maybe he's just got the runs."

# CHAPTER 34

"What do you mean, they're holding on to the body?"

Bobby Singh's tone never wavered, even in anger. It was a point of pride for him to know that nothing and nobody ever affected him to the degree that he lost his temper. Controlled anger was healthy, but rage was indulgent.

*"That's what I heard. And now they're looking into Priory Developments."*

He could hear the note of panic at the other end of the line, and smiled.

"What's the party line?"

*"They're calling it an accidental overdose, just like we planned."*

"You're probably worrying about nothing, then. Our little helper in the Major Crimes Team has been given very clear instructions about what to do, and he knows the consequences if he fails to comply."

*"But…if it was ruled accidental, Ryan would have handed it over to another team. Wouldn't he?"*

Singh was quiet for so long, they thought the connection had been lost.

*"Hello?"*

"I'm still here," he said.

*"Well? Don't you think he would have passed it over to another team, if he thought it wasn't murder?"*

Now that he thought about it, Singh had to admit it was true. Ryan was, in many ways, as single-minded as he was, himself.

"We're being deceived, it would seem," he said, after another long pause. "Our little helper hasn't been so helpful, after all."

*"What do we do now?"*

More panic.

"You do nothing," he said. "Your past dealings have caused enough trouble as it is. The deal will be going ahead, without delay. In the meantime, I have some more of your mess to clean up."

"I'm sorry, I had no idea he would ever find out—"

The conversation over, Singh disconnected the call and then walked to the bedroom window to look out at his brand-new swimming pool in the garden below. The rain continued to fall in fat droplets against the surface of the water and he watched it for a few minutes, before turning away again to issue the next order.

He sent a short message to Ludo, which read:

JL NOT COMPLYING. INSTRUCT PACK DOGS TO TERMINATE.

After the message was sent, Singh walked through to the dressing room he'd shared with Rochelle for two years. Now, half of the shelves were empty of her clothing and shoes, her make-up and underwear. Anything she'd ever touched had been destroyed, as if she had never existed.

First thing Monday, a crew would be coming in to remodel the entire house, so he would no longer see her fingers touching the worktops, or smell her scent lingering in the carpets and curtains. The company he'd started in her name would be liquidated, and the women she'd worked with would find themselves out of a job.

Then, he'd start looking for her replacement.

---

Jack Lowerson pulled into the staff car park at Northumbria CID and heard a message *ping* onto Ludo's burner phone. He turned off the engine and reached for it, shoving aside the distasteful memory of how he'd gained access to the device in the first place.

He opened the message and, when he read what it contained, it was as though somebody had walked over his grave.

*JL not complying…instruct pack dogs to terminate…*

Ludo had created a WhatsApp contact group on his burner phone, which contained three members. Each member went by a non-identifiable nickname, but the group itself had been named 'PACK DOGS' and the content suggested that they were police officers.

Lowerson therefore understood that Singh was giving the order for Ludo to instruct the bent coppers on his payroll to kill him.

Just as his thoughts began to spiral downward, dwelling on all the gloomy possibilities that lay on the horizon, the automatic doors at the front of the building opened and he spotted Ryan, who emerged like an avenging superhero. Lowerson would always remember that moment, and always be grateful that, at his lowest ebb, there had been someone there to help—his mentor, his hero, his boss, and, most of all, his friend.

Jack flashed the headlights, to attract Ryan's attention.

A moment later, he let himself into the passenger side of the rental car and pulled Lowerson in for a brief, hard hug.

"What the bloody hell has been going on?"

Lowerson wondered where to start.

"Ludo's dead," seemed as good a place as any. "I found out where he liked to go every weekday morning, and tailed him there. He made me, and drove like a madman out of Washington Services, straight under a lorry."

Ryan drew in a deep breath, then let it out again.

"I thought we agreed you would get in touch before making any moves."

"There was no time," Lowerson said, and it was probably true. "Besides, if things turned bad, I didn't want you there. You've got Anna to think about."

Ryan didn't know whether to hug him again, or punch him.

"Jack, for Christ's sake…will you never learn? We work as a team, not as lone wolves, and you don't need to worry about me. Yes, there's Anna, but every officer has someone who would miss them, should anything happen."

Ryan realised that, deep down, Lowerson didn't feel he had anybody.

"For starters, you've got your dad, your brother…me, Phillips and MacKenzie. And you've got Melanie Yates, too."

"No, I don't."

"Not right now," Ryan conceded. "She's angry and hurt— and rightly so. You lied to her, and to all of us. I understand the reasons why, but she doesn't. That's something you can correct, and maybe she'll forgive you."

Lowerson didn't dare to hope.

"If she finds out about this business with Rochelle—"

"You'll have to explain that, too."

Jack nodded.

"I've made some bad mistakes, but I think I've found a way to redeem myself."

"I'm all ears."

Lowerson reached for Ludo's burner mobile and wallet, which he'd taken to stall the traffic police making an identification too quickly.

"These belonged to Paul Evershed," he said. "I took them, before the traffic police arrived, and then lied about who he was, to buy us a bit of time."

"And why do we need more time?"

"Look on the phone."

Ryan spent several minutes scrolling through old and new messages, his face becoming more and more thunderous with each new outrage.

"So, Singh wants you dead," Ryan said, clasping the inoffensive piece of plastic in his fist. "But he doesn't know Ludo hasn't received the order, and he doesn't know Ludo's dead."

Ryan thought of the personal cost and presence of mind it must have taken for Lowerson to keep Paul Evershed's name a secret, amidst the carnage of such a serious road traffic collision. There would only have been minutes in which to act, and he knew that he would have taken the same decision, if the situation was reversed.

"You did the right thing," he said. "Because you were brave, Jack, we've got an opportunity now to bring the whole house of cards crashing down."

"I thought…maybe we'd be able to set something up, now we know how to contact them," Lowerson said.

"Exactly. If we can get these people to incriminate themselves, we've won."

"So long as Singh doesn't find out that Ludo's dead."

It was a genuine risk, since the man had sources everywhere.

"I'll put a call through to Pinter and ask him to handle Evershed himself," Ryan said. "That'll minimise the risk of leaks. He's already done me a favour, this week, so we might as well make it two for two."

"The traffic police will find out, soon enough, that I lied about Ludo's identity."

"Don't worry about that, now," Ryan said. "It'll come out in the wash. The priority is to draw these people—these *pack dogs*—out, and expose them for what they are."

"How?"

"By following through Singh's orders," Ryan said, with a slow smile. "Let's beat them at their own game."

Lowerson nodded. This wasn't just a crusade to prove himself or even to defend himself anymore; he'd finally come to understand that his career in policing had never been about Jack Lowerson. It was, first and last, about protecting others and protecting what was right. It had been a long and painful lesson to learn, but he had learned it.

"There's more on there," he said. "Times, dates…if we play it right, we might be able to bring Singh down with the rest of them."

Ryan flicked through a series of messages containing plans for the next shipment of drugs, and shook his head, mutely, at the audacity of it.

"They need to believe we know nothing," he said quietly. "And we'll play along."

"We don't know who to trust," Lowerson started to say, but one look from Ryan silenced him.

"We've always known who to trust."

# CHAPTER 35

An emergency briefing had been arranged that lunchtime for the taskforce of Operation Watchman, once again convened in the largest conference room Police Headquarters had to offer. Ryan had gone to town, providing a buffet lunch for all the hardworking men and women of CID, many of whom had never heard the old saying that they should be wary of Greeks bearing gifts.

"Thank you all for coming at short notice," he said, casting his eye around what was, by now, a sea of familiar faces. "The reason you're here is that we've had a breakthrough, thanks to the efforts of our colleagues in the Drugs Squad."

Ryan looked across to where DCI Coates and DS Gallagher were seated, looking pleased with themselves.

"I think the next part would be best coming from them, so I'll invite DCI Coates to fill us all in."

Paul Coates sauntered to the front of the room.

"As Ryan says, we've had a breakthrough," he said. "My team have been working around the clock, chasing down leads to get a handle on how the drugs are coming into the region. This operation might be about tackling county lines, but it's also about stopping the source, before it gets that far."

There were nods around the room.

"This morning, we received intelligence to say there's going to be a big delivery via the Port of Tyne, late tonight."

Coates paused, for dramatic effect.

"Our source tells us that the ship isn't due to be unloaded until the morning, but the drugs will be taken off sometime after dark and then loaded onto a lorry for onward transportation."

"Do we know which lorry to look for?" Phillips asked, between mouthfuls of egg mayonnaise.

Coates shook his head.

"That, we don't know. But any lorry that arrives after dark should be treated as suspicious," he said. "It's imperative that no move should be made until the goods are transferred from the ship onto the lorry; in other words, once its driver has taken possession of the contraband."

"Who was the source?" MacKenzie asked. "Are they reliable?"

DCI Coates gave a thin smile.

"We are not able to divulge the identity of our sources, as I'm sure you're well aware, DI MacKenzie. However, I can say that the intelligence they've provided to us in the past has been reliable."

"Thank you, DCI Coates."

Ryan stepped forward again and faced the room.

"Our plan is to be there when the shipment is unloaded," he said. "There'll be a tactical firearms unit, squad patrol vehicles to manage exit routes and a police helicopter on standby, if things go south."

He picked up a sheet of paper, on which was printed a detailed map.

"You should each find in front of you a copy of this map, which shows the Port of Tyne complex. DCI Coates will be commanding the operation this evening, assisted by DS Gallagher, and he has set out a number of rendezvous points which will provide the most cover and maximise visibility for those on the ground."

"At this point, I want to thank our colleagues in Drugs Squad again for their fast and efficient work, which, with a little bit of luck, will help to reduce the flow of drugs at all levels."

Coates and Gallagher nodded, looking even more pleased with themselves.

"In terms of the wider investigation, as many of you will know, our effort to apprehend the man known as 'Ludo' proved unsuccessful in Biddlestone, the other day. However, we remain optimistic that, with a bit of old-fashioned detective work, we'll bring him in sooner rather than later."

Ryan's eye caught the snatched glances between some of the officers in the room, and smiled grimly. They thought they were untouchable, he realised. They believed they were above the law.

They'd be disabused of that notion, soon enough.

---

While MacKenzie remained at Police Headquarters, it was Phillips' turn to do the school run.

It was a bit of a shock to the system, having to implement a new childcare routine, where none had existed before. It took some getting used to, especially for somebody like himself, who had spent the best part of fifty-five years being answerable to nobody.

Yet, for all that, it was no hardship.

Despite missing the opportunity to take spontaneous decisions, he was coming to understand that parenting Samantha was enriching his life in ways he'd never imagined.

For instance, he was learning much about rare equestrian breeds, which seemed to be of great importance in the life of a ten-year-old girl.

*Unicorns.*

"I bet they're real, Frank. They just live in really far off places, where people can't find them."

Whilst he was ninety-nine-point-nine-nine percent certain they were merely the stuff of myth and legend, Phillips would never be the one to trample on a person's dream.

"Aye, maybe you've got a point there," he said, as they followed the road home from school. "What kinds of far off places, d'you reckon?"

Samantha made a humming noise as she thought about it.

"Well, it depends if the unicorns like hot or cold weather."

"Let's say they like both," Phillips put in, enjoying the game.

"Oh, well—that's easy then," she said, knowledgeably. "Some of them live in Outer Mongolia, and others prefer to live in the Gobi Desert or the darkest rainforests."

Phillips wondered if they'd had a geography lesson today, by any chance.

"You'll have to take a trip, one day, and let me know if you see one."

"You could come too," she said, and brought a lump to his throat, as easy as that.

"Aye, maybe I will," he said, and, when he spotted a golden 'M' up ahead, decided it was high time for an after-school treat.

"Fancy a milkshake and some nuggets?" he asked.

"Is the Pope Catholic?" she replied.

"Atta girl."

---

Once they had fortified themselves with thick strawberry milkshakes and Happy Meals, they were back on the road again and the conversation changed to more mundane topics.

"You seem a bit more cheerful, today," he remarked. "How'd school go?"

"Better," she said. "I took your advice and set some new boundaries for the girls who were nasty to me, yesterday."

Phillips wasn't sure he liked the sound of her 'setting new boundaries'.

"I see, and what kind of new boundaries did you set?"

Samantha looked mischievous all of a sudden.

"Well, they kept calling me a 'gyppo', so I told them they should be careful because gypsies know magic, and spells. I said, if they didn't stop calling me names, I'd put a curse on them so they wouldn't grow any boobs."

Phillips almost choked on the rest of his milkshake.

"You—you said that?"

Samantha nodded.

"They're the ones who are desperate to have all that stuff, so it scared them a lot. They didn't say anything nasty for the rest of the day."

Phillips tried to find something to fault in her approach, but all he felt was pride.

"You handled yourself, kid. Now they know not to mess with you, without you having to lift a finger. I'm proud of you."

"You are?"

"Course, I am!"

"Nobody ever said that before."

Phillips smiled.

"I reckon there's going to be lots of times when I'll be saying that to you," he said, and made the turning for home.

# CHAPTER 36

John McDougall had been a fisherman all his life.

As a boy, he remembered going out on a little red boat with his father, who taught him everything there was to know about the oceans and their secrets. He taught him to love the sea and to respect it; and, if he did, the sea would be kind to him. John had tried, but he'd found that loving the sea was not enough. There were bills to pay and mouths to feed, neither of which he could do without bringing in a good haul and selling it for a fair price, which was becoming harder and harder every day.

John shut the front door to his white-painted cottage with a soft *click*, then began to make his way down to the harbour, where his boat was moored. It had blown a relentless gale earlier in the day, the rain battering against the town walls of Berwick-upon-Tweed with all the might of an angry god. But now, the rain had stopped, leaving behind a warm breeze that brushed against his face as he followed a well-worn path.

As his footsteps sounded against the cobbled stone streets, John told himself he had no choice; that circumstances had led him to this and, if the sea had been kind to him as his father had promised, he would never have been driven to accept.

*And, why shouldn't he accept the man's offer?* he thought, defensively. It was a good offer, one that would clothe and feed his family for a long time to come, without any of the stress that came with his usual lot in life.

*What about all those people...*

No!

He wouldn't think of that, or of anything but the job in hand. It was just one more trip. One more load, and he'd be set up for months, if not years.

He'd be a fool not to.

As he reached the harbour, John spotted his fishing boat, the *Annie-Mae*, bobbing on the water. The afternoon sun showed up every peeling crack, and made a mockery of his father's stern warning that a fisherman was only as good as his boat.

There'd been no money to keep it properly maintained, let alone to buy a new one.

*But now...*

Now, he could buy a gleaming new vessel, one that would put all the other boats in the harbour to shame.

John stood for a long time by the water's edge in England's northernmost town, formerly one of its greatest strongholds since it was situated less than three miles from the Scottish border, on the River Tweed. He could hear their accent in his own, which was a diluted version unique to that corner of Northumberland, and their traditions were shared. John was proud of his town and of its heritage, and it gave him no pleasure to think that he would be despoiling that heritage, in any way.

His thoughts circled back around to his wife, Trina, and their two girls. There was nothing he wouldn't do for them.

John looked out at the open water, and then back at the tired little fishing boat.

Time to go.

———

It was after five by the time Lowerson retrieved his things from the dingy airport hotel and returned the hire car, then drove back home in his own car. The garden flat he'd lovingly renovated and restored felt alien to him now; a place filled with unwanted memories and ghosts of people from the past; a place where he'd lived in fear.

Perhaps, that would change.

He stepped inside the hallway and locked the front door behind him, setting his small bag on the floor. He took a few minutes to wander around the rooms, re-acquainting himself with its shadows and edges, noting all the things that could be used as a weapon, if need be.

Then he sank down into one of the armchairs and stared out of the big bay window in his living room, watching people bustling past at the end of the working day. Soon, the street would be quiet again, those people tucked safely inside their own homes, never knowing what might be happening on their doorstep.

The rain had stopped, and the early evening skies were awash with blue.

It was a good day to die.

# CHAPTER 37

The Port of Tyne was the navigational authority for the tidal reaches of the River Tyne, all the way from the mouth of the river to Wylam, seventeen miles west of the sea. It was a deep-sea port, handling all manner of regular and bulk cargoes that came to berth and be unloaded on its docks for onward transport, as well as serving the cruise liners that came to visit for a day or two. There were two piers at North and South Shields, respectively, but it was to the south that DCI Coates and DS Gallagher made their way to intercept the arrival of an enormous cargo of illegal drugs.

The sun was making its final descent into the horizon by the time they took up their position beside *The Starry Night*, a long, low cargo vessel designed to carry bulk container storage.

"This'll do," Coates said, as Gallagher reversed his car into the alleyway between rows of offloaded containers from other ships.

Coates spoke into his radio and received confirmation that his team were in position; squad cars from the local police were standing by in the network of smaller streets leading out of the main entrance to the port, ready to close off local roads upon receiving his order. The firearms unit were also in position, with officers stationed at strategic points with a clear view of the vessel and its bulkhead.

"What now, sir?" Gallagher asked, popping a Murray Mint into his mouth.

"We wait," Coates said, checking the time on his watch.

*Eight-thirty.*

It wasn't fully dark, yet.

"Keep your wits about you," he muttered.

---

Lowerson checked the back door again to make sure it was securely locked, did the same at the front, and then paced between the kitchen and living room.

He'd given up trying to sit.

Singh's message to Ludo played through his mind, again and again.

*Terminate.*

*Instruct pack dogs to terminate.*

Singh wanted him dead before he could clear his name, so the world would believe he'd died a murderer. The plan to intimidate him into submission had failed, and Lowerson was of no further use to him, except for one loose end.

*Rochelle.*

It was growing dark, now.

They'd be coming for him soon.

---

MacKenzie drove through the gathering darkness with steady hands and a clear head.

She did not think of Frank, or of Samantha. She thought only of the job she'd been tasked to do, and of the team that relied on her to execute it with the professionalism she was known for. The countryside passed by in a flash of green and blue, and she flipped down the sunscreen to protect her eyes against the last of the sun's rays before it fell off the edge of the world.

Behind her, a cavalcade of marked and unmarked police cars followed; an army of specialist police staff drafted in from DCI Blackett's own hand-picked and trusted team, some of them having travelled from as far afield as London.

It had taken less than fifteen minutes for Ryan to explain the position, and less than fifteen seconds for her and Frank to understand his predicament. Ryan had spoken to them when he was ready and able, and when he'd needed people he could trust without reservation.

That was all they ever needed to know.

---

As darkness fell, the shadows lengthened in Lowerson's ground floor maisonette.

The streetlamps on the pavement outside flickered into life, shining their artificial glow through the panels in the front door like yellow fingers, stretching out along the hallway floor to where Jack stood, waiting.

He did not have to wait any longer.

He heard the distant squeak of metal as somebody opened the front gate, and then soft footsteps making their way to the front door.

A figure appeared.

Jack's heart slammed against his chest in one hard motion and his stomach churned.

They'd come for him.

---

At the Port of Tyne, DCI Coates and DS Gallagher waited inside their parked car, eyes trained on *The Starry Night*, which was berthed directly ahead of where they had concealed themselves. Shipping containers were stacked in high walls around their heads, like miniature skyscrapers, and the water glistened like navy-blue ink against a backdrop of twinkling lights as the city came to life on the northern shore.

Coates checked his phone, then slid it back inside his breast pocket, growing impatient.

"Nothing here," Gallagher muttered, and it was true. There had been no sign of any lorries arriving to take possession of the ship's cargo.

Coates said nothing. He was getting too old for this, too long in the tooth to be gadding about the town late at night on a fool's errand.

"D'you hear that?" Gallagher said, in an undertone.

There was a rumbling sound, distant at first but growing louder as it drew nearer.

It was a lorry.

---

Jack Lowerson stared at the figure beyond the door, wondering which of his fellow officers had answered the order; which of them had fallen so far as to take another life.

He watched their arm raise to the door knocker, and three loud taps rang out like a death knell in the silent hallway.

The blood rushed through his veins, pumping fast as he told himself to stay calm. To get the job done.

Lowerson walked slowly towards the front door, and reached out to unlock it.

"Jack?"

His arm froze, and he looked up sharply in confusion.

"Jack! I know you're in there. I can see you through the glass!"

*Melanie?*

Lowerson swore softly, then unlocked the door with shaking fingers to find Yates framed in the doorway.

"You could at least let me in," she said, her eyes shooting daggers at him.

Lowerson took a quick survey of the street and saw no other signs of life.

"Quickly," he muttered, and tugged her inside the house.

"Hey!" She yanked her arm away and planted her feet in the hallway. "I want to know what the hell's going on with you, and I'm not going to be fobbed off anymore."

"Mel, please. This isn't a good time."

"When is it ever a good time?" she exploded. "I'm sick to death of all your long looks and sad smiles, Jack. I want some straight answers, and I want them *now*."

"Look," he said, casting another nervous glance towards the door. "This really isn't a good time."

"Oh, I see," she said, in a dangerous tone. "Already moved on to the next victim, have we? What's her name?"

It was an unfortunate choice of words, and he turned pale at the thought.

"No, it's nothing like that," he said urgently, and grabbed her arm again. "Look, I know you deserve some answers, and I want to give them to you. But *not now*."

"Get your hands off me!" Melanie shouted, more upset than angry. "I don't understand all this, Jack. I wish you'd explain…"

In that moment, Lowerson would have taken on fifty murderous bent coppers rather than have to see the hurt in Melanie's eyes.

"You're not going to be very happy about what I'm going to do next," he warned her. "But you'll understand why, very soon."

She had no time to react before he plucked her off the floor and up into his arms.

"Jack! What the hell? *Put me down*!"

She began thrashing and kicking as he mounted the stairs, and Lowerson swore viciously as she almost toppled them backwards.

"Watch it!"

"What are you doing?" she said, with a touch of fear. "Where are you taking me, Jack?"

But she knew where he was going. He was taking her to his bedroom.

She began thrashing again, but Lowerson was saved from any further injury when the door to his bedroom opened to reveal a roomful of surveillance officers, DCI Blackett and DCI Ryan, all of whom were trying very hard not to laugh.

Lowerson marched through the lot of them and deposited Melanie in the centre of the bed, where she bounced a couple of times and then sat up, looking furious.

"*See*?" he said, gesturing to the people crowded around the room. "Now do you see why it's not a good time?"

Yates looked around their faces and felt a flush work its way up her neck.

She needed to leave, before she could be humiliated any further. She scrambled off the bed and made to barge past them all, but Ryan put a gentle hand on her shoulder.

"Mel," he said. "Stay here with us. We're on the cusp of something very important, and we can't risk scuppering the operation, not just now."

Yates cast a final, fulminating glare in Lowerson's direction.

"I'll stay until it's over."

Ryan gave Lowerson a nod, and the door shut behind him. A moment later, they heard his footsteps retreating down the short flight of stairs.

Yates looked around the room at the men and women with microphones and headsets.

"I don't understand what's going on."

"I know, Mel. I wanted to tell you, and so did Jack," Ryan said. "All you need to know is, things aren't as bad as you might think, and neither is Jack."

He reached for another set of headphones and handed them to her.

"Listen for yourself."

# CHAPTER 38

Coates and Gallagher watched the lorry pull up with a low rumble and a squeal of brakes in the loading area beside *The Starry Night*. Two men got out and walked around to the rear, where they let down the back of the lorry and made it ready for loading.

Gallagher spoke quietly into his radio, telling the local squad cars to move into position and set up roadblocks at every exit to the port.

Coates typed a quick text and then slid his phone back into his pocket.

"We should move," he said.

"Sir? Surely it's best to wait until they've loaded the goods onto the van?"

The bust would be meaningless, unless they'd handled and taken possession of the drugs.

Coates fell silent, but his fingers drummed an irritable rhythm against the side of the car door.

Soon enough, the two men emerged from the ship carrying what appeared to be large laundry bags along the gangway, which they hauled onto the back of the lorry. They watched them walk back and forth, until they were done.

"Now, sir?"

Coates felt for the phone inside his jacket pocket, but there had been no answering message.

"Now," he agreed, and followed Gallagher as he jumped out of the car, shouting down his radio for all units to move in.

---

The interlude with Yates had served as a blessing in disguise, because Lowerson no longer felt fearful, but oddly...joyous.

She had come to find him, which meant there was still hope.

He was grinning like an idiot, when he heard the scrape of a knife jiggling the lock at the back door. Simultaneously, there came a similar sound at the front door, and he remained in the hallway, waiting for them to find him.

His mouth ran dry as he heard the lock give way on the back door, and a gust of air rushed through the flat as it swung open. A moment later, he heard footsteps moving through the kitchen, into his living room and then, before his eyes, the first of them appeared in the doorway.

Then, two more appeared at the front door, their faces cast in shadow.

---

"It's nothing but laundry," Gallagher exclaimed, from his position in the back of the lorry. "There's nothing in here except dirty sheets. This one's filthy!" he added, in disgust.

"I told you, we're a laundry company," one of the men protested. "We collect the cabin bedding and towels once a week, when *The Starry Night* docks. We do the laundry overnight and have it back with them first thing in the morning. We'll be late, now!"

Coates stood a short distance away, holding back a smile.

"Guess our source must've made a mistake," he said, and worked up a bit of anger about it. "Total waste of our time."

"Are we free to go?" one of the men asked. "Only, we've got a few other pick-ups tonight."

"Aye, bugger off," Coates said, and waited for Gallagher to jump off the back of the lorry. "Can't win 'em all, Tim."

Gallagher raised his radio to his lips and gave the order for all officers to stand down.

"Could be another lorry coming in," he suggested. "Maybe it hasn't arrived yet."

"It's possible, but now they've seen all of us pouncing on that laundry van, they're unlikely to want to risk it, are they?"

Gallagher nodded.

"I'm happy to keep watch here, sir."

"Very diligent of you," Coates said. "But I'm going home."

He'd been a party to this farce for long enough.

Lowerson stared at the faces of the three police officers and, despite everything, found that he was disappointed.

"I didn't think it would be you," he said, to Detective Inspector Anika Salam. They'd worked together countless times on cases involving fraud.

"Don't make this any harder than it needs to be," she said.

"I'm not allowed a few last words?"

"Shut up, Jack." This, from her partner, DS Harry Tomlinson. "You brought this on yourself."

"Howay, man. Let's get it over with." DI Terry Prince stepped forward, from the Vice Squad.

Lowerson turned and hurried upstairs, in the direction of his bedroom.

The others let out a cruel laugh.

"There's nowhere to run," Tomlinson called out, and their footsteps thudded on the stairs as they came to find him.

Salam turned the handle on the bedroom door, and came face to face with Ryan.

"Surprise," he said, softly.

---

John McDougall guided the *Annie-Mae* around the pier and safely back into the harbour at Berwick-upon-Tweed. Nothing stirred on the water except the gulls, and he was glad to see the glittering lights of the town guiding his way back to shore. It had been an arduous journey—despite the rain having stopped over the mainland, the wind had whipped up a storm over the deeper waters out at sea. The Northumbrian coastline was infamous for its treacherous waters and hidden rock beds, and there were countless shipwrecks lining the ocean floor like a mariner's graveyard.

The waves had crashed around the rickety old fishing boat as he'd reached the stronger currents of the shipping route, where larger vessels made their way to and from Scotland, or further afield. Even as an experienced sailor, he'd been afraid.

It had been a risky manoeuvre to run up alongside the larger vessel and collect the goods, without going under beneath the force of the waves.

Now that home was in sight, relief washed over his exhausted body.

———

His relief lasted right up until he laid anchor and set his feet back on the jetty.

"Mr McDougall?"

John spun around to see figures materialising from the arches, their torches shining on the slick wooden floor.

"Who're you?"

An attractive, red-headed woman stepped beneath the single light at the end of the jetty and held up a warrant card.

His stomach performed a slow somersault.

"DI MacKenzie, Northumbria CID," she said, nodding towards his boat. "Been out for a midnight jaunt?"

His eyes skittered over the scores of other police officers standing behind her, their faces little more than stony masks of contempt.

MacKenzie cut through the small talk and cautioned him, before producing a warrant giving her permission to search his boat.

John closed his eyes, and nodded.

MacKenzie gave the signal for a couple of officers to board the boat, and there was a short, awkward silence while they completed a preliminary search of the vessel.

"Looks like it's clear, ma'am."

John thought he had misheard.

"Check under the fish," MacKenzie told them, her infallible nose for criminal behaviour never having failed her in the past. She'd have the whole boat dismantled if necessary, but her instincts told her that McDougall wouldn't have bothered with any elaborate attempts at concealing his illicit cargo.

Sure enough, the two constables amended their earlier, hasty conclusion.

"Ma'am, you need to see this," one of them said. "This is the biggest haul I've ever seen."

MacKenzie boarded the boat and walked over to where they had lifted part of the wooden deck to reveal the ice storage unit, and were now shining their torches down into the crevice.

At first, she saw nothing but dozens of glazed, dead fish-eyes, staring up at her from their icy grave. But then, she saw the vacuum-packed bags, stacks and stacks of them concealed beneath the top layer of fish under the ice.

While officers held John McDougall on the jetty, MacKenzie took a pole from the floor of the wooden deck and used it to scrape away the top layer of fish and ice. What she found beneath made her breath catch in her throat, because there must have been nearly two hundred kilograms of cocaine or other substances piled in a heap, with a conservative street value of over twenty million pounds.

MacKenzie looked across to where the fisherman held his head in his hands.

"Book him."

# CHAPTER 39

Officers surrounded Lowerson's address, closing off any escape route from the front or back doors and leaving DI Anika Salam, DS Harry Tomlinson and DI Terry Prince cornered. Ryan marched them downstairs to the living room, where DCI Blackett stepped forward to perform the arrests on behalf of the Anti-Corruption Unit.

"Detective Inspector Anika Salam, I am arresting you on suspicion of conspiring to commit murder, and as an accessory to murder," he said. "You do not have to say anything, but anything you do say—"

"Sir, you've got this all wrong," she said quickly. "We were, in fact, on our way here to place Detective Constable Jack Lowerson under arrest."

The other two smiled, bolstered by her ability to think on her feet.

"We received a series of anonymous text messages, containing photographs of DC Lowerson in a compromising situation with a woman we believe to be Rochelle White, the girlfriend of Bobby Singh who has recently been reported as missing. Even more harrowing, we received photographs of Ms White, clearly deceased, and apparently taken very soon after her liaison with DC Lowerson."

Yates turned to Jack with uncomprehending eyes, and he simply reached down to take her hand.

"No, I didn't," he whispered, in answer to her unspoken question. "But Ludo staged it to look like I did."

"We believe those photographs to be highly incriminating," Salam continued. "Furthermore, we understand that evidence has either gone missing from the Evidence Store or been tampered with."

She turned to Lowerson.

"Ask him if he denies it."

"You should really be asking me, since I'm the one who switched the evidence bags," Ryan said, and was gratified to see her face fall. "DCI Blackett and I have been aware, almost from the start, of an attempt by an organised criminal gang to impugn DC Lowerson's character, in order to place him under duress and to extort sensitive police information. This was in exchange for not sharing photographs which appeared to show him in a sexual assignation with Rochelle White, a woman who was in the process of becoming a police informant.

"The request by the criminal gang, we believe to be the Smoggies, to have DC Lowerson remove, destroy or otherwise tamper with primary evidence linking Rochelle White to the late Daniel Hepple, thereby creating a link to her partner, Bobby Singh, was an attempt to induce DC Lowerson to incriminate himself further. Having been made aware of this situation, I, with the approval of senior members of staff including DCI Blackett, re-arranged the evidence and removed one item to a safe place. The evidence therefore remains completely intact."

Their faces were mirror images of dawning horror.

"You say you were coming here to arrest DC Lowerson?" Blackett said. "We believe you came here on the orders of a man named Paul Evershed, street name 'Ludo', who, in turn, received an order from Bobby Singh to kill DC Lowerson before he was able to clear his name of these spurious allegations."

"That's utter nonsense," Tomlinson blustered.

Blackett turned to one of the constables standing behind him.

"Search them," he said.

Within seconds, various items including a firearm, nitrile gloves, a length of rope, plastic sheeting and duct tape they would commonly associate as being part of a murder/suicide kit, were pulled from their pockets and from the small bag DI Terry Prince had brought with him.

There were also three burner mobiles.

As a final nail in the coffin, Ryan pulled out the mobile belonging to Paul Evershed and typed a single word:

NICKED.

Seconds later, all three phones buzzed against the carpet.

"Well, well. Look at that," Blackett said, and then to his sergeant, "Get these three scabs out of my sight."

# CHAPTER 40

*Friday, 14<sup>th</sup> June 2019*

Paul Evershed's mobile phone contained the clues to the identities of a further fourteen corrupt officers across command divisions in Northumbria, Durham and Cleveland, including DCI Coates, who was arrested at his home in the early hours of Friday morning by DS Tim Gallagher, who had been working undercover in Coates' team for over twelve months, in his role as a special agent for the Ghost Squad.

The drugs bust in Berwick-upon-Tweed caused an overnight sensation, and was widely reported to be the biggest haul ever intercepted by a UK police force.

In the media and bureaucratic whirlwind that followed, it would have been easy for Ryan to forget that there remained another important visit he needed to make. By now, it had become clear that Sally and Mike Emerson had been taking kickbacks in respect of large-scale property deals with off-shore companies they strongly suspected to be owned and operated by Bobby Singh. Unfortunately, as Priory Developments was held under a Nevada Trust, they were unable to access the details of its beneficiaries in order to make the evidential connection.

It was clear that Simon and, possibly, Alan Watson, had died at Ludo's hand on the orders of Bobby Singh, but it was unclear whether this related to his prospective property investment near Penshaw, or whether the order came via a member of their own family.

Ryan made it his business to find out.

He and Phillips made the drive down to Durham Hospital, knowing that Sally Emerson was due to speak at the rally organised by her brother against Universal Credit later that morning, while Mike Emerson was due to be at his office for the rest of the day.

It gave neither man any particular pleasure to know that their visit may lead to further heartache for Joan Watson, who had suffered more than her fair share already. However, it was their job to avenge the dead, who could not speak for themselves, even if it meant inflicting a measure of pain on the living who remained.

"Joan?"

She looked up at the sound of Ryan's voice, and became very animated, her hands searching around the bedspread for the notepad and pen she'd been given the previous day.

"Do you need this?" He held it out for her.

She nodded, miserably.

"Cnt spk," she managed, and tears pooled in her eyes.

"Sorry to have taken so long to get here, Joan." Ryan reached across to place his hand gently over hers. "We were hoping to speak to you about Simon..."

He trailed off when Joan clutched the pen between her two good fingers and began, painstakingly, to write a message.

Phillips leaned across to read it out.

"I know...I know... what she did."

The two detectives exchanged a glance.

"Sally?"

She wrote another message.

"Sally...Mike...talking here."

"Here in the hospital?" Ryan wondered aloud. "You heard them talking?"

Joan nodded again, and managed to write another word.

"Worm," Phillips said. "You think Sally's the worm?"

Tears rolled down Joan's face, but she nodded, and Ryan leaned forward.

"In the papers your husband requested from GCHQ, it mentioned that the handler who'd been in charge of communicating with their mole in Penshaw—the person people came to call 'The Worm'—had been reprimanded for improper behaviour. I wondered whether there might have been an affair of some kind. Do you know anything about that?"

"Mcdge," Joan said, and shook her head when they looked blank. "Miscrdge."

"Miscarriage?" Phillips asked.

"Sally had a miscarriage, and it wasn't Mike's baby?" Ryan said.

Joan nodded, and collapsed back against the pillows, grey with the effort.

"Rally," she said, very clearly, and Ryan understood what she was giving him permission to do.

Unable to find the words to express his sorrow, Ryan stood and leaned down to press a gentle kiss to the old woman's forehead.

"We'll be back to see you soon," he whispered, and she patted his hand with her bandaged one.

---

It seemed that the entire population of Penshaw and the surrounding villages had turned out for the Rally Against Universal Credit, which was Simon Watson's greatest legacy. A microphone and enormous speakers had been erected beside the monument, and hundreds of people were sitting and standing on the hillside so that, when Ryan and Phillips arrived, it bore an uncomfortable resemblance to the Sermon on the Mount.

"There she is," Phillips muttered.

Ryan looked up and saw Sally Emerson walk to the podium amidst the friendly cheers of the people she'd known since childhood, and whom she had promised to serve in public office.

"*As many of you know, we lost my brother to a fatal drug overdose only a few days ago,*" she was saying, and her voice rang out across the fields, echoing around the village where she'd been born. *"He was a kind and loving man, who battled his own demons over the years, but managed to overcome every challenge. Before he died, he organised this rally, ahead of a Jobcentre Workers' Strike, as a peaceful platform to raise his deeply-held concerns about the implementation of Universal Credit. As a former resident of Penshaw and a daughter of this region, it gives me great pride to—to—"*

Sally stumbled over the words she'd written, as she spotted Ryan and Phillips, dressed in their best suits and flanked by two police officers in full uniform, making their way through the crowds to where she stood, at the base of the monument.

*"—to, ah, to be here, today."*

As the four police officers passed through the crowd, which parted to let them through, the whispers started.

*Why are the police here?*

*Are they here for Sally?*

*Why would they want to arrest Sally?*

Ryan held eye contact with the woman holding the microphone, as they drew nearer.

*"Please,"* she whispered, and it echoed around the hillside. *"Not here, please."*

When Ryan and Phillips reached the podium where she stood, Sally Emerson fell silent, and the microphone dropped from her hand with a heavy metal thud.

"Sally Emerson, I am arresting you on suspicion of soliciting the murder of your brother, Simon Watson. I am further arresting you on suspicion of fraud, conspiracy to defraud and of misconduct in public office," Ryan said. "You do not have to say anything, but it may harm your defence if you do not mention when questioned something which you later rely on in court. Anything you do say may be given in evidence."

"The murder of my *brother*?" Sally replied, with feigned indignation. "Why on Earth would I have wanted my brother dead?"

"One very simple reason—he had found out that you were 'The Worm' and probably threatened to expose your other illicit dealings. You would do anything to prevent your betrayal from being made public."

Ryan watched the colour drain from her face and she cast her eyes to the ground, a broken woman. He looked across to the two constables, both from the local station, and gave a short nod for them to step forward.

Handcuffs might not have been strictly necessary, but there was nothing he could charge her for in relation to her moral crimes against her family and the people she'd deceived for so many years. There was no law against betrayal, the kind that cut to the core of a community, or the treachery of a daughter implicating her own father to protect herself, consigning a good man to a life of shame and hardship.

But it gave Ryan solace to know that, for a woman such as Sally Emerson, there was no greater punishment than the contempt of her peers, some of whom were recording the event on their smartphones and broadcasting it on social media, for all to see.

Sally Emerson's wailing cries could be heard as she was marched down the hill towards a waiting squad car, but, before she reached it, an incredible thing happened.

*Scab*, the crowd whispered.

*Worm*, they said. *Worm, worm, worm.*

One by one, the hundreds who had turned out to stand up for the vulnerable and the weak turned their backs on Sally Emerson, who stood for nothing and nobody but herself.

# CHAPTER 41

Before the morning was out, Councillor Sally Emerson had sung like the proverbial canary. She provided detailed accounts of her conversations with Bobby Singh to the police, which enabled officers from Operation Watchman to apprehend him as he tried to board a private jet bound for Rio de Janeiro.

Mike Emerson was charged as an accessory, although his charge was reduced in exchange for the disclosure of significant records kept throughout the time he was bankrolled by Bobby Singh. He was also delighted to give evidence against his wife, Sally, upon learning not only that she had been 'The Worm', but that the baby they'd lost all those years ago, and for whom he'd grieved, had not been his own flesh and blood. Even morally bankrupt criminals were not above a bit of hypocrisy, apparently.

Having obtained a search warrant, Lowerson and Yates made their way to Singh's mansion with Faulkner's team of CSIs in order to complete a thorough search of the property and, in particular, the brand-new swimming pool that had been laid in such haste.

"I still have no idea where Ludo took us, after I got into the car," Lowerson said, as they watched the police contractors excavate the site. "The tech team are going to use Ludo's burner mobile to work backwards and, hopefully, triangulate its position last Wednesday and Thursday. We should be able to locate whatever holiday cottage or farmhouse he used, once we know that."

"Even if you don't, it doesn't matter."

He turned to look at her.

"Without a crime scene, there's no chance of me clearing my name. It would always hang over me…"

"They wouldn't—" Yates started to say, but fell silent when he shook his head.

"You don't need to say it. I know it was stupid to arrange a meeting with an informant without telling my partner. I put myself in a dangerous position and opened myself up to extortion, which is exactly what happened."

He looked away, thinking of how stupid that had been.

"Mel, I can only give you my word that nothing happened with Rochelle. I was knocked unconscious and, while I was out, Ludo probably threatened her into posing next to me on the bed. That's all I can think. But, look, I wouldn't blame you, if you'd had enough," he said quietly. "I've messed you around too many times to ask for another chance."

Yates gave a small sigh.

"I put in a transfer request," she told him.

Jack was shocked.

"Mel, please, there's no need for that. I'll move, if you can't stand to work with me. You shouldn't have to move anywhere—"

"I cancelled the request this morning."

Lowerson smiled beautifully.

"Why?" he asked.

*Because I think I love you, you stupid great lump,* she was tempted to say.

"Because, although you were foolish, you were also brave," she said, carefully. "Without you, we wouldn't have been able to bring in the biggest drugs haul in living memory. We wouldn't have toppled the Smoggies, or Bobby Singh—and Joan Watson might have lived the rest of her life never knowing who really killed her husband, thirty-five years ago."

"Don't you mean, last Friday?"

Yates shook her head. "Although Simon Watson was certainly murdered by Ludo, and we have the messages on Ludo's phone to prove it, Ryan and the pathologist both believe Alan Watson had a heart attack and dropped his cigarette, which subsequently caught fire on the living room carpet. It wasn't murder, but it still turned out to be a catalyst for all the rest."

"God rest him," Lowerson murmured. "His last act was the FOI request that finally cleared his name, but he never knew it."

Yates nodded, and they shared a quiet moment.

"Detective Constable? I think we've found something."

They both turned as one of the police contractors called across to them from where they had been digging up the foundations.

Lowerson and Yates both said a silent prayer, and made their way across the lawn to pay their final respects to Rochelle White.

# EPILOGUE

*One month later*

Joan Watson passed away peacefully in her sleep, whilst under the care of the doctors and nurses at the hospital in Durham. Before she died, she spent considerable time and energy writing a complete account of all she remembered overhearing her daughter and son-in-law say whilst they were at the hospital, which was duly attested and entered as a statement into evidence.

Joan had never been a wealthy woman, but what little she had, she bequeathed to a local charity who worked exclusively with recovering addicts and who had worked tirelessly with her son, before he died.

The Penshaw Village Association thought long and hard about how best to honour Alan and Joan Watson, both as an apology and in recognition for all Alan had tried to do, to maintain the way of life and to improve living and working conditions for the miners, ex-miners and their families.

After the scandal surrounding the housing contract between the Emersons and Priory Developments, plans for three hundred new homes to be built on common land forming part of Herrington Park were scrapped. Instead, the Village Association petitioned the council to erect a small memorial in Alan Watson's memory, which was agreed by a unanimous vote of the council's representatives.

Ryan and Phillips were invited to attend the ceremonial unveiling of the memorial plaque, which was placed near to the existing miners' memorial garden in Herrington Park, to serve as a symbolic reminder that Alan Watson had, and would always be, a man of the people.

"Lovely ceremony," Ryan remarked, on their way back to the car. "Must've been three or four hundred there, at least."

Phillips nodded, and paused to look out across the parkland, which had once been a very different landscape entirely. Children played on the swings or played football while their parents spread picnic blankets on the grass, enjoying the simple pleasures of fresh air and sunshine.

"Nobody expects the world to stay the same," he said, after a minute or two. "Nothing ever does. All they ask is for a little compassion during the transition."

Ryan nodded, and gave his friend a manly slap on the back.

"Quick pint?"

"Aye, go on. You've twisted my arm."

# AUTHOR'S NOTE

*Penshaw* was inspired by the real village and monument of the same name, which I always watch out for on the train home to Newcastle from London. The historic Penshaw Colliery, which features in the book, is of course entirely fictional. Although not from Penshaw, my father grew up in a pit village with uncles and grandfathers who worked in the mines. My overriding impression is of a close-knit community life, where people looked out for one another and helped wherever they could. In the North East, where I am from, people are still feeling the effects of the mine closures and remember the Miners' Strike of 1984-85 as being a very difficult time, during which they felt abandoned by the state and misunderstood by those who did not work in that industry. Whilst I do not intend to make any political remarks about whether the mines should or should not have closed, I think it is important to reflect, to the best of my ability, some of the feelings and emotions of those caught up in that strike and in the subsequent closures, as with my character of Alan Watson, whose tears I shared when writing the prologue to this story.

LJ ROSS
July 2019

# ACKNOWLEDGMENTS

As with every new book that I write, I find myself utterly blown away by the kindness of my readers, who not only spend their hard-earned pennies on reading my stories, but who also take the time to leave lovely reviews on Amazon, to e-mail me, or send a message on Facebook. I'm so grateful for all your positivity and generosity, which is the sole reason why I continue to enjoy writing the characters I know and love, in the region where I was born. It is down to you, that *Penshaw* became a UK number one bestseller within twenty-four hours of its release on pre-order and, in so doing, became my tenth UK number one.

I feel so lucky to be able to write stories for a living, and I have a lot of people to thank for their continuing love, support and encouragement in that endeavour. First and always, my wonderful husband, James, whose love for and faith in me, has been pivotal in my writing career and in our lives together as a family; my son, Ethan, for his laughter and mischievous nature, and for keeping me 'young';

my mother, Susan, for her love, vivacity and hilarious one-liners that often find their way into Phillips' conversation; my father, Jim, for his quiet wisdom, humility and excellent taste in music; and, finally, Rachael, whose bubbly sense of humour and loving spirit are all I could wish for in a sister.

# ABOUT THE AUTHOR

LJ Ross is an international bestselling author, best known for creating atmospheric mystery and thriller novels, including the DCI Ryan series of Northumbrian murder mysteries which have sold over five million copies worldwide.

Her debut, *Holy Island*, was released in January 2015 and reached number one in the UK and Australian charts. Since then, she has released a further eighteen novels, all of which have been top three global bestsellers and fifteen of which have been UK #1 bestsellers. Louise has garnered an army of loyal readers through her storytelling and, thanks to them, several of her books reached the coveted #1 spot whilst only available to pre-order ahead of release.

Louise was born in Northumberland, England. She studied undergraduate and postgraduate Law at King's College, University of London and then abroad in Paris and Florence. She spent much of her working life in London, where she was a lawyer for a number of years until taking the decision to change career and pursue her dream to write. Now, she writes full time and lives with her husband and son in Northumberland. She enjoys reading all manner of books, travelling and spending time with family and friends.

If you enjoyed reading *Penshaw*, please consider leaving a review online.

DCI Ryan will return in
BORDERLANDS: A DCI RYAN MYSTERY
Keep reading to the end of this book for a sneak preview!

# BORDERLANDS

## A DCI RYAN MYSTERY

# LJ ROSS

# PROLOGUE

*Helmand Province, Afghanistan*

*August 2009*

He wore flip-flops, the day Naseem died.

As the sun beat down upon the desert plains of Helmand Province at the end of the bloodiest summer of the Afghan War, he and his friend seated themselves on the banks of the Shamalan Canal and looked out across its muddy brown waters.

"One day, I'll show you my country," Naseem told him, in broken English. "When all of this is over, we'll take a boat and sail along the river. I'll show you what we're truly fighting for."

It was a pretty thought, and he allowed himself to imagine it. He saw a friendship that spanned continents and lasted a lifetime. Their wives would meet, their children would play, and they'd reminisce about their combat days over the thick black coffee Naseem liked to drink, and that he couldn't stand—especially in the stifling desert heat.

*Pie in the sky*, as his gran used to say.

"You should come over and see my country, too," he offered. "It's colder than here, but there are mountains and streams, and meadows of green grass…"

He trailed off, embarrassed to find a lump rising in his throat.

"It sounds beautiful," Naseem murmured, and then narrowed his eyes to look around what was left of his own war-torn land. "There were meadows here too."

They fell silent for a moment.

"We'd better be heading back. I'm on duty in an hour," he said, and reached for the rifle lying limply by his side.

The Black Watch—or, to give their infantry battalion its full title, the Black Watch, 3rd Battalion, Royal Regiment of Scotland—had been stationed on the canal since June of that year. It lay to the north of Lashkar Gar, the capital of Helmand Province, and had been wrestled from Taliban control during 'Operation Panther's Claw', one of the largest combined infantry and air assault operations undertaken by NATO forces. Coalition troops had succeeded in ousting the Taliban at three major crossing points on the Helmand River, hobbling their supply routes and forcing them further back into the dusty mountains.

While the fanfare resounded back in Whitehall, the Black Watch remained to guard the canal alongside their comrades in the Afghan National Army. Over the weeks that followed, the fighting became less fierce, daily attacks from the Taliban dwindled and, slowly, they began to relax.

*Enough to wear flip-flops.*

"We have time enough," Naseem replied. "Do you hear that?"

His body went on full alert, and he cocked his ear to listen for the sound of gunfire.

"I can't hear anything," he said, eventually.

"Exactly," Naseem replied, with a smile.

The two men stayed a while longer, telling tales about home while the insects buzzed in the undergrowth, until Naseem let out a small sound of surprise.

"He's back!"

A small, skinny-looking dog with the face of a wolf and a big, lolling tongue skipped its way through long grass further along the canal, stopping here and there to sniff the scorched earth.

Naseem rooted around his pockets until he found the small package of food he'd saved, and pushed to his feet, letting out a low whistle.

"He never comes when you make that noise," he said, brushing the dust from his shorts.

The animal was a stray and had never learned to come to a master's call, but he'd developed an understanding with the gentle Afghan captain who shared his food and ruffled his ears.

"He is proud," Naseem declared, and set off towards the reeds while his friend waited.

He cast his eyes over the canal, then back over his shoulder to the camp, which awaited their return. It had been a long summer, and an even longer tour, this time around. He'd seen too much destruction—too much for his soul to bear—and he was ready to go home.

*One more month,* he told himself. *Just one more month.*

In the early days, he'd believed in the cause; in fighting for Queen and Country. Now, he was tired, and bone-weary. He hated the sand and the heat, the blood and the toil. He longed for peace, that elusive thing they fought for, but feared would never come.

Suddenly irritable, he turned to leave.

"I'll see you later!" he called out.

Glancing back, he saw that Naseem was crouched a short distance from the reeds. His palm was outstretched, and he spoke softly to the dog, who raised his snout to the air and took a couple of tentative steps towards the food that was offered.

The soldier's breath caught in his throat.

As the dog emerged from the grass, he saw that a small improvised explosive device had been strapped to the underside of the animal's belly.

He watched in horror as it trotted over to his friend.

*"Nas! Look out! Nas!"*

He lunged forward, but an explosion of heat threw him back. He smelled his own burning flesh and began to roll, writhing around the dusty floor to extinguish the flames that licked his skin. There was a ringing in his ears; a deafening bell that drowned out all else, even his own howling cries of pain.

Across the sand, a small cloud of smoke rose up into the sunlit morning, taking his friend with it.

# CHAPTER 1

*Otterburn Army Training Ranges, Northumberland*

*Friday 16ᵗʰ August 2019*

"CONTACT!"

When the Range Conducting Officer's voice broke into the quiet night air, Private Jess Stephenson threw herself to the valley floor with a thud, the force of the impact driving the air from her body in one hard *whoosh*. Unlike in a real combat scenario, no enemy shots were fired, but the section was supposed to role-play during the night-time live-fire tactical training exercise, because learning to react quickly could mean the difference between life and death on the battlefield.

Jess lay there in the bog, her body tensed and ready for action. Only when she heard the order did she haul herself up and continue onward, her boots squelching over the uneven ground. The darkness was almost overwhelming;

the blackness so deep it seemed to close in and contract around her, as though it were a tangible, living thing. In the daylight, she knew there would be sweeping hills rising up on either side of the river, with the mighty Cheviot towering above them all. There would be forests in shades of green, and barren moors in a patchwork of brown and gold, littered with the carcasses of abandoned tanks and artillery weapons, now rusted with age.

The Otterburn Ranges were situated in a remote corner of the world, covering ninety square miles of the Northumberland National Park, which was an area of outstanding natural beauty in the northernmost uplands where England met the border with Scotland. It was 'Reiver' territory; a wild frontier where battles had been waged hundreds of years before, and where men from both sides had slipped over the misty hills to pillage and rustle cattle from their neighbours by the light of the silvery moon. Now, the Ministry of Defence followed the tradition of warfare in that region by training its soldiers on its vast, open moorland.

But, without the moon to guide their way, the small section of the 1st Battalion, The Royal Welsh Fusiliers relied on their knowledge of the terrain and the night vision equipment attached to the front of their helmets, which was designed to track thermal heat. Somewhere out there was a moving target—a thermal contraption operated remotely by a Target Officer—and they were tasked with finding and neutralising it before sunrise.

Scanning either side of her, Jess counted two slow-moving figures to her left and another three to her right. She knew their names as well as she knew her own, but in this vast space of land and sky, they were little more than faceless, androgynous entities, just as she was.

She could feel herself beginning to tire, the muscles in her arms and legs burning with the effort of remaining upright, and she hiked the rifle up a little higher in defiance. She'd had enough well-meaning advice from family and friends about her decision to enlist—according to them, the army *wasn't suitable for a woman* and she would never have the physical strength or endurance required to be a soldier. No matter that she'd completed marathons and Ironman competitions, aced her basic training, and managed to outdo most of her male peers in the process.

Remembering that, she shifted the pack on her back and dug in her heels for the duration.

The section hiked over fences and through glens, along sodden burns and over rocky outcrops, clearing abandoned buildings as they went. It was slow, painstaking work, and her legs were trembling by the time the first, palest hint of dawn began to creep into the sky. It was little more than a lighter shade of navy blue, so it scarcely provided any respite and only served to remind them that they needed to find their target before the sun came up.

By mutual accord, their footsteps quickened, and they came to a flat, open range with a forest on one side. The section separated into a line and scanned left and right, tracking every knoll, every shadow and rock for a heat source.

Suddenly, there it was.

Through the night vision goggles she wore, Jess saw a flash of thermal imagery streak onto the horizon, about fifty yards up ahead.

"TARGET FRONT! CONTACT!" she shouted, and raised her weapon to fire.

Reverting to training, the outermost members of their section peeled away to move quickly around the side of their axis of advance, while she and the other central firers continued straight ahead.

Her finger curled around the trigger, and the first shot exploded into the night.

---

After the RCO called out, "STOP! STOP!", the small section locked their weapons and began the process of self-congratulatory back-slapping that was traditional at the end of a training exercise. Jess held back, finding herself preoccupied with a small, niggling doubt that wormed its way into her mind.

*The target had gone down too quickly.*

Normally, in exercises such as these, the RCO didn't press the electronic button for the target to fall until the section had expended most of their rounds trying to bring it down. But, in this case, the target had fallen almost immediately.

She slid her night vision goggles back on and peered through the gloom.

The target was still showing up as a heat source.

A slow, creeping feeling of dread began to spread through her body, and she shivered beneath the layers of protective armour she wore. Electronic thermal targets stopped emanating heat when they were switched off, as this one should have been.

Slowly, she began to walk towards the shadowy heap lying up ahead in the darkness, the toes of her boots scuffing the rocks at her feet. Behind the towering hills on the eastern edge of the valley, the sun rose higher in the sky, casting a thin, first light over the small group on the plains below.

"Hey! Where you goin'?" one of her section called out.

Jess ignored them and continued to walk towards the target, her heart hammering against the wall of her chest as she drew nearer.

As the first shaft of daylight burst down into the valley, she saw the target clearly.

"Oh—Oh, God, no—"

There came the sound of running footsteps and a moment later the RCO, a security officer and the medical officer puffed their way to where the section were standing in a rough circle.

"Packs and weapons on the ground, exactly where you're standing," one of them barked, while the other two ran ahead to where Jess stood frozen.

"Stephenson! Stand aside, and return to the section—that's an order."

Jess took a faltering step backwards while the medical officer went to work administering CPR, and the RCO made a hasty call back to camp, urgently requesting the emergency services.

But there would be nothing they could do, because it wasn't a mechanical target they'd fired upon; it was a woman, whose body now lay crumpled on the ground.

Jess looked down at the rifle she still held and let it slip from her nerveless fingers.

# CHAPTER 2

When the call came from the Control Room shortly before six a.m., Detective Chief Inspector Maxwell Finlay-Ryan awoke instantly. There was no groggy fumbling as he reached for the phone on his bedside table, nor any bleary-eyed struggle as he processed the news that a life had been lost. There was only the same, aching sadness he felt every time; a sense of impotence at the waste, and the knowledge he could do nothing to change it. He could not bring back the dead.

*But he could avenge them.*

Ryan looked across at his wife, Anna. She was sleeping peacefully, but he knew that, somewhere under the same sky, another woman had not been so lucky.

He leaned across to brush his lips gently against hers, careful not to wake her, and then rolled out of bed to get dressed. Soon after, he was on the road, covering the short distance from his home in the picturesque village of Elsdon to the Otterburn Army Training Camp, six miles further west in the Northumbrian heartland.

---

An hour earlier, in the pretty market town of Wooler, Detective Sergeant Frank Phillips had thrust out an arm to quell the persistent ringing of his phone and banged it smartly against the metal edge of his new campervan.

"Yer *bugger*!"

"I beg your pardon?"

The question was delivered by his wife and boss in all things, including the police hierarchy. Having been rudely awakened, Detective Inspector Denise MacKenzie now regarded him from the other side of their bed with a cool, green-eyed stare.

"Sorry, love," he muttered, still rummaging for the phone. "I'm trying to find the blinkin'—"

A moment later, another irate female head appeared, hanging upside-down from the top bunk of the double bunk beds he'd fitted inside the vintage VW camper.

"What's all the racket?" Samantha asked, yawning hugely.

"Never you mind," Phillips grumbled. "I'm lookin' for—"

"Is this it?"

Samantha dangled the phone between her fingers, and he didn't bother to ask where she'd found it. The campervan might be small, but things had an uncanny knack of going missing, including most of the shortbread biscuits.

When he saw who the caller was, he threw back the covers and grabbed his coat, before taking it outside. Some things were not appropriate for young ears to hear, calls about murder being one of them.

---

The road was scenic and winding, taking Ryan along the underside of the Northumberland National Park and through the Cheviot Hills to the ancient village of Otterburn, thirty miles northwest of the Northumbria Police Headquarters in Newcastle upon Tyne, and a mere sixteen miles from the Scottish border. In days gone by, it had been the site of a major battle between the English and the Scots, but nowadays it serviced a large army community as well as tourists, hikers and wildlife enthusiasts who flocked to visit the area.

Ryan passed through the village and followed the road north until he came to the turning for the camp. There had been no other traffic on the road but, as he neared the military entrance, he found himself caught behind a slow-moving Volvo that he recognised on sight.

With a smile playing around the corners of his mouth, he punched a speed dial number on his hands-free system and waited for the driver up ahead to answer.

"Mornin'!"

Detective Sergeant Frank Phillips' unmistakably gruff voice boomed out of the car speakers, and Ryan hastily adjusted the volume control to avoid permanent damage to his ears.

"Are you nearly there?" he asked, wickedly.

"Aye, I'm on my way. Nearly at the entrance to the camp."

"Did you get stuck behind a tractor, or something?"

"For your information, I'm driving at the national speed limit," Phillips said, with dignity.

Ryan glanced at the speedometer on his own vehicle, which read less than thirty miles per hour, in a sixty zone.

He leaned on his horn, and gave a casual toot.

"Some joker behind is in a bleedin' hurry—" Phillips complained, and then glanced in his rear-view mirror.

Ryan waved at him.

"Oh, har bloody har," Phillips said, good-naturedly. "I s'pose you think you're funny?"

Ryan grinned.

"Shake a leg, Frank. This joker wants to get there sometime before nightfall."

---

They left any humour at the large security gates, which were manned by a pair of serious-looking armed guards. Once they'd been cleared for entry, the two detectives made their way along another winding road across undulating moorland until they reached Otterburn Training Camp. It was an extensive site, consisting of a collection of one and two-storey utilitarian buildings which had clearly been designed with functionality in mind, rather than style.

They proceeded directly to the guardroom, where they were met by a small welcoming party.

"I'm Detective Chief Inspector Ryan, and this is my sergeant, Frank Phillips. We're from Northumbria CID," he said, drawing out his warrant card for inspection.

A clean-cut, uniformed man of around fifty stepped forward and extended his hand, which Ryan took.

"Thank you for coming so quickly," he said, in a soft Scottish burr that was common in the borders. "I'm 2nd Lieutenant Pat Dalgliesh, and this is Corporal Amanda Huxley. I was the Range Conducting Officer for last night's live-fire tactical exercise and Corporal Huxley was one of our safety supervisors."

Ryan nodded politely.

"Thank you for meeting us," he said. "What steps have been taken, so far?"

Dalgliesh indicated that they should walk and talk, and began to lead them from the guardroom towards a battered-looking army jeep parked in the forecourt nearby.

"At around oh-five-twenty hours, a section from the Royal Welsh came across what they believed to be a thermal target, and opened fire," he said.

"The point of the exercise was to locate and neutralise two moving thermal targets, simulated at a running speed," Huxley put in. "Without any natural light source, the section relied on their night vision equipment which picks up thermal energy. They found the first target as planned, and then proceeded to look for the second. The locale was very dark and otherwise deserted. At that hour, I don't think anybody could have expected to find a civilian on the ranges. It's a terrible tragedy."

Ryan made no comment, but thought privately that it seemed the army had already begun to close ranks to protect its own.

"Both myself and Corporal Huxley attended the scene immediately and called a stop to the exercise when we became aware of the false target," Dalgliesh said, after he'd settled himself behind the wheel. "We called in the medical officer, who was with us, and then radioed back to camp, who called the emergency services immediately. We moved the casualty via stretcher around half a mile further east, to be nearer the access road, and I believe the paramedics arrived shortly before six."

Neither Ryan nor Phillips queried the time it had taken the ambulance service to arrive on-scene. The Northumberland National Park was a vast area of land, much of which was largely inaccessible other than on foot or with an all-terrain vehicle. He also happened to know that the nearest air ambulance helicopter was based in Hull, and wouldn't have arrived any sooner—even if it had been authorised for night service in the region.

Dalgliesh sighed, and started up the engine.

"Our soldiers are trained to act quickly, and according to instructions. As Corporal Huxley says, it's extremely regrettable, but that's why the controlled access area is clearly marked with red 'danger' flags and signage to the public not to enter."

"Where is the victim now?" Ryan asked, and the other two exchanged an uncomfortable glance at his descriptor.

"The scene of the incident is approximately twelve miles north of here, near Witch Crags, which is roughly in the middle of the controlled access zone," Dalgliesh said, and steered the car along one of a network of smaller roads giving access to the more remote parts of the training ranges. "Having been pronounced dead at the scene, the casualty was transported by ambulance to the larger mortuary in Newcastle."

Ryan nodded, and made a note to contact the police pathologist.

"What about the trainees?" Phillips asked.

"When we stopped the exercise, they were instructed to remove their packs and to set down their rifles," Huxley replied, looking over her shoulder from the front passenger seat. "It's protocol whenever there's an incident like this, to mark the position of firers on the range."

"Makes sense," Phillips said. "We'll need to confiscate the gear and the weapons, for ballistics."

She nodded.

"We've got an investigator on the way from Defence AIB," she said, referring to the Accident Investigation Branch responsible for conducting independent inquiries into service-related fatalities and other major incidents. "They should be here within the hour. They'll be able to unload and hand over the weapons for testing."

The Defence Accident Investigation Branch fell under the remit of the Defence Safety Authority, which in turn fell under the authority of the Ministry of Defence. Its investigators were supposed to defer to the primacy of the regional police Major Crimes Unit, but in Ryan and Phillips' limited experience of army-civilian fatalities, this wasn't always the case.

"Has the forensics team arrived?"

Dalgliesh shook his head and made a sharp right turn along another barren road, where the wind blew in across the fields and buffeted the sides of the car as it made its lonely way over the moorland.

"We've given directions for the CSIs to use the army access roads, and I've stationed soldiers at checkpoints to guide them in from the main road at Harbottle when they arrive," he explained. "In the meantime, we transported the section back to base as they were beginning to display signs of shock. Their clothing has been confiscated and held in plastic bags, and they've been given a warm meal alongside some debriefing."

*Quick work*, Ryan thought, and ample opportunity for members of the training section to confer, as well as for commanding officers to 'debrief' along party lines, if they wished to.

Perhaps he was growing cynical, in his old age.

Time would tell.

# CHAPTER 3

An hour before dawn, Imam Aayan Abdullah had left the modest terraced house he owned in an area of Newcastle upon Tyne known as 'Arthur's Hill' and made his way towards the Central Mosque. It lay to the west of the city centre, overlooking rows of residential houses and shops running all the way down to the banks of the River Tyne, in a vibrant, multi-cultural area where people of all skins and faiths flocked to enjoy the best sugary *dodol* that side of the Indian sub-continent.

The sky was still a deep, navy blue speckled with stars as he made his way through the quiet streets, but he knew that, before dawn, the streets would bustle as men—and women—of his faith flocked to the mosque to say their Fajr Prayer, the first of five daily prayers in the Muslim faith. The Imam was proud of the community he served; of the way it pulled together in times of hardship to offer free food and clothing to the needy, and of its outreach programme that aimed to break down barriers and show people that the true followers of Islam practised peace and submission, not hatred.

He allowed himself to hope that, in a few more years, he'd be able to walk down the street without seeing fear and mistrust in the eyes of his neighbours. His mind was pleasantly occupied with these optimistic thoughts, when he heard what sounded like an enormous firework exploding somewhere nearby.

With a sense of foreboding, he hurried along the main road to where a small crowd of people had gathered.

And then, he saw what they saw.

The mosque they'd worked and saved so hard to build was burning, orange flames crawling over its carved wooden doors like serpents. A large black symbol depicting three interlocking triangles had been spray-painted on its white walls, alongside the message, 'MUSLIMS GO HOME'.

In the distance, Abdullah heard the sound of sirens approaching, and knew that one of his brothers or sisters must have called for help. Around him, the community stood solemnly and looked to him for guidance, so he set aside his personal sadness and drew on his strength to counsel forgiveness and love.

Behind the burning building, the dawn began to rise, and his heart was heavy as he prepared to tell those who shared his faith to go back to their homes, and pray there instead.

But, before he could speak, he felt a hand on his shoulder.

"Come and use our hall," the priest offered, and nodded in the direction of a small, Christian community hall tucked behind the main road. "It might be a squeeze to get everyone in, but you're welcome."

The Imam held the man's hand in both of his own.

"*Jazak Allahu Khayran*," he murmured. "Thank you, my friend."

---

Detective Constable Jack Lowerson was otherwise *very* pleasantly occupied when the call came from the Control Room to attend the scene at Newcastle Central Mosque and, for the first time in his career, he found himself torn between a desire to serve and an even greater desire to stay exactly where he was, possibly for the rest of his life.

"Who was that?" a sleepy voice asked, and he turned to smile into the eyes of his newly-promoted colleague and—he dared to say—*girlfriend*, Detective Constable Melanie Yates.

"Control," he replied, while his eyes roamed over her flushed skin and spiky cap of blonde hair. "There's been a hate attack on the Central Mosque. Ryan's already attending an incident up in Otterburn with Phillips, so this one's ours."

Melanie's eyes clouded with sadness, and she sat up straighter in bed.

"What kind of attack?" she asked.

"Arson," he replied. "The fire's still raging now."

"That's dreadful," she said, softly. "Was anybody hurt?"

"Not that they know of," Lowerson murmured, and curved an arm around her shoulder when she laid her head against his chest. "That makes two attacks on non-Christian places of worship, in as many weeks."

She nodded, and the top of her hair brushed the underside of his chin.

"Arson in both cases, too. D'you think they're connected?"

"There's only one way to find out," he said, and threw back the covers so the cool morning air hit them both in a rush.

"Time to go to work," he declared.

But, before he padded towards the bathroom, she tugged him back to her and bestowed a slow, thorough kiss.

"To be continued," she murmured.

It took his brain less than a second to reject that option, and her eyes widened when he plucked her off the bed and up into his arms.

"On second thought, it'll be much quicker if we shower together, don't you think?"

"Very sensible," she agreed, and broke into a wide smile.

# CHAPTER 4

The sky was a bright, bold blue by the time the Jeep reached a small mass of water known as 'Linshiels Lake', on the eastern edge of the Controlled Area and not far from the village of Harbottle. A number of other army vehicles were parked nearby, as well as a plain, unmarked van they knew belonged to Tom Faulkner, the senior CSI attached to Northumbria CID.

"We have to go on foot from here, but it's not far to walk," Dalgliesh said, and slammed out of the vehicle. "All of this area falls within the controlled zone, but the lake is protected from fire since there's a dam attached to it. The training plan for last night's exercise took the section through the middle—between the lake and Witch Crags, a couple of miles further west. That's the direction we go from here."

At the thought of having to walk for at least a mile, Phillips looked down at his comfortably worn-in hiking boots and then made a surreptitious inspection of Ryan's feet, half expecting to find them clad in a pair of fancy suede shoes. Instead, he was surprised to see a pair of scuffed, top-of-the-range boots in their place.

Noticing the direction of his gaze, Ryan's lips twitched.

"The last time we were called out to the middle of nowhere, I seem to recall I almost fell arse-first over Hadrian's Wall," he explained. "I learned my lesson."

"Glad to know some of my good sense is rubbing off," Phillips said. "We'll move on to your southern mispronunciation of the word 'scone', next."

Ryan snorted, and looked out across the wide, open space.

There was both beauty and isolation in that part of the country, which had allowed rare species of birds and mammals to flourish without man's interference—and the hills and crags, burns and lakes provided endless opportunities for quiet contemplation for those who sought it. However, it was also a detective's nightmare; an enormous mass of gullies and caves, of abandoned buildings and woodland where dark deeds could and probably *did* happen.

"It's a logistical nightmare," Ryan murmured, as they waited for Dalgliesh and Huxley to finish having a word with one of the sentry officers standing guard over the vehicles parked at the side of the road.

Phillips nodded, and screwed up his face against the sun as he looked out across miles of untamed wilderness.

"Aye, and I can't help wondering what somebody was doing all the way out here, at that hour of the morning," he said. "Anybody planning to come out here would know which areas to avoid, and we've seen how hard it is to wind up in this neck of the woods purely by accident."

Ryan agreed.

"It's too far from any campsite or tourist destination to be accidental," he said. "Therefore, we have to assume the visit to the Controlled Area was planned, or for some other reason, as yet unknown."

"*Suspicious*, you mean," Phillips put in, with his usual forthrightness.

Ryan smiled, and nodded.

"You know what struck me, Frank? From the outset, both officers have been very keen to tell us how accidental and tragic the whole thing is. That may still be true, but they also told us the section was given orders to neutralise a moving thermal target, simulated to run. You know what that means?"

Phillips nodded grimly.

"It means the lass was running, when she was hit."

"Exactly," Ryan murmured. "And we need to find out what she was running from, or to."

There was a short, meaningful pause, and then Phillips heaved a long sigh.

"Well, there go my plans for a peaceful few days at the holiday camp," he said.

Ryan gave him a bolstering slap on the back, and they began to follow the two army officers, who set a brisk pace across the moorland.

"Chin up, Frank. You'll be back with Sam and Denise toasting marshmallows before you know it."

---

It may not have been toasted marshmallows, but Phillips would have shed a manly tear if he'd known that, at the very moment his boot connected with a large pile of sheep dung, Denise and their foster daughter were tucking into a couple of bacon stotties, fresh out of the oven from a mobile van that passed through Wooler every morning.

"I think I like the ones from *The Pie Van* best," Samantha declared, between bites of bacon smeared in ketchup. "I'm particular about my bacon sandwiches."

"You're getting as bad as Frank," MacKenzie chuckled, as they made their way towards the swimming pool. "It's a shame he's still on duty, but at least we can spend a bit of time together."

Samantha felt a warm glow spread through her belly. Never, in all her life, had anybody told her they were happy to be spending time with her, until now.

"Are you looking forward to going back to school?" MacKenzie asked.

There hadn't been much in the way of a regular routine for Sam, and the process of starting school and making new friends had been a challenge, to begin with. But, soon enough, she'd made a nice group of friends and they'd been relegated to little more than glorified taxi drivers to

Faulkner," he said, and then turned back to the CO. "We appreciate your cooperation."

With that, he turned and strode purposefully across the moor.

**BORDERLANDS will be available in all good bookshops from October 2020!**

# LOVE READING?

## JOIN THE CLUB...

Join the LJ Ross Book Club to connect with a thriving community of fellow book lovers! To receive a free monthly newsletter with exclusive author interviews and giveaways, sign up at www.ljrossauthor.com or follow the LJ Ross Book Club on social media:

 #LJBookClubTweet

 @LJRossAuthor

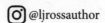 @ljrossauthor